ML PRESTON

Cover Design—T.E. Black Designs; www.teblackdesigns.com

Interior Formatting—T.E. Black Designs; www.teblackdesigns.com

Editing—The Indie Author's Apprentice

W HERE DID I GO WRONG? How did we go from being the King and Queen of the court to miserable and divorced with a child? See, Corey was the highly sought-after sophomore, Vice-President of his fraternity, and captain of the basketball team in college. Me? I was a freshman pledge for the dominant sister sorority. This was nothing like how it was depicted in Spike Lee's joint, *School Daze*, but it could've been at some point. I remember the first time we met. It was rush week and during the party Saturday night, we had to perform a line routine in adult-sized footed pajamas. My line sisters and I wore our hair in pigtails, had novelty sized pacifiers around our necks, and giant bottles.

Amongst all the other pledges, both male and female, we were the last to perform. We worked the routine with precision because our leader was not having her name being tarnished on the campus. We won the dance competition, took the battle trophy for that year, and I won the hottest guy strolling around. After I graduated, we got married. Nine months after that, the real love of my life was born. My beautiful baby boy, Xavier. Perhaps I was so into my child that I never saw the break in our relationship. I mean, we still acted and functioned like a family, a couple, but once he made partner at his firm, those hot exciting times came once a month, if at all.

Then, our 7th anniversary came. He called earlier in the day to say he was going to be working late to close out a big case for the company. I thought it would be a nice surprise to show up at his office wearing only my red heels and a long trench coat. The surprise was on me, however. I exited the elevator and went to his office where I knew he would be. As I approached, I heard noises, moans and groans, followed by laughter. I thought surely it was another partner working late with company. I mean Corey and I never got busy in his office. So, this wouldn't have been unusual except, this was coming from my husband's office.

Hearing those familiar grunts and moans caused the pains in my stomach to increase and the tears roll before I even had a chance to hold them back. I leaned against the door trying to keep my composure knowing on the other side was the end of it all. I put my life and career on hold to raise our child and now I had to go out and start over. Take my child from the life he knew to one of uncertainty. I mean, who'd hire a forensic accountant with no experience nearly eight years after she graduated? The tears became pain and anger. When I swung that door open, I caught him, balls deep, in Vanessa, his assistant. I had a feeling this day was going to come. The way she carelessly flirted with him at the company Christmas party made it all too obvious. Who's to say that this was their first time? Maybe this was the time they got caught. He was at his moment of eruption when he looked up and saw me standing there. The look of anger I gave him stopped him from his thrusting motions and he hung his head low.

"Corey, baby, what's wrong?" That's all she had managed to muster out of her mouth before she turned her head to see what he was staring at. I looked to her, then back to him before snapping a picture and emailing it to my friend Gary, who was also an attorney. The subject line read: Print the divorce papers NOW!

"Happy Anniversary, Corey. You can expect to be served within two days." That was all. After eight years and one child, I turned on my heels and walked out of my marriage.

Chapter
ONE

"All I'm saying is that you could come work the casino with me. Victor is doing interviews today for a new cocktail waitress. It'll get you out of the house *and* out of your funk," Jewel, my best friend, says before taking a bite of her salad. Since my divorce, I've been holed up in my house with Xavier, except the times that are necessary, like the grocery store, school, and basketball, both practice and games. She's been trying to get me a part-time gig, so I won't be so mopey.

"I don't know. What are the hours? I'm not dressed for an interview. Should I go home first?" I ask while stirring the juice from my lemon in my tea.

"I chose to only work the nightshifts. The crowds are generally bigger, and the tips are more generous. Lots of big ballers and potential sugar daddy's if you're interested. Plus, you wearing shorts is perfect. Our uniforms consist of short shorts and a sparkly vest. He'll need to see those legs and that chest to make sure he has an outfit available or if he'll need to order you one."

"See, I'm not looking for another man, sugar daddy, or part-time lover. They can all burn in hell if you ask me." I may still be bitter about my divorce. Corey and Vanessa married three months ago and are surprisingly having their first child in a few months.

"Oh, my Gloria! Tiff, please get a hold of yourself. Corey was a dick and he doesn't speak for all men. Yes, you're still tender, and I'm not saying that you should go get you some. I'm just saying get out the house."

"You're right, sis. I'll come meet your boss."

"Thank you." We go back to eating our lunch and all I can focus on is the sound of the silverware meeting the various plates, bowls, or glasses. I stab my pasta before swirling it onto the fork and shoveling it into my mouth.

"I mean, if you happen to find some good dick, that's a bonus," Jewel adds.

I laugh so hard I nearly choke. The waiter, who has been eyeing me since we were seated, rushes to my aide with a glass of water.

"Are you okay, miss?"

"I'm fine," I respond. "My friend has poor comedic timing."

I throw my napkin at her as she continues to laugh hysterically. "Could you be anymore bold?" I question as she finally calms down from her laughter.

"Well, the mood was becoming so serious, I needed to break the tension."

"You know what, I do need to move on from the past. That reminds me, I got the decree and final papers the other day that I need to send to Gary."

"Oh, really? What's in them?"

"Well, it's the final settlement. I own the house outright since it was paid off early. He also has to continue to make the payments on the car. Not to mention child support, healthcare, alimony, school tuition and any extracurricular activities."

"Damn, girl. Did you at least leave him his drawers?" Jewel jokes.

"Oh, yeah. Those are Vanessa's dirty drawers to deal with now. Gary made sure that Corey lived up to his promise of til' death do us part." The waiter brings us the check and I hand him my debit card to settle our tab.

"Most women have a *Waiting to Exhale* type of celebration when they get their freedom papers. What are you going to do?"

"Here's your receipt, Ms. Lang," the waiter says as he places the black booklet into my hand, holding my gaze with his. I knew this guy was flirting with me, but I guess this is a last-minute attempt to seal the deal. He licks his full, plump, bottom lip and flashes me a killer smile. His cocoa brown skin is smooth as silk and those honey brown eyes could melt the panties off any woman, but not me.

"Thank you. Great service today. I'll make sure to give you a nice tip."

"Well, why don't you give me your number instead?" he asks. Jewel looks on not missing a thing. I bat my eyes, flash a little smile of my own, and gently stroke the back of the hand that's holding the restaurant receipt. I glance at his name badge and run my finger playfully across it.

"Well, Detrick. I'm not sure you'd want to tangle with me, because, you see, I've been a bad girl. My friend and I just killed a man and now we are on the run. I'll give you my number if you help us dispose of the body." His eyes change from fun and flirty to scared and nervous.

"Uh, I don't think I can help you with that," he replies nervously.

"Good, 'cause I can't help you with this." I point threateningly at his crotch area and he jumps a little. Jewel loses her shit laughing loudly. "A little advice don't let your dick lead you through life. It'll cost you in the end." I sign the check and leave him a nice tip. After all, he is cute. I grab my wristlet, and we head over to the casino to meet with her boss, Victor.

WE ENTER THE CASINO MEETING room where there are a few other younger, bouncy-boobed, women waiting to be interviewed. Long legs, round asses, various hairstyles, and diverse across the board. *How am I going to compete with this?* I take a seat in the last chair. Jewel crosses the room and goes through a door to where her boss is located. I can feel the curious, judgy looks from the other women, sizing up the competition. I pull out my phone and distract myself until I hear my name called.

"Tiffany Lang?" A deep boisterous voice calls, and all eyes shift to the back of the room where I'm sitting. I stand and make my way toward the tall, balding, slightly round man. His eyes stay fixed on me the entire time, glimmering with approval.

"Hi, I'm Tiffany Lang," I say, extending my hand for an introduction.

"Hi, hon. You're hired. When can you start?" The immediate acceptance leaves me exhilarated and thrilled. I feel like I'm taking the first step into my new life.

"Wow, Thank you so much. Well... I'll need to square away arrangements with my ex-husband for our child. I'll make sure he can help me get a babysitter. So, two days?"

"Two days is perfect. That's enough time to run your background check. We got one of our high rollers coming into town and he spends big on the crap tables. This will be a great experience for you. I'll put you with Jewel. She's his favorite." I assume he wants me to follow him down the hallway, since he turns and starts walking while talking.

"Sounds great. Is there some kind of training program or anything?" I say, struggling to keep up with his fast-paced walking.

"You'll get all the training you'll need in your orientation on Thursday. Not much to it, really. Take drink orders, keep the guests happy. If it's a VIP client, they'll let you know. If in doubt, Jewel can point them out." He hands me a packet that contains all the rules of the casino cash office and bar staff.

"Sounds great," I say, trying to retain the information he is firing off at me.

"Also, heels are a requirement, and looking at those calves I don't think you have a problem with that." I glance down at my shapely legs and bump into him when he abruptly stops in front of a room with lockers and a computerized time clock on the wall. He directs me to go in and look around while he sorts through the clean uniforms in the room across the way. I stroll in and spot a few girls changing out of their street clothes into their uniform

"Hey, green eyes, what size are you in the waist and top area? No, I'm not hitting on you, it's for your uniform," Vic calls from the door. He doesn't enter, you know, because of privacy. I meet him back in the hallway and we go to the room where he has the uniforms.

"Um, I'm twenty-six inches in the waist and I wear a thirty-six C bra, without padding."

"What about your hips, dear?" he asks while slipping on his glasses to check the tags. He pulls out three sequined vests; one in red, blue, and black, before turning to me for an answer. distracted by the sounds of the casino, the chatter from the girls about some high roller who's coming in next week as they walk by, the uniforms, and realizing all of this is becoming real at the break-neck speed of Vegas. "If you need to slip into the room to check your tags, I can wait," he says directing me back to him.

"Oh, uh, thirty-six. I have a thirty-six-inch hip."

He smiles at my reply as he hands me the three vests and matching sequined short bottoms. "Here, step inside and go try these on. There are adjustment tabs on the inside incase the vest needs to be adjusted. As for the shorts, we either have to order or alter if there's an issue." He directs me with an arm signal and I go into the dressing room. As I put on the last one, I stare at my reflection in the floor length mirror. I see a person who has to find herself again. She only lives for her son and herself now, and this starts her mission of erasing the pain of her past.

"Oh, nice ass," Jewel says as she smacks me on my cheeks. I didn't see her enter when I was self-reflecting. I turn to get the side view, so I can make sure my butt isn't exposed and the shorts make it flattered not faulted.

"Meh, it looks okay," I reply.

"Wow, your ass looks great in those shorts. Is it real? Oh, and your breasts?" One of the ladies says as she catches me checking out my goodies. She's not curvy like me so I can understand why she takes a keen interest in my shape. "I'm thinking of some surgery for myself, actually," she continues.

"Oh, well, yes. I'm all natural. I personally think you have a great body. It fits your frame. You just need to make it work for you. Not that it's any of my business what you do with your own body." I always find myself giving out unwanted advice to others.

"Hey, Tiff. Come on babe let me show you around," Jewel says, interrupting my conversation with the young lady. "Vic had to get back to the cage." I change back into my regular clothes and pick out a locker for me to keep my uniforms. Jewel hands me an extra lock for me to use.

"I see you're making friends already. I told you that this would be a good thing," Jewel says as we slow stroll across the casino floor. The flashing lights, sounds of the machines, and bells ringing for a big win catch my attention. I look around at the building taking notice of the design and colors that attract customers in to play. I refocus and answer Jewel.

"Yeah, but now I have to discuss this with Corey, so he can help with a sitter or getting our son from school if needed. And you know I hate talking to my ex."

"Do you need me to go with?"

"Nah, I got it. I have to go pick up Xavier from his house today anyway so, I'll bring it up then."

"If you need me, just call. I still owe him an ass whooping for what he did to you anyway." She takes me to each of the bar station on the casino floor and the private poker rooms introducing me to the bartenders that are currently on duty. She leaves me at the cage where I fill out my employment package and they take a picture for my employee badge.

"Okay, doll face, that's all for today. If your background check is clean, you will get your register key and handheld on Thursday for training," Vic says as he hands me my company ID.

"Thank you again for the opportunity."

"It's no problem. You have a good evening." He heads back to his office and I go to my exes, wondering how this conversation will go.

Chapter TWO

I had to pick up Xavier from his dad's house today since he had practice and it was Corey's day for carpool. I pull up the new home that he now shares with his new wife and their soon-to-be bundle of joy. Upon my arrival, I see her waddling and carrying a shopping bag into the house. She spots me but doesn't try to say hello. I don't blame her. If I was the man stealing whore that she is, I wouldn't greet me either. No sooner than she enters, he exits. I'm confident that she alerted him to my presence. I step out of the car to see my son running toward me.

"Hi, Mom," Xavier says, still in his practice uniform. I wipe the crumbs from his mouth as he gives me a kiss on my cheek.

"How was practice?" I ask, grabbing his backpack and putting it in the backseat.

"It was cool. We had to run extra laps if we missed free throws, but I didn't miss any, so that's on them." My son is always striving to do better each day. Instead of me looking at him with pressed lips, I accept his moment of gloat.

"Hey, Tiff." The words are like acid being poured into my ears to hear him call me Tiff.

"It's Tiffany, Corey. We don't have that kind of relationship anymore." I stand from my stooped position to face him. I catch him staring longingly at my legs since I'm in my short-cuffed tan shorts. A white sleeveless tee and heels completes the ensemble, like Mr. Vic observed.

"Now, we were together for a while. I think it's okay that I still call you Tiff." I refrain from making this conversation turn ugly, especially when I need to secure funding for a sitter.

"Corey, I need to ask for some assistance. I got a job today and we need to discuss child care arrangements."

"A job? What do you need a job for? I make sure you are taken care of."

"No. You make sure that our *child* is taken care of. The alimony is just a bonus paid up front for all the times you won't be there in the future because you will be too busy with your new family."

"Don't do this in front of Xavier," he pleads.

"Xai, get in the car baby and buckle up." He says bye to his dad climbs into his seat and straps in before I turn back to Corey.

"Now you want to pretend like his feelings are important? Were you thinking about him when you were fucking your then assistant on our anniversary?" This is the lane I didn't want to be in, but certain words trigger my emotions. "Now, like I was saying, I have a job that starts on Thursday. I'm not sure of the hours but I will be in the afternoon-evening time frame. I need to get a sitter, vetted of course, to care for him while I'm working, or he can stay here, if that's not a problem with the misses." I catch her looking out the storm door before darting off to the shadows.

"Fine, Tiffany. I will pull some names from some of the companies the others use and shoot them to you in an email. I will also set up a different account that will have money to pay the sitter and you will have access to verify funds and transactions."

"Thank you. I mean it. This helps me feel more confident about my decision."

"Where will you be working?"

"At the casino with Jewel."

"Oh, a cocktail waitress? What about your degree?"

"Well, not many jobs in the banking industry and not many willing to hire someone with no experience, but I'll be happy here. The boss is 'real nice', like Jewel always says."

"I'm glad you're getting back out there. I know I've said this time and time again, but, I'm sorry." He takes my hand in his and for the first time since our divorce, there's closure. Then I see it. That spark he had the night we met back in school. This road is closed, but at least I still have him as a friend.

"Corey, I think the baby is coming," she calls from the porch. For someone in 'labor' her face is as calm as the wind.

"Well, thank you again. I'll text you with the details of my schedule and you'll forward the information on the sitters." I turn to get into my car when I hear a subtle whistle from his lips. I ignore him but can't help but smile when I pull off watching him in my rearview.

"Mommy are you and dad fighting?" I see my child's reflection and his eyes tear me apart on the inside. I let my pettiness get to me and that was wrong.

"Honey, we let our anger get to our words before we had a chance to think. I'm sorry. We know better than that."

"I think you need to go to your room and think about what you could've done differently." Never thought my child paid that much attention to what I say to him when he's in trouble.

"Well, if I go to my room, how are we going to get ice cream? You can't drive us there," I reply.

"Mmm, okay. You can go after ice cream."

"Wait, did you eat at your dad's?"

"Mmhmm, we had chili dogs with cheese and French fries. I had two."

"Two? Well, that sounds like you get two scoops of ice cream."
His smile melts my heart and I'm convinced this is the right
thing.

We pull into the local ice cream shop and head in to order our
guilty treats. Well, guilty for me. The cashier was kind enough to
bring our sundaes to the table. His eyes light up at the mountain of
whipped cream and toppings covering his two scoops of chocolate
chip ice cream. This is definitely my kid.

"Hey, Xai. Mommy got a job today."

"You did?" he mumbles with his mouth full.

"Mmmhmm. I'll be working with Auntie Jewel."

"You'll be working at the casino making big men pay you lots of
money?" Note to self. Ask Jewel what she told my son she did for a
living.

"Well, I will be serving them drinks and they will give me tips if
I do a good job."

"So, will you be giving the girl who bought us our ice cream a
tip? I think she did a good job." I can't argue with him, especially
since I'm trying to explain my new duties are the same as the
workers in this establishment.

"Yes. I will allow you to give the pretty girl a tip before we
leave. Will you be okay with a sitter or spending more time with
your dad?"

"Yeah, that's okay. Can I help choose the sitter? I need to make
sure they can play Minecraft."

"Sure, you can be in on the decision." He smiles at my answer
and bares his soon to be missing tooth. I stare at my child and I
can't help but think that he has that same sparkle his dad has. I
scroll through social media while he finishes scarfing down his
treat. I receive an alert from Jewel. .

Jewel: Girl, the whole back room is buzzing
about you.

Me: How? I was only in there for like thirty minutes.

Jewel: Well, Erica couldn't stop girl-crushing over you. Then Vic was telling some of the guys that you start Thursday. See, I told you, with that body and those eyes, melting hearts and taking their money is easy.

Me: Girl, please. Thank you for the assist. I got the okay for a sitter and he's even looking for one.

Jewel: Yeah. He probably already fucked her.

Me: Stop!

Jewel: LOL! What are you doing?

Me: Having dinner with this handsome young man.

Jewel: Tell my baby auntie says hi. Talk to you later.

"Are you ready to go, Xai?"

"Yes, ma'am." I hand him two dollars and walk him to the counter where the lovely young lady stands waiting to take the next order.

"Here you go. My mom said that it is always a good thing to tip those who serve you and they do a good job." A small group of onlookers 'ooo' and 'ahh' at his gesture. The young lady says thank you and comes from around the counter to give him a hug.

"Yeah, I have that effect on all the girls," he says as he puts his shades on and we walk out the door. This kid will be breaking hearts before too long. I better get some repellant. We get into the car and head home.

ONE THING THAT CAME FROM my divorce is the fact that he paid for the house that was supposed to be ours forever. It's still ours, except that means mine and Xavier's. My ex purchased this home when he won his first major case before they made him a partner. The case was a multi-million-dollar suit against major corporation and they settled for twenty million plus court and attorney fees. He made 1.5 of those millions and on my birthday, he surprised me with this house. We drove out to see it once and I told him how nice it would be to have it as our forever home. Then, one day when we walked in the door, he had balloons, rose petals, champagne, and wings from my favorite place. Right next to the wings, was the deed and highlighted places for me to sign of course. We had to have it to the title company the next day. But now, that memory is the only thing that I have of our marriage.

Sure, I have other memories, but that is the one that means the most.

"Mom, we're out of chocolate milk," my young Prince calls from the kitchen.

"Okay, add it to the list. Carefully write it down." To say I have a little genius on my hands is a mommy brag, but hey, I have a little genius on my hands. For an almost eight-year-old, he's in the accelerated class program at his school. Plus, he has a desire for anything science related and I'm glad. I didn't want him to follow in either of our footsteps. I always wanted him to make his own.

"Mom, can we go star gazing this weekend? My teacher said that we should be able to see a lot of meteors."

"Um, well, sure. If I don't have to work."

"Oh, yeah. You have a new job. I forgot," he says joining me on the couch while I sort through the mail. I put the mail down and give him my full attention.

"Hey, I don't have to go if you want me to stay home, cupcake."

"Mmm, cupcakes. Are you going to make your cupcake some cupcakes?" He's so corny and clever.

"Yes, I will make some tomorrow, so we can interview the new sitter."

"Okay, you got a deal." He extends his tiny hand to shake mine and I mentally add baking cupcakes to my morning to do list as I walk to my pantry. I go through the shelves to make sure I have all the ingredients that I need or if a store run is in order when my cell phone alerts me to an incoming email. I grab my phone and head to the refrigerator to write down the few items I find that we need and see the email is from Corey.

Here are the names of a few people my colleagues recommended. Here is the banking information also to pay for the sitter's service. As you can see, I opened a line of credit for this account and it will be deducted from my bank account. Be sure, whomever you choose, has my contact information as well. Oh, by the way, congratulations on your new job.

I shoot back a reply thanking him for the info and the account information. I grab my tablet to have a better view of the suggestions that he sent over. I don't like leaving the care of my child with another person, let alone a stranger, but I understand that there are times when I will need someone because of Corey's ever-changing schedule and now my job schedule unpredictability. The first applicant is Meghan. She's a junior in college, majoring in business administration. She works part-time for the law firm, and she's not available weekends. Weekends may be requested, so I pass on her. The second applicant is Brianna. She's also a college student studying drama theater. She's available some weekends in the morning only and that eliminates her. *This is not looking good,* I think while pulling up the last candidate. Her name is Ashley and she's a senior in college. Her degree will be in child development and hopes to open a youth learning center one day. *"Promising,"* I utter softly and then print her information to gather her contact details. I check the time and then dial her to set up a time to speak tomorrow.

"Hello," a sweet young female voice calls from the other side of the phone.

"Hi, am I speaking with Ashley Hamilton?"

"Yes, you are. Who is this?" she replies with a hint of uncertainty.

"My name is Tiffany Lang. My husb- I mean former husband works for Bailey and Banks law firm. You were recommended as a part-time sitter for our child." I'm usually a calm person, but I've never had to hire anyone, let alone set up a meeting.

"Oh, yes. I watched the Banks' children last summer. You need a sitter?"

"Um, yes. I start a new job on Thursday and we are looking for someone who will be able to watch our son. Since my schedule isn't set, it will be on an as needed basis, sometimes without much notice since his father's schedule is unpredictable too. Would that be okay?"

"That'll be fine. I usually ask for at least a two-hour notice. I'm currently not working anywhere while I concentrate on finishing my classes, so that's not an issue."

"Great. Are you available to meet me and Xavier tomorrow evening?"

"Yes, I am. What time works for you?"

"How about 5 p.m.?"

"Oh, that's perfect. Can you text me the address?"

"I sure can. I thank you so much for being available to meet with me on such short notice."

"No, thank you for considering me."

"See you tomorrow." We disconnect, and I shoot Corey a text to see if he wants to be part of the process tomorrow.

Me: Hey, I scheduled an interview with Ashley Hamilton for 5 p.m. tomorrow. Do you think you'd be able to join Xai and I?

Corey: I will have to check the status of this case tomorrow. If we aren't going to court, then yes, I will be there. I figured you would choose her.

Me: Why?

Corey: She's majoring in child development, so she must be good with kids.

Me: Well, that was a strong plus. Okay, I won't tell Xai that you're coming, in case you don't. TTYL.

I always end the conversations so that he won't try to keep me longer than needed. After that fateful day, I try to keep him at a distance. Like I said before, this lane is closed. I head to the theater room where I see Xavier watching his favorite movie.

"Well, kiddo. It's time for bath and bed. Do you need me to help you with anything?"

"No, ma'am. I got it." He takes the remote and turns off the DVD player and the projection screen ascends back into the ceiling. I follow him to his bathroom and start the water for his shower while he gets his jammies. He brushes his teeth first and starts to undress for the shower.

"A little privacy here, please?" he says as he begins to pull off his little polo boxers. I hold my hands up and go take his uniform from the closet and place it on his bed for school tomorrow, keeping me within an earshot distance in case he needs anything. He emerges fifteen minutes later wrapped in his blue plush robe, and slippers to match. I think my kid is a reincarnated old man. He takes his robe off showing off his TMNT night wear before climbing into his bed and under the covers. I grab the towel from the hook in the bathroom and dry his hair a little more. My little person is really growing into his own and he will be eight in a few months. Before too long, he'll be ten and time will continue to pass. These little moments become just a memory and I begin to wonder if I'm doing the right thing.

"Mommy, are you happy that you got a job?" Xai asks, probably picking up on the expression sitting on my face.

"I am, in a way, I just worry about you. I don't like the thought of another person being around."

"Mom, it'll be fine. I can tell if she's a good fit or not. I'm sure dad checked her out since he's a lawyer." He yawns, signaling my young prince is ready for bed.

"Okay, kiddo. The timer is set for 30 minutes, then lights out. Okay? I love you, cupcake." I kiss him on his forehead and head to start my night regimen.

"I love you too, pudding," he says sleepily as his eyelids flutter the dance of night. I secure the house, checking all doors and turn off all the lights before setting the alarm and heading to my room. I can't help but continue to worry about the path I'm taking, wondering if I'm doing this out of spite for my ex or if I truly believe I'm ready to start again. I turn on my shower, undress, and use a make-up wipe to remove the small traces of makeup on my face. Then I brush my teeth. When I open the door to my shower, the steam escapes, enveloping me in its warm mist. Stepping in, I sink to the floor and allow the hot water to cascade down my back hanging my head low. The jets massage the tension and worry in my muscles. I rotate my neck to allow them to heal me from different angles. I shampoo my hair and put the conditioner on before I lather up. I remove the shower head to aid in my leg shaving.

The water jet gently kisses my clit as it makes a pass through when I rinse the clipped hairs from my area. This reminds me of another issue I haven't faced. I haven't been with anyone since the day I caught Corey dick deep in his now, wife. Our divorce was final 7 months later. Sure, I have my special toys, but I miss the warmth of a body attached to that appendage. Before I get carried away, I turn the water to cold, freezing my temptation to get off with my shower head. I dry off and sit at my vanity and proceed to detangle and comb out my hair, blowing it dry, and putting it up making it easier to put my wrap over it for the night.

I lie in my bed in complete silence wondering what the next few days are going to be like. I begin to think about all my errands tomorrow, the store, the nail shop, and the wax bar. I was looking at how Jewel dresses and the styles of some of the other girls and added a trip to the MAC counter. I guess if you work on the strip, you need to look the part. All this thinking allows the sandman to creep in and soon, I'm drifting off to sleep.

"Xavier, Ashley is coming up the drive," I call out while arranging the cupcakes on the carousel.

"Okay, mom. Can I answer the door when she knocks?" he asks as he runs to the kitchen standing by the Alexa show. He's been excited about this all day. The teacher said that he told her he was getting a new employee to make sure he did his homework when his mom wasn't available.

"I will go to the door with you." The doorbell rings and he rushes to answer it with the Alexa.

"Yes, who is it?" he asks energetically.

"Hi, I'm here to meet Tiffany Lang," she replied.

"Oh, sure, she's expecting you. One moment, I'll let you in." He hops down from the stool and rushes to the door and I'm on his heels with a paper towel to clean off my hands. I squirt some sanitizer and manage to get it all rubbed in before the door swings open.

"Hi, I'm Xavier Michael Lang." He extends his little hand and she's taken immediately.

"Well, hello there. I'm Ashley Hamilton. I'm here about a caregiver position," she says shaking his hand. I laugh and the playful exchange between these two. In my opinion, she's hired.

"Come on in, Ashley. Thank you for meeting with us on short notice."

"No problem. I love your house."

"Thank you."

"Mommy, can I give her a tour?" Xai asks. I can tell he likes her already and he is a good judge of character. Corey walks in from the garage carrying a bag distracting me before I could answer.

"Hey, Xai," he says calling out to his son. He runs over and gives his dad a hug, while peeking in the bag pulling out a new project car for them to work on together.

"Cool you got the Corvette we looked at. Thanks, dad." He gives him another hug before showing me the car.

"Ooh mom, a new car for my collection."

"That's nice baby. Why don't you go put it in your room and your dad and I can ask Ashley the hard questions and you can come ask her the even harder ones."

"Okay." He races to his room to put his car on his bookshelf that is only for his projects. We all turn to look towards each other and Corey tries to put his arm around my shoulder. I casually slide from beside him and walk to the kitchen.

"Ashley, please come have a seat here at the island. Would you like a cupcake or something to drink?" I ask deflecting my annoyance to something more positive.

"Um, I'd love a cupcake, but can I take it home instead of eating it here? I hate having food stuck in my braces during an interview. I just had them tightened so something is bound to get stuck." I smiled at her pleasantly giving her appearance a once over. She's about 5'7, with glossy blue eyes and is a natural ash blonde with a dusting of freckles along the bridge of her nose. She has an innocence about her and that makes me comfortable.

"Sure, you can take a few home. That may help push you through those late-night study sessions like Tiffany went through when we were in college." Why is he talking about that? I roll my eyes and grab a treat box from my pantry.

"Sure, Ashley. Just fill this box up with what you want to take home. Corey grabs her a water from the fridge and hands it to her before taking a seat next to me.

"So, Ashley, if needed, could you start tomorrow?"

"Uh, yes. If needed. What time do you need me here?"

"Well, we're not sure yet. Just wanted to be sure just in case. Now, you are majoring in Child Development, what spurred that choice?"

"I actually have been child sitting since I was a sophomore in high school. The parents always loved that I was more than a warm body to watch their child while they were out for the evening. I always made sure that the child expanded their mind when with me. I made sure to teach them something or work on homework with them before playing." Corey and I sit with a blank stare on our face because most sitters just watch the child and not become more involved.

"Well, I'm impressed," he says. A smart comment was brewing

but it's not something I should allow to fly out my mouth at this time.

"Yes, impressive. Can you cook? Do you have a problem with light cleaning duties? Meaning, making sure to clean the kitchen should you and Xavier cook or make treats."

"Yes, ma'am. I can cook a few basic, kid friendly things and have no problem making sure the house is still standing when you return home." Xavier enters back into the kitchen and I notice he has his notebook that we call his think pad. He uses it to right down questions and thoughts that he may have.

"Can I ask my questions now?"

I waive my hand opening the floor to him.

"Ashley, do you have a game system at home?" He places a check mark next to that question.

"Yes. I have an X-Box S."

"Okay. Do you like Minecraft?"

"Of course!"

"Can you put model cars together?"

"I have built a few of them over time, so yes."

He has a check mark next to each of these questions. "Okay, thank you, Ashley. You are hired."

"Whoa, little dude. Let me and mommy talk that over first. Take Ashley on a tour of the house. Show her your putting skills on the mini golf course." Xavier hops down and takes her hand showing her the house.

"Well, baby, what do you think?" He grabs my hand and gently strokes the back of it.

"Um, I think you need to let go of my hand and stop calling me baby," I say snatching my hand from his grasp.

"I'm not making moves on you, I'm just trying to be here for you and Xai." My patience is running thin with his fake kindness.

"You know what? You've been acting too nice lately. What's up?"

"What, just because we aren't together I can't show you love?"

"No. You want or need something. We were married, after all."

"It's neither. I'm just thinking about how I fucked up my good thing. Remember what we did the day we moved in to this house?" There he goes grabbing my hand again. My heart begins to palpitate as his simple touch sends electric pulses through my body straight to my neither region. I'm sure it's lust since this pussy belonged to him and only him for many years.

"Corey, stop touching me," I plea and turn to grab a water from the fridge. When I turn back, he has me cornered with his arms extended above me.

"Those eyes have always hypnotized me," he says before dipping low to steal a kiss. I quickly find a path out of his grasp before our lips connect and hips make a fatal mistake.

"Corey, go home to your wife." I walk away looking for Ashley and Xai and find them outside at the mini golf setup. They are playing and he's having fun with her.

"Yay, another hole in one! Wooooooo!" They high-five each other and I laugh as Corey joins me at my side.

"I'm sorry. I let the past become my present for just a moment. I didn't...," he offers up an excuse and I gaze at him. I can tell he came there with one goal in mind. For starters, he's wearing basketball shorts. Grey, basketball shorts. I can see his imprint through all that mesh. Secondly, he's wearing my favorite cologne. The one that I couldn't get enough of when we were in college. Thirdly, he's recalling the day we signed the deed. We fucked all over this house, inside and out. Nine months later, my prince was born.

"I don't think we should talk about this right now," I say while returning my focus to Ashley and our son. My body is conflicted with what it's feeling. I'm torn between, head, heart, and pussy.

"Mommy, can we hire Ashley, please? She's awesome. She plays golf, and she helped me organize my cars on the showcase shelf, and she plays Minecraft. Can we, please?" He bats his lashes and I can't say no to that. I was just about to speak when Corey decided to weigh in on the question before me.

"Ashley, do you mind keeping an eye on him for about two

hours this evening? Consider this a trial run." I turn to him and he finishes. "We're not going to be far. In fact, we are just going down to the bar for a quick drink. It's about a seven-minute drive."

"I'll be taking my car because Corey has to get home to his wife," sending him a clear signal that one drink was my limit and that's all.

"Sure. I'd love to play a few more rounds of golf with this little guy."

"Cool! Come on Ashley. This time you can go first." He drags her back to the golf course and they begin to play. I turn back to Corey he's smiling like that Disney cat.

"One drink, that's all. Nothing else."

"Great. Are you really going to take your own car?"

"Yes, I am. Let me go grab my purse and write down our numbers for Ashley. I'm going to leave all emergency contacts on the kitchen island," I shout out to her advising of my intentions.

"Yes, Ms. Lang. See you shortly." I walk in the kitchen, take the pad on the refrigerator and jot down my cell, his two cells, and Jewel's number in case we can't be reached. I grab my wristlet, freshen up my gloss, jump into my car and back out of the driveway, following him to his choice of location.

Chapter
THREE

W E PULL INTO THE SANTA Fe Station which is a Hotel and Casino. I start to turn around and go home, thinking he's really trying me, but I did say one drink and there are a few bars inside. We enter and take a seat in a semi secluded and visibly obscured booth in the corner. An average height, blonde haired, big blue-eyed woman, dressed in the establishments choice of uniform, a cowboy hat, tie front plaid crop top, and daisy dukes, approaches us for our order.

"Hi, Welcome to the Santa Fe. My name is Kailee and I will be your server tonight. What can I get you?"

"The lady will have a peach sangria and bring me a Corona with lime and a tequila shot." Ordering my favorite drink? He's really up to something.

"So, what's really going on, Corey. Why are you being so nice?"

"Tiffany, to be honest, I want my family back."

"You have a family. Vanessa is pregnant with your child and she's due in a few months. That's your family, now."

"No, you and Xai will always be my family. " The server places our drinks on the table and we continue our conversation.

"Corey, our ties were severed the day I caught you fucking..."

"I know, Tiff. I know. I can't apologize enough for that. I didn't fight you over what you wanted in the divorce and I made sure to set you and Xai up comfortably, so you didn't have to work."

"Oh? Is this what's it's about? I have a job now? Trying to re-establish my identity?"

"No, that's not it. I'm proud of what you are doing. It reminds me of the Tiffany I fell in love with. Determined, beautiful, sexy as fuck, independent. All the things that I lost because I couldn't control my dick." He takes a swig of his beer and comes to the side of the booth where I'm sitting.

"I had everything I ever needed with you, and I'm sorry. I wish I had fought for us. Don't get me wrong, I'm not hurting for cash and if you need more, I'd give it to you no questions asked. I just wish I did more to save our marriage." He takes another pull and signals for our server.

"Do you folks need another round?"

"What about it Tiff, another round?"

I'm going to regret this, but I agree anyway.

"Sure, another round." We continue to talk and laugh about the good times that we had in school. It's a nice evening filled with laughter, bad jokes, and reminiscing. I look up and I've had four peach sangrias to his six pack. I also notice a lot of touching going on between us as well, but I'm not pushing him away.

"Oh, well, I guess I should go home," I say. A tall slender man brings Corey an envelope and he signs a tab for the drinks.

"Come on, let's go upstairs. I got a room comped for one night." He begins to kiss me along my exposed shoulders. I can't help but fall into my desires. He stands with his hand extended. I get up from the table and we head upstairs to the room. Once in there, we begin making out like our first time all over again. He strips down showing his bare essentials and my pussy aches even more when I see his member thick, veiny, and waiting for me. He sits on the edge of the bed standing me in front of him. He pulls my dress down and it falls to the floor exposing my black strapless bra and matching thong panties.

"My god, I forgot how fucking fit you are. Your body is amazing," he quips between placing kisses on my belly and along my panty line. He slips his fingers into my already primed pussy lips causing a knee-jerk reaction that sends me over the moon. I moan and gasp as his fingers play and bring me to near orgasm. He stands and backs me into the wall kissing me with purpose.

"Stop," I plea.

"What?" He asks between kisses.

"This is wrong, Corey. Stop." He backs away holding up his hands.

"Why, Tiffany? Why'd you stop? Baby, we both want this. Let's make this right."

"Corey, you fucked me over almost a year ago when you fucked Vanessa. And although, nothing would please me more than to get her smug ass back for fucking my husband, I'm not her and I'm not going to stoop that low." I pull my dress back up and check my appearance in the mirror. I grab my wristlet and head toward the door. "Oh, there's lotion over here so you can finish off that hard on." I pull off my thongs and toss them at him too. "You can use these to help you through the moment. Thanks for the sitter." I walk out of the room and the hotel, get into my car, and head home where B.O.B and I will have a long night.

THAT NEAR RELAPSE PROVED TO be very tiring. Once I got

home, I officially gave Ashley her welcome speech, copied her ID, and took pictures for her files per Corey's last text to me after I left. I also gave her a key card to bypass the alarm system. I don't like giving out codes because even that person can share with another person. A key card can't be shared or duplicated. Once Ashley headed home, and I put Xavier to bed, I used my special toys to cool the ache my ex caused. It was so tremendous I almost called him back over, but I had to push away that weakness inside.

Today I begin my new job and I'm kind of excited. Vic messaged me yesterday and asked me to be in at noon and told me that it's only about a two-hour orientation. I arrive at 11:30 a.m. and knock on his door to announce my presence.

"Hey, green-eyed doll. Wait a minute, why aren't you in uniform?" He asks looking over my dress for the day. I'm wearing black dress pants and a white button up shirt.

"Oh, I didn't think the uniform was required for orientation."

"It's usually not, but I'm going to put you on the floor with your friend after you get all your papers signed, your cash out key, and employee badge."

"Oh, I'm sorry. I didn't know."

"That's okay, beautiful. I should've mentioned it in my text. I ordered you a gold uniform in case you have to work some private events. It's in your locker. By the way, here is the combination." He hands me an envelope with numbers written on a piece of paper tucked inside.

"Now, go get changed and go to conference room A for orientation." Vic moves and talks at such a fast pace, it takes a minute for all the information to process.

"Aye, Vic. Big Tex is asking for an advance," A gentleman calls over the 2-way radio sitting on his desk.

"How much?" I'm intrigued by the conversation being held.

"Five-hundred large. Said he'll be here all week. Need the confirmation from his bank, Vic." Vic types in some numbers into his computer database and calls back some numbers to the gentleman on the other end.

"Okay, he's a go. Tell him his favorite girl is working today."

"He said tell his Jewel to find him at the floor tables." They both laugh and I'm not sure if they just pandered my friend for favors.

"Okay, doll. If you have any questions, ask Jewel or find me."

"Okay, Mr. Carbona." I turn and head toward the locker room and change into my gold sequined vest and black shorts with gold sequins lined down the side.

"DAMN, GIRL. THAT ASS IS FAT in those shorts," Jewel says as she comes sauntering in for her shift.

"Is that too much? Do I need to tell Vic to get them bigger?"

"Bish, no. That's a guaranteed tip." She smacks me on my ass as she opens her locker which is next to mine. Thankfully. "Here, let me see something. Bend over."

"Bend over?"

"Girl, don't act shy and shit. Bend your ass over." I do, and she walks around and stands in front of me.

"Hmm. Those tits look good in case you have to bend over to pick up something or even if you have to stoop down to pick up something. You're giving enough of a show for them not to be upset. Also, when you bend over, you can see your pussy print from the back side of those shorts. These big ballers love that shit. They tip big when they can get a little imagination going on about what's in these shorts." I feel conflicted and cheapened at the same time.

"Do these men asks for sexual favors?"

"Oh, they'll try that shit, but Vic has a strict rule of not mixing business with pussy. Some of these house players drop some major coins in here and he doesn't want that fucking with the church's money. If you fuck with his money, you are immediately out of a job."

"Makes sense," I say putting my heels back on. Jewel takes me by my hand and we continue to talk as we go to the conference room.

"Now, on the other hand, he will allow you to sit with a customer at their request. Nothing private and no money exchanged. If a customer feels that you are a good luck charm, he'll likely ask you to sit with him or her. We got some boss bitches in here too, so don't exclude the ladies. If you choose to sit with them, Vic pays you comp time, especially if they start winning big, because we all know that if the customer is winning, the bank is winning because the customer is tipping."

"Oh, that's why Big Tex calls you his favorite," I add thinking about the conversation overheard earlier.

"Texie is here? Ooo, yes. That's vacation money there. You'll meet him today when you work with me on the floor."

"Hey, Jewel baby, how are you?" A tall, olive skin tone, medium build, Caucasian man, with dark hair and smoldering light brown eyes, says as he enters into the conference room. He is luscious. His tan skin tone only accents that dazzling white smile. I think I hear a faint hint of an accent too.

"Hey, my love. I'm doing you later, hopefully." They laugh and I'm not sure if I missed the entire joke or if that's just an inside thing.

"Oh, I'm sorry. Tiff, this is Casey McIntyre, the bar master and the trainer for today." I extend my hand to shake his and he's locked in on my face.

"Hi, nice to meet you," I speak as we greet each other.

"Nice to meet you too. Your Jewel's friend that everyone is talking about."

"I guess." I can tell he's flirting a bit, especially since we continue to shake hands. Jewel jumps in between us and continues her conversation breaking our hand grip.

"I think Tamara will be here too. She's the bar bitch. Like she's cold with her mixing and the guests love her. She will not sugar coat anything unless it's the rim of your glass and you better be on your *A* game." A few other people enter wearing their all black uniforms reminding me that I already messed up. I think really fast and text Corey to see if he's getting Xavier today. His reply is a short, 'yes'. I guess he's still mad at me.

"Okay, new hires, let's get started. This is going to be a crash course in the order and cash out systems," Casey says. I take my seat and he looks toward my direction flashing a smile making me blush. Jewel slips out and tells me to find her on the floor after orientation. As she leaves out, a short, mocha skinned, but statuesque woman enters the building carrying an iPad with a scanner and a box of empty key cards like the one I have for my home security.

"This is Tamara, or we call her Tam. She's one of the other lead bar bosses. If you work a different shift, you may meet a few more but the process is the same." Casey and Tamara tag team the few of us that are in attendance. They give information on how to put in an order, the proper way to key it in the system and how to turn in your tip chips at the end of your shift. While the other person called us one by one to have our picture taken and receive our key card to be used to clock-in and to also ring at a register. At the end of the orientation, we were released and given our station assignments.

"Hey Tiffany, you're coming with me. Jewel is working my station tonight," Casey says as he walks beside me down the hallway to the casino floor.

"Oh, okay." My reply is soft and obviously gives away my nerves.

"Are you nervous? You don't have to be. It's fairly easy."

"Sure, if you say so." My sarcasm rolls off my tongue without second thought causing him to laugh.

"No, seriously. Jewel is good at showing the newbies the ropes. And with you being her friend, I'm sure you won't have a single problem tonight. She won't let anything happen to you."

"Hey, you, don't be trying to steal my work boyfriend," Jewel says as she approaches us at the bar station.

"Trust, I'm not looking for any kind of in-office romance," I reply without taking notice that he was kinda feeling my vibe.

"Well, with an attitude like that, you won't be getting many tips. Flirting can always earn you an extra buck or two. Ain't that right, baby." She gets in his face with merely a micro inch between them. He swallows hard and then backs away with a huge grin on his face and begins to prepare his station for the evening.

"So, what's the deal between you and Casey?"

"Hmm. What deal? There is no deal."

"Sure, looks like one. He practically melted when you got nearly lip to lip with him."

"Girl, Casey and I are complicated. I'm not gonna lie and say that we haven't done anything, because we have, and it's so good, but, I like it the way it is. Non-serious." Jewel is a champion flirter and a semi serial dater. It doesn't surprise me that she isn't looking to make "settle" moves, but I can tell there's more. I catch them making eyes at each other until a voice pulls them from their discreet stare down.

"Do you have those drinks for me, babe?" Her voice reminded me of a person sucking on an inflated balloon. Cute for the moment but will grate your nerves if you're around it too long.

"On the way, Charlotte," Casey answers back.

"Oh, so is this the fresh meat everyone is talking about?" She comments as she sizes me up with her eyes. I'm not passing judgement, but I wonder if her brain is floating around on helium. She's the Barbie doll all men want. Blonde hair, big tits, blue eyes, and what appears to be a cosmetically enhanced ass. I'm not going to touch it to test my theory. I'll just stick to my wondering.

"Hi, I'm Tiffany," I say, extending my hand to shake. She turns up her pointy little nose and skips the introduction.

"Sorry, newbie, I have sticky hands from a soda I spilled. Casey, can you hand me a wipe, please?" She leans over, squeezing her breasts together, and giving Casey an eyeful.

"Um, the dispenser was just refilled right behind you. You can grab a wipe from there." I guess he doesn't buy into her damsel in distress routine.

"Oh, really. I didn't notice that. Thank you, Casey." He slides the tray to her with her drink orders and she skips off to her waiting customers.

"Not a fan of black people?" I say with an implied questionable tone.

"Girl, please. She has banged every big black dick that has strolled up in here."

"But I thought no mixing business with pleasure."

"That's true, but she found a way to meet these guys offsite and they have to promise not to report her. She takes pictures in case she has to hand them over to security to ban them for entering. Now, come on. Let me get you introduced on the floor."

"Bye, Casey." I wave as I'm being led away by my eager friend. We walk around, and she introduces me to a few other people. Some dealers, letting me know their preferred drinks when they are on and off duty, some of the maintenance staff, and the cage crew. When we are all done, we go to work.

"Now, here's your hand held for the night. You put in the drink order, note where the customer is, and if they have a frequent guest card, you can just jot down that number and you'll be able to find them should they move after you take the order. Hit enter, and the bartender will have your order ready at the station. Grab a tray, load them up, and voila, simple. Here I'll let you take Tex's order." We walk over to a semi-large man with a white cowboy hat and an even larger mouth.

"Well, there's my prized Jewel," he says loudly taking her in for an embrace.

"Hey, my Big Tex. How are you darlin?"

"Well, shit, doing better now that my lucky charm is here. Who's this with them ol' leprechaun eyes?"

"Oh, this is my best friend, Tiffany. She just started here tonight. Tiffany, this is Big Tex."

"Well aren't you pretty. Like a stream of melted caramel my grandson puts on them there, green apples back home for the fair. Well, come give Tex some love." He embraces me with his other hand with a force that cause me to giggle a bit.

"Yes, yes. Two of the prettiest fillies in here. Hey there, dear. Do you mind taking a picture of me with these gorgeous ladies?" He calls to Charlotte as she passes by. She looks at us and subtly rolls her eyes. I catch Jewel sticking out her tongue and I laugh. I slide her the finger as I scratch my eyebrow.

"Sure thing. Anything for my Big Tex." She takes his phone and snaps a few pictures of us bent over and his hand prominently on our ass. He's a big teddy bear and super sweet. This is all in fun, of course, and I'm enjoying it. After our photo shoot, I take his order.

"So, what can I get you, Tex."

"Oh, darlin' you can call me Texie like Jewel and bring me a Jack and Coke. Double on the Jack." I input the order and send it to the station.

"Okay, I'll be right back. " I head over to the station being mindful of the area and picking up the empties along the way making a few heads turn when I walk through the crowd. I know I'm cute, correction, fine, and my eyes have a lot to do with that, but I'm more than what is seen. I guess in this line of work, nothing else matters. I see Charlotte playfully joking around with the men gathered around her. She's playing up to their adoration and it's kind of nauseating. I decide to change up their tempo a bit and stroll by her little crowd.

"Well, I think you are quite, uh, uh, um?" One of her admirers' stumbles over his words seeing me walk by and make brief, but long enough, eye contact. I giggle walking over to the station listening to whistles from her band of not so loyal followers. This isn't social media after all.

"Hey, Casey. Do you have Texie's drink?"

"Yep, just added his cherry. Here you go?" I place his drink on the tray and go back to Jewel and the Texan. I approach them with a smile on my face but receive a little nudge and my balance is compromised. I stumble and spill his drink all over him.

"Oh, I'm sorry newbie. I wasn't paying attention to where I was going," Charlotte's snide comments were begging for me to snatch her and her extensions down on the ground, but I remained calm and focused on Tex. I take my bar towel and gently start patting his shirt down to his pants and batting my eyes at him.

"I'm so sorry, Texie." He didn't bat an eyelash or move a muscle. He kept his eyes pasted on my breasts that I purposely put in his view.

"Well, honey. It's - it's okay, really. Tha-that is perfectly normal for first day." If only that was a first day incident.

"Are we good, baby? Let me go get another drink for you okay?" I wink and go back to the bar.

"That Charlotte is going to cause me to lose my job," I scream approaching Casey who is topping off the replacement.

"She's one to watch out for. She never tried Jewel, but they are not friends either. You need to be assertive with her. No fighting just show her you are not to be played with." I spot her with a tray full of drinks and decide this is my chance. I take the drink and walk in her direction, which is just a row over from my destination and skillfully bump her with full causing the customers to be showered.

"Oops, I'm sorry. My hips got in the way." I serve Tex his drink and he hands me a $500 chip.

"Now, that's entertainment, my dear," he chuckles. I think I'll do just fine.

Chapter
FOUR

A FTER A FEW WEEKS I really came into my own. I had a set schedule that allowed me to go to all my son's games and gave me at least one of the weekend days off. Charlotte got over her Barbie personality and came around too. She apologized after she found herself cleaning that couple she showered and realizing that I'm not a meek individual. Now we tag team a section if we see the other person is overwhelmed. Friday night on the strip means tourists, big ballers, and lots of drinks to be served. I arrive about twenty minutes early to help with bottle service set up before changing into my outfit. I decide to put on my red sequined uniform. There's something about the color that makes my eyes pop and the tips bigger.

"Hey, girl!" Jewel shouts seeing me enter the dressing room. I'm surprised she's here so early since her shift starts an hour after mine.

"Hey. What are you doing here so early?"

"One of the VIPs is coming in for his monthly private poker night in his Villa Suite. I work his parties and he tips very well.

That's how I bought my godson that expensive backpack for school." She makes great tips which puts her in the high five-figure salary range. She also spoils my Xai every chance she catches me slipping. I never lacked in support, especially since the divorce. Between her and my family, Xavier has never wanted or needed anything. The child support that I do receive goes into a bank account for him and him only. My alimony pays the bills and provides creature comforts. This job goes into our vacation fund.

"I didn't know they have private events," I reply. "What are they like?"

"Well, for starters, they are long and exhausting depending on how many of his friends and associates are coming. But, it's pretty chill. You can watch them play or sit and watch some TV, read, or listen to music. But you have to keep the drinks coming or make cash runs to the cage for him. Oh, and food. Can't forget about the food."

"Is he from Texas like your casino boo?"

"Oh, no, honey. He's a Cali boy, well, man. He's a successful LA entertainment attorney, with a major client list. He's usually in town because of them or he needs a break," she says.

I shrug off my interest and put my street clothes away before applying my make-up, what little I do wear. I have a matte red lipstick that accentuates my lips and I pair it with some pale pink shadow and the bat-winged eyeliner.

"Wow, you looking for big tips tonight?" Jewel comments as I apply my glittered lotion on my arms and the top of my cleavage.

"Since you will be hobnobbing with lawyers, I will be working the slots. Every little bit of accent helps." We both laugh and head out to sign in and go to our designated stations. I walk over to the cage where she's grabbing setups for the party interested in what she normally has to go through.

"Hey, beautiful. How'd you like to make some extra dough?" Vic asks when he sees me coming.

"Natalia, one of the girls that usually works with me, called out sick. It'll be fun for you and can help earn for that vacation fund," Jewel adds trying to convince me to say yes.

"No, thanks. I'm comfortable where I am. I haven't even worked the poker rooms on the floor," I remind them. It doesn't work.

"Girl, this is a cake walk. Trust me. You want this gig. It's real chill." Vic nods his head emphatically.

"Ugh, I guess." I sigh.

"Jewel, make sure Carter doesn't scare her away," he says smiling. I look to him then Jewel with a questioning expression.

"Oh, girl. Don't listen to Victor. He's messing with you. Carter is a sweetheart. He can get you into sold out shows, concerts, pro games. He's *that* type of connect. Here, carry these setups and I'll push the liquor cart." She hands me about five of the standard high roller setups. Each person has about ten thousand in chips and each setup houses five people. That's two hundred and fifty thousand dollars in my hand. Shit, I think to myself as we leave the main casino and head out towards the private villas. These are some heavy hitters and I'm not sure if I will fit in with this crowd.

WE COME TO THE TOWER Suites entrance and after scanning our ID badges, we are given a key to the suite where we go to set up for the game. We are casually discussing random things when we get to the room and hear a man's voice from the other side of the door.

"Hmm, he's not supposed to be checked in yet," Jewel says as we approach the door. You can hear him shredding the other person on what we hope is the phone.

"I don't give a fuck how much he's paying me, you tell him to stop getting in these fucking predicaments and we won't have to keep spinning his bullshit." His voice is even louder as Jewel opens the door and we quietly enter. He sees Jewel and waives us on in pointing to the bar. I don't make any eye contact, I just follow closely behind her. We stop at the bar and I help her stock and make sure we have enough glasses taking count of what we do need. His conversation continues and he excuses himself to the bedroom where he kindly slams the door.

"Fuck! I'm not sure about him. His temper is..."

"Girl, don't worry. He may be having issues with his job, but he's not like that." Knowing she has a penchant for hot guys, I ask her that one question.

"You fucked him, didn't you?"

"Carter? Girl, no. We just flirt a lot. He likes me 'cause I don't take any bullshit from him or his guests. Put them all in their big dollar places. That's why you don't have anything to worry about." He walks back into the common area headed straight for the bar his phone still in his hand.

"Fix me a coke with a splash of jack please?" he openly asks. Jewel nods to me and I shake my head no.

"Sure thing, Carter. My friend Tiffany will bring it right to you." I gasp for a minute before glaring at her as she fixes the drink.

"You can at least introduce yourself since you're going to be with me tonight." If she wasn't my friend, I swear I'd bust her in her mouth. She hands me the drink and pats me on my ass. I walk to the living area where he is sitting on the couch, his tie undone, and shoes off his feet. I didn't see it earlier, but damn, he's fucking hot. I'm so caught up in his looks and my nerves that I trip on the edge of the rug and spill his drink all over on him.

"Goddammit!" he exclaims. I look at him with shock and his glare is of surprise.

"Fuck, Mr. Carter. I'm so sorry. My, uh, heel caught the rug and made me lose my balance." I take the napkins and frantically wipe him down not paying attention to the fact that my boobs are in his face as I lean over.

"Damn, Tiff. Move your tits so the man can see," Jewel says adding comedy relief as she hands me a towel. He stands, and I notice he's at least 6'3". He has smoldering grey eyes with a salt-n-pepper like scruff adorning his chiseled jawline and chin.

"Donna let me call you back. Suddenly I need to go change." He presses end on the phone and takes the towel from my hand.

"You're new, huh?" he asks.

I try to find something to distract me. "Um, not really. I usually work in the casino on the main floor for about the last four weeks."

"Well, welcome. Jewel, I'm gonna go shower. Tell the others when they get here to pay the new girl. She can run the cash count tonight. You can handle the drinks." He smirks and heads to his bathroom. My heart is racing, palms sweaty, and breathing has returned to my lungs.

"Um, no. Hell no. This is so fucking embarrassing, J. I'm not doing this shit. Call Vic and get someone else." I move to the door when Carter calls out.

"Jewel?" I try to pull away from her grasp as she answers.

"Yeah, babe," she replies. We are passing hand swats while I steadily make my way to the door.

"Tell the new girl I want her working with you at every party." Suddenly the hand exchanges stop, and I stand there with my head turned to the side.

"Okay, boo. I'll add her to your list." She sticks her tongue out at me and I try to grab it.

"Maybe he likes the way you rubbed him down," she jokes. I punch her in the arm and go back to the bar area and take it among myself to set up the poker chips, putting the extra setups away.

Jewel and I are sitting at the bar chatting and laughing when Carter comes out joining us. He's in a white Polo shirt with khaki shorts that show off the hair on his tanned legs and his well-maintained feet, for a man anyway.

"What are you two giggling about?" he asks, signaling Jewel for a drink. I turn my attention away from the direction of his gaze and focus on my friend.

"Oh, Tiffany was discussing how rock hard your chest was when she was wiping you down." She passes him his drink and laughs out loud.

I'm gonna fuck her up tonight, I think.

"Oh, well, thank you." He tips his glass to me and takes a swig of his drink. "Ooh, yeah, that's a drink there. That's why I love you, baby. You always take care of me," he says placing a kiss on her cheek. I absolutely am not letting her crash at my house tonight. Our friend sleep over has been officially cancelled. She looks at me with doe eyes and I subtly flip her off pretending to scratch my eyebrow. A knock at the door alerts me to new arrivals so I walk behind the bar and take my position.

"So, you not talking to me?" Jewel asks face to face trying to fake me out. I just stand there and appear dead pan, unmoved by her funny faces or chewing her gum loudly, which is one thing I can't stand. Just as Carter and his guests come around the corner she catches me with a kiss.

"Girl, what the fuck are you doing?" I said breaking my vow of silence as laughter erupts.

"I can't have my best friend mad at me. I'm just trying to get you to loosen up a bit. You know, be fucking Tiffany motha-fuckin Lang! This snobby bitch, I don't like her."

"Whoa, Carter. Do we pay extra for this? Cause I'm all in," a gentleman said witnessing our exchange.

"Baby trust me. You don't have enough money to see me do anything. But what you can do is hand me your dollars and I can give you your chips for the night." I hold open my hand waiting for his deposit and he hands me a bank bag. Carter looks with a smile spanning from ear to ear as his other guests do the same. I hand them each their chips and Jewel gives them a drink before they go to the table.

"Oh, shit. I forgot my chips," I hear Carter say as they chatter about my no money for nookie comment. Feeling more comfortable, I step into my role.

"Mr. Carter, I got you," I say sashaying my sweet, untouchable ass over to the table. I place his chips in their slots for him and take up all the trays before returning back to the bar.

"That's my bitch," Jewel says while wiping down the counter and putting the snacks in their individual serving dishes.

"Well, I had to let them know this pussy isn't for sale, period." I peer out at the table and see them laughing and conversing about random things, but then he catches my unintentional stare and I can't break his hold. He smiles as he returns his focus on the game.

"Tiffany, did you hear me?"

"Uh, no. I was um, thinking about..."

"Carter? Don't fucking deny it. I see how you're looking at him. I see how he looks at you."

"What do you mean?"

"Let's just say, I've worked with Carter for about five months now and I've never seen him look at anyone like he stares at you. Not even me and hell, I'm a fucking ten plus ten." If Carter never checked my friend, who, by the way, makes dime pieces seem like pennies, the way she says he gazes at me, then something is wrong with him. But I had to take the bait.

"How does he look at me?"

"Like, you intrigue him, and he wants more." I give her the side eye. That's not what I expected to hear from her mouth. "What, I have to be fucking crass all the time?"

"Yes, you do," I reply with a bit of snip in my tone. I see Carter take the last swig of his drink and quickly fix him another one. Jewel stands there with a quiet smirk on her lips as she watches me take him his fresh replacement. The guys are quiet until one of them speaks up.

"Yo, C, man, aren't you going to introduce us to the new girl?" A gentleman with smooth mocha skin, pearly whites, and salt-n-pepper waves, asks smiling at me like I'm the last ribeye steak in Nevada. He has a distinguished appearance, in fact they all do. I figure they must all work together.

"Oh, um, I just met her, but I do believe her name is Tiffany. Tiffany, this is Damien, Jim, Micah, and Walter. They work for me at my firm."

"Hi, nice to meet you all. Can I refresh any of your drinks?" I shake each guys hand as we are introduced.

"Yeah, I'll have another beer."

"Make that two."

"I'll take a slow screw," The mouthy one, Walter, said while flashing his sexy smile.

"Well, that sounds like something your wife should be able to handle." They all laugh at my quick comeback. I can hear the comments like, 'man she's funny' or 'damn she's fine' and my favorite, 'how close are her and Jewel?' Probably thinking back to that quick kiss we shared when she was trying to get me to talk to her. I collect the drinks from Jewel and take them back to the table and hand them out per request. As soon as I hand Carter a glass of water with a lime and cherry, he gets a card dealt to him and he wins. By my calculations, that hand was about five thousand dollars.

"Wow, C, how'd you pull that Ace? That's almost an impossible hand to get."

"I guess my luck is changing." He looks at me and smiles. I take his empty glass, and bottles, clearing the table. Jewel brings the snack bowls she put together.

"The Jewel of the Nile," Micah says as he slides his hand across her firm round ass. She takes a seat in his lap and I witness him padding her bra with a few dollars from his pocket. I take it this is the guy she talks about on occasion but didn't introduce me to him or even give me his name. I return to the bar area and clean the glasses. She joins me shortly after, taking a seat on the other end, while watching the guys continue their poker night.

Throughout the evening, into the early morning, we continue to bring them drinks, exchange barbs, and flirt with the players. It did seem that every time I served Carter, which became frequent, he did win that hand. He gave me a one-hundred dollar chip each time. By my last count, I had seven of those black chips. I checked the time and it was nearing 3 a.m. and the guys were tapping out. They turn in their poker chips and receive their cash in exchange and I bid them good night, or day, as it is.

"So, you probably guessed that Micah is the other guy I kinda see. I know Vic's rule about dating guests, but we just couldn't help it. My car was in the shop one night and he gave me a lift home. We stopped, grabbed something to eat along the way, and we've been close ever since. " She looks at me expecting a snide comment, but I smile instead. As long as we've been friends, which has been since freshman year in college, she has bounced around from one guy to the next. To see her settled, somewhat, is an upgrade.

"Jewel, you ready?" Micah says as he stands at the bar. He's handsome, I must admit. All of them have that LA look about them. Like they should be in movies playing a lawyer and not actually, you know, lawyer-ing. Micah is tall, slim, with almond skin tone, light brown eyes, and dark hair. Okay, he's swoon worthy. I get why she's stuck on him.

"Sure, Micah. Let me grab my purse and take the bar total down to the cage."

"Okay, I'll pick you up out front. It was nice finally meeting you, Tiffany. You're all she talks about." He kisses her on the cheek and says bye to the others.

"Yeah, we're gonna head out too, Carter. See you next game night," Damien says as he, Jim, and Walter cash out. I lock the cash in the bag and begin to clean up as everyone exits, leaving me alone with him.

Chapter FIVE

I COLLECT THE POKER CHIPS, count them down so I can separate how much money goes back into his house account and put the rest back in the setups. I can feel his eyes on me and I want to ask him if there's something he needs, but I don't want to draw attention to myself. After all is complete, I grab my things, so I can get to the cage and then head home. This has been a long and exciting shift for me.

"Wait, come have a seat," he beckons.

"Uh, Mr. Jackson, I don't think that's a good idea." He shrugs his shoulders nonchalantly and his stance shifts to a defensive position.

"Why not?" I want to lay into his cocky attitude but since I already spilled a drink on him, I think I should save it for later and go for the subtle answer.

"For starters, I'm here in a work capacity and I don't want people to think I'm vying for special treatment or fraternizing." He laughs at my comment in a way that makes me feel insulted. I give him the "what's so funny" stare and he quickly retreats.

"Oh, you were serious. I understand how you'd think that may pose an issue, but I'm just asking you to have a simple drink with me. I mean, you deserve it after all the luck you bought me in tonight's game. I never win against those guys. So, come, sit. Let me pour you a drink and try not to spill it on you."

"Thanks, but the tips you gave me is gratitude enough," I reply.

"Please?" he says.

I hesitate for a moment, but the look in his eyes is enticing, inviting even. I close my eyes and convince myself one drink won't hurt before I sit in one of the chairs.

"Thank you. Now, what would you like to drink?" He asks as he relieves me of my purse and jacket.

"Um, I'll take a water with lemon," I reply.

"Tiffany, I asked you to sit for a drink, not a glass of water. Let's try this again. What do you want to drink?" His eyes are stern, and lips are pressed tightly.

"Tequila with pineapple, please."

"Now, see. That wasn't so hard," he says as he goes to the bar to fix the drinks. "I'll have my usual." He returns to me with drink in hand. "What music do you like to listen to?" he asks handing me my beverage. I take a sip and allow it to consume me for just a moment. It is the perfect blend of liquor and juice and by perfect, I mean more liquor and less juice.

"Um, I'm fine to listen to anything you want." His eyes roll slightly, and his lips begin to part but I quickly interject. "But I do love Jazz and R&B." I don't want to fall under his scorn again.

"Great, I like those too. Let me put some on to help you not appear so rigid." He plugs in his iPhone to the built-in stereo system and the sounds of soft, slow jazz begin to billow through the room. I continue to sip on my drink and he must notice that my glass is near empty and he brings me another one.

"I think you are trying to get secrets about the cash room out of me and I don't have them so no need to continue this alcohol assault." He laughs, and I can't help but chuckle.

"There's that sense of humor I saw earlier. What else?"

I take that as an invitation to tell him about myself. I pull a small sip from my glass before speaking.

"Well, you already know the main things, like I'm a woman and I work here. What else do you want?"

"Are you married?" He wastes no time getting to the big questions. I forgot he's an attorney.

"No. Divorced about eight months now." I take another sip hearing myself say those words for the first time to another person and the sound is surreal.

"Any kids?"

"Yeah, just one. His name is Xavier and he's seven."

"Seven? How long were you married?"

"Eight years. Yeah, after we got past the seven-year itch, I thought we had it made, at least that's how the old saying goes."

"Mind if I asked why it ended? I mean that's a long time to be with someone then just quit."

I become uncomfortable answering these questions that are so personal I decide to switch it up. "Yeah. I don't know you that well so, let's change the dial. Are you married? Any kids?"

He smiles at my redirect and raises his hands in surrender fashion. "Um, no never married and no kids. I do date often, or at least I did but I've never been in a seriously committed relationship." He downs the last of his drink and I watch his Adam's apple move with each swallow. My mind wonders to a sexy thought and I shut it down.

I glance at my watch to redirect my concentration and realize I need to get home. Xavier will be up soon, and we have our day planned. "It's getting late. I should get home to my sitter and son. Thank you for the drinks. Will you be here next weekend?" I use this as a way to establish boundaries, employee and guest.

"Actually, I'm in town for the next month or so due to various client obligations."

"Wow, you must be some lawyer. I've checked the cost of this villa per night and even with my discount, I still couldn't afford to stay here for one night, let alone two. But a month?"

"You're right. The at cost rate is high, but my clients bring a lot of business to this hotel. The type of clients that have multi-million-dollar contracts and or deals. Plus, my game nights bring in a fair amount of money as well."

"Well, it's something that I'd never be able to afford. Not anymore, anyway. Well, have a good night, Mr. Jackson," I say turning on my heel and head toward the door to leave. The brief stop to open the door allows him enough time to catch up with me.

"Tiffany, uh, I'd be lying if I didn't say I do have an ulterior motive of asking you to stay a few minutes and that my line of questioning didn't have purpose."

"Okay. Did you need me to work an event for one of your clients?" I say presumptively. He smiles and shakes his head slightly before looking back to me. I notice his cheeks are flush and he seems to be somewhat nervous.

"No. I wanted to ask you if you'd join me for dinner sometime this week? I realize that you don't know much about me except that I'm an entertainment lawyer, unattached, with no kids, who likes to play poker. I get that you are a divorcee with child, that works here as a cocktail server and my personal good luck charm. I understand if you say no, but please be aware that I won't stop until you say yes. So, will you?"

"Why do you want to take me out to dinner?" I ask with caution. The debate is still at war in my mind.

"Well, I like to eat, and I prefer to do it with the company of a beautiful woman."

I blush and turn my head giving away my innocence. When I return my attention toward him, he's standing closer but leaning against the wall. His shirt is untucked from his shorts and his belt is undone. He has dimples in his cheek when he smiles, and those lips of his are plump. *What the hell was in that drink?* I think to myself as I realize I'm aware of his looks.

"Mr. Jackson…"

"That's another thing, call me Carter. Mr. Jackson is a bit too formal," He interrupts.

"Mr. Jackson, you just told me that you date often, so why would I go out to dinner with you?"

"Because you're hungry and I asked." He smiles.

I tilt my head to the side like I was staring at a science project. *He must bleach his teeth* I think continuing to inspect this man standing before me. I remove my detective mind and focus on the question before me. "How about I counter with coffee instead?"

He looks at me with a smile when I present a different option. "Fine, coffee it is. When do you want to go?"

"I'll meet you Sunday morning, 9 a.m. at the spot on Sunset."

"Great. That's one of my favorites when I come to town."

"Mine too. I usually go there after I drop my son off at school and gain some perspective."

"Wonder how I've never seen you before." His eyes grab my attention and for a moment hold me captive.

"Who knows, we might have but didn't notice." I reply. There's a significant surge of electricity pulsating between us, and I want to follow its path. I instead, smile and put a little more distance between us allowing the charge to fade.

"I really need to get going. See you Sunday?" I question for certainty but mainly to remove the tension.

He pulls out his phone. "Here, put your number in my phone and I will call so you will have my number," he requests.

I pull out my phone and hand it to him. "Okay. Seems easy enough." I enter my number and press dial. My phone rings capturing his number, and he saves it in my contacts and I lock in mine on his before we exchange phones.

"Okay. I got you all locked in. Sunday," he says taking a step back with a sigh of relief.

"Okay, Sunday." I turn to open the door, but he interferes and opens it for me.

"Well, drive carefully," he says finding a reason to extend this moment. This has turned pleasantly awkward.

"I will. Thank you. I look forward to your call." I reach to shake his hand just as he was attempting to come in for a hug and I accidentally brush up against his junk. Now if things weren't already uneasy they have now just skyrocketed to embarrassing.

"Oh! I'm so sorry. Oh, my God, you must think I'm a moron or something. I swear I wasn't trying to touch your package." He begins to laugh while I'm standing in complete shock.

"Tiffany, it's okay. You didn't junk punch me, so it's fine. No harm no foul." He extends his hand and I carefully meet his with my own and we shake. My eyes can't help but glance at the area I nearly assaulted and he has a little bulge showing. I wonder if I caused that reaction.

"Well, goodnight, Carter," I say as we continue to shake hands.

"Goodnight, Tiffany. See you soon." I pull away and head toward the main casino.

"Tiffany!" A voice calls. I pause with my hand on my pepper spray and turn to see that it is him.

"Yes, Carter."

"Can I ask you to at least text me to say you made it home safe? I don't want to sound crazy or anything."

"Yes, I will let you know when I make it home. Thanks for the concern."

"Well, I have to make sure you'll be able to have coffee with me."

"Yes, of course. Good night." I enter the main casino where I turn in the unused poker chips and cash in my tips before heading home.

"Ms. Lang, you are home a little later than usual," Ashley says.

"Oh sorry. We discussed an event for the upcoming week and lost track of time."

"Oh. Is it a special event?" I hand her the pay for the evening plus a little extra. I think about my impending date on Sunday.

"No. Nothing special. Are you available on weekend mornings, if needed?"

"It's possible. Just let me know, Ms. Lang. I'm sure I will be available." I glance around and notice that the Lego's were out tonight and can't help but wonder what they created.

"Thank you for watching Xai. Was he a good boy?"

"Of course. His father stopped by for a few minutes to bring him a new backpack."

"Oh, that Iron Man bag he ordered must have come in finally."

"Yeah, that and he left this letter for you." She hands me a white linen envelope with my name written in the middle.

"Goodnight, Ms. Lang," she calls from the foyer. I rush to meet up with her and to ensure that she gets into her car safely. We live so far out from anyone the only threat is the occasional wildlife wondering by. I close and lock the door and proceed to continue my usual check of the house securing all doors and windows before peeking in on Xavier. I see him sleeping wildly in his bed with his new backpack on the floor full of the things that came from his other bag. I pull his door halfway then go to my room where I undress and throw on my jammies thinking I'll shower in the morning. I retrieve the mysterious envelope from my nightstand and open it to read its contents.

My eyes slim and I feel my mouth tighten reading over the words spilled onto the paper in my hand.

I can't believe he's doing this. Corey has decided that he will not be able to take Xavier to his games on Saturday since his new wife signed up for Lamaze classes. This now means that I will have to plan for the sitter to possibly take him or give up my Friday nights at the casino. I fall back onto my pillow in angst wanting to call him and give him a piece of my mind until my message alert goes off breaking my anger.

Carter: I take it you made it home or you are stranded somewhere.

I smile when I see this message and I can't think of anything but him. I actually thought of him all the way home. His smile, his wit, his generosity. Of course, his looks.

Me: I think you're stalking me.

I wait to see if he replies and after five minutes, I counted, he did.

Carter: LOL! I want you, but not like that.

Me: Then how? Wait, don't answer. We just met. We can talk more over coffee, Sunday.

Carter: Oh, so you're not going to back out?

Me: No. I'm a woman of my word.

Carter: Okay. I'm going to hold you to it. Goodnight.

Me: Goodnight.

Chapter
SIX

XAVIER AND I SPENT SATURDAY VEGGING out at home. I needed the rest and he wanted to work on his free throws in the back yard instead of going to the movies, which was fine with me. I explained to him that I had a coffee date this morning, and he was happy. He said that his mom should go out and meet a new man. Sometimes I wonder who the parent really is in this relationship.

"Mom, you can't keep him waiting. That's rude," he says as he enters my bathroom and sits on the edge of the counter watching me put on my minimal makeup. I already showered and dressed in a pair of jeans that fit just right, a cold shoulder embroidered top, and paired it with some black, strappy-heeled sandals.

"You don't even know this guy," I say to him in an argumentative tone.

"I know that if you said yes, he must be nice," he says back to me in defense.

"He is," I say in response conceding that my kid is right.

"So, hurry up. Nice guys don't like to wait." I look at the little rugrat and figure he's trying to hide something from me.

"What are you up to, little one?"

He shrugs his shoulders and shakes his head from side to side. "Mom, I'm not up to anything. I just want to see you happy like dad's happy." I pull him in for a hug. Maybe he doesn't have a hidden agenda. The doorbell rings and he takes off running down the hall.

"Hi, Ashley," I hear him say when he swings the door open and I walk out to greet her. She comes in with her backpack and dough-nuts from the shop near the strip. Now I see why he was excited as she pulls a new Lego expansion set from her backpack.

"Good morning, Ms. Lang. I hope you don't mind but I bought Xavier something for his collection.

"Morning, Ashley. That's fine. I appreciate you coming on a Sunday morning."

"It's okay. I'm usually studying anyway. That's why I bought my books with me." She gives me the once over and smiles when her eyes meet mine again. "Wow, you look great for just a cup of coffee," she comments.

"Oh. Is it too much? I don't want to give the wrong impression."

"No, ma'am. Maybe this will turn into a lunch date."

"It's not a date. It's just coffee." I keep making a fuss with my hair and then remove my lip gloss and reapplying one with a tint.

"Mom, go," Xavier says as he urges me toward the door. I grab my wristlet and key fob before walking out. Once I get in my car I sit and think for a moment. *Do I really want to go through with this?* I'm not being indecisive, but this is a big step, even if it is just coffee. Fuck it! I push the start button on my car and pull out heading to the cafe on Sunset.

CARTER JACKSON

SHE'S NOT COMING, I THINK checking my watch. I stir my coffee for the fifth time since it was delivered ten minutes ago. I take chances with my clients daily. Advising them on what to do, what not to do, how to avoid public embarrassment and I get paid well for my services. I represent some of the hottest stars in the entertainment and sports industry today. I have my own firm and can date any woman I want, but here I am sitting in a small coffee shop waiting like a lovesick loon.

The ding from the bell hanging over the door alerts to its opening as guests enter or leave. I watch eagerly hoping to see her green eyes, but like I've done the last one hundred times, I turn away when I learn that the bell is not ringing for her. I have no idea why I'm acting this way. Hell, even she questioned my motives. I don't even know what I'm going to say if she does come. I absent-mindedly go back to stirring the now cold coffee.

"Ahem. Do you always keep your head down in a public place?" That sweet voice beckons to me and I tilt my head toward its direction. *She's here.*

"Oh, I didn't see you come in. Please have a seat." I stand and pull her chair out allowing her to sit before pushing her in slightly. Taking my seat, I signal for the waitress.

"Thank you. Sorry I was running a bit behind. I had to stop and gas up. In my laziness yesterday, I forgot. Should've text you so you wouldn't worry or think I stood you up," she explains.

"I must admit, I was beginning to think you did. No matter how difficult that is to believe."

"What? No woman stands up Mr. Carter Jackson?" She smiles, and my heart skips a beat looking at her plump lips.

"No, not really." I joke.

She laughs, and I can tell her body relaxes a little more.

"Hi. What can I get you?" The waitress asks Tiffany.

"I'll have a mocha latte with a drizzle of caramel please," she requests.

"Okay. Sir want me to touch up your coffee?"

"Uh, no. I'll have a fresh one, please. I think I killed this one with all the stirring I was doing."

"Yes sir." The waitress scoots off to retrieve the coffee orders and I try to figure out what to say. I mean I asked for this. Actually, I asked for dinner and *she* suggested coffee.

"So, tell me about your firm, Carter. What do you do, exactly?" This is the question that will tell me if I even remotely have a chance with her or if I'll be used to get to one of my clients, which has happened on occasion.

"Well, as we briefly discussed, I'm an entertainment lawyer. I represent some of the music and sports industries top names or brands, if you will."

"Oh. I thought that you like did business with the casino bringing clients to them. Well, that job must keep you busy."

"It does. That's why I come here during my down time so that I can relax and do some non-work-related things."

"That's right. You live in LA. Well, it goes to reason you're involved in the industry since that is where you live."

"Isn't that geography-ism? Assuming that because I live in LA, I must be involved with entertainment things?" We both laugh and now I'm becoming more relaxed.

"I think you mean regional discrimination, and yes, it was wrong of me to assume that you'd be involved with Hollyweird based on the sole fact that you live there. I apologize." She flutters those beautiful green eyes in a playful attempt to look innocent and suddenly I pray that she's a bad girl.

"Actually I don't live in LA," I reply.

"You don't? Where do you stay?" Her eyes widen with anticipation as she waits on my answer.

"I live in Pasadena, actually. I wanted to get away from all the busy hustle and bustle."

"Oh, yeah. Pasadena is nice. I have a few relatives that live out there. Can I ask you a question?" The open dialogue is flowing smoothly, and she seems to have a genuine interest in me.

"Shoot," I respond curious to know what's on her mind.

"If you're here, who's minding the store?" *Oh yeah, she's interested.*

"I have partners, like those you met Friday, paralegals and other associates that help my business run smoothly while I'm away. Plus, I'm always available." She bobs her head in understanding and I delve further into her mind. "Oh, what about you? I can tell cocktail waitress was not your first choice of occupation."

"Yeah, you're right. My degree is in forensic accounting. If there is money to be found, I will find it. But, since I graduated college, I've only mastered being a stay at home mom. Not that I don't mind. Best seven years of my life. I also didn't plan on getting a divorce either." I can still see the hurt in her eyes when she speaks of her marriage ending. She told me it has been eight months since it was final, but you can tell that it still bothers her. I want to find the fucker and thank him for letting her go, because it's obvious he didn't deserve her. Then kick the shit out of him for hurting her. The waitress brings our coffee and Tiffany takes that first sip and closes her eyes as she allows it to awaken her taste buds. She put the cup down and has a bit of a caramel, whip-cream, mustache going on. I chuckle a bit until she looks at me with a questioning glare.

"Um, you have leftovers on your lip." She licks her upper lip slowly trying to remove the sugary trail from her lip. Little does she know, she's lighting a fire trail in my pants.

"Mmm...is it gone?" she asks. If she's speaking of my chub, no. But the coffee is.

"Yes, you managed to get it all." I pass her a wet nap from my side of the condiment tray on the table to help with the cleanup.

"Thank you," she replies as she accepts. "I have to admit. I had reservations about this coffee thing and almost backed out. But really, that's not why I was running late. I thought about this all day yesterday and my son convinced me I should go."

"Smart kid. I like him already," I gloat seeing how it was that little push that got her here today.

"You do? You'd think differently if you knew him." She laughs.

"Well, tell me about him, if you don't mind." I can see the hesitation in her eyes, but it soon dissipates as she begins to talk about her son and his interests. She mentions that he loves basketball and I happen to represent one of his favorite players, JD or James Durant. I make a mental note to get him here for a talk with the little league basketball team and a few photo ops with Xavier. I don't mention it to her because I have to get him to agree and I want it to be a surprise.

"He sounds amazing. You say he's into science?"

"Yes. I love that he has such broad interests than I had growing up. What about you? What are your interests?" This may be my one chance to tell her that nothing has had my attention the way she does. I'm not trying to run her off, though.

"Well, my clients keep me going. Each day is something interesting. In fact, how would you like to go with me to a pop-up party? It's a 90's style soiree so dress accordingly."

Her eyes actually light up. "Yes! I'd love to go." Those words spill out like musical notes from a symphony.

"Gr- great!" I stammer out. I was expecting a hard no or another counter offer with coffee. I can tell she's very guarded of her heart and her family, so this really shocked me. I glance at my watch and see that we have been sitting here for three hours making mindless conversation, talking random facts, and getting acquainted with each other. She catches my glance and checks her phone in response.

"Oh, my. I didn't expect to be out this long. I guess time does fly when you're having fun."

"Well, we can hang out longer. There's this great restaurant nearby. We can go grab lunch, if you want."

"I would, but my sitter has other plans for the evening. So that means I should be heading home now." The sting of her leaving me hits me a little and I give, this time.

"Okay. Let me walk you to your car."

I place enough money on the table to cover the coffee and tip and escort her outside, cautiously placing my hand along her back. She doesn't move or ask me to stop. I separate once we reach the parking lot away from the crowd of people making their way inside the establishment. I can tell that we have approached her car when the parking lights flash twice as the remote start is engaged.

"Wow, you're in a hurry to leave me, huh? Am I that bad of a date?" I ask, making light of the fact she started her car.

"No way. That's out of habit when I leave a public place. When I'm within a certain distance, I start my car, so I don't have to fumble around with the keys to open the door. You are actually a pleasant date."

"Since you liked the first one, how about we go on a real one. Dinner sometime this week? Well, not Saturday. That's when the party is happening."

"I'd have to check my son's practice schedule and make some arrangements, but sure. Dinner sounds good." She smiles big and it melts my heart. *Am I wrong for thinking that this woman is into me?* I wonder internally. She hits the unlock button on her door and I open it allowing her to climb in, strapping her seat belt on, and positioning her hands on the steering wheel before I gently close the door. She lets down the window and we exchange our final words.

"I guess I'll see you this week sometime," I say, leaning into her window space dragging out the inevitable goodbye.

"Yeah. Maybe I'll see you around the casino," she replies. I don't normally go to the floor when I'm in town. I usually don't have time, but if it means I get a chance to see her, I'll try to come out of hiding more often.

"Or you can come visit me," I suggest.

"I could if you were having an event or something, but not socially and definitely not while I'm on the clock." She reminds me of the policy of not getting involved with the guests.

"But you will have dinner with me this week, right?"

"Yes. And go to the 90's party as your guest. I'll be off the clock and no one can say anything." She pats my hand and allows hers to linger on top for a few seconds. I take her hand and put it to my mouth placing a soft gentle kiss on the back of it before letting it go. I see a streak of pale pink flash across her cheek bone as she turns away and hides from her smile.

"Okay, then. I'll see you around." I back away from the window to allow her to leave.

"I'll text you when I make it back home," she says before pulling off and heading down Sunset. I watch her make it to the traffic light at the intersection before I walk to my car and go back to my room to get some work done for the evening.

Chapter
SEVEN

TIFFANY

"Hi, mommy. You were gone for a long time. Did you have fun?" Xavier greets me when I enter the house.

"I did have a pleasant time. How did you behave for Ashley?"

"On my best behavior, of course." He grins his little snag a tooth smile which catches me by surprise since he had all of his teeth when I left home earlier.

"What happened to your tooth? Did it finally come out?"

"Yes! When I was eating my apple, I bit down, and it took it right on out. It didn't hurt." My little man is growing up right in front of my eyes. It makes me think that I do need to start thinking about dating. Carter is definitely a man I'd date. He seems nice, gentle, caring and lawd is that man is fine. I try not to be obvious of my attraction when I'm around him, but I'm sure that is not going over well.

"Ashley, thank you for watching my little cupcake. Here is your pay for the day. What is your schedule for this week and Saturday?"

"No mommy, not Saturday. I'll be at dad's this weekend." Xavier kindly reminds me. That helps ease the pressure of going out.

"Oh, so do you have another date?" Ashley says as she smiles big.

"In fact, I do. Two this week. Dinner one day during the week and a party on Saturday."

"Ooh, is it with the coffee man?" Ashley asks. I can't help but laugh at her innocence and attempt at humor. She's a young adult, but I choose not to share too much with her. But then again, in the event of an emergency, she'd need to know some key information.

"Yes, it will be with the coffee man. I will share his details with you once our date is confirmed in case something urgent comes up."

"Okay. I look forward to your call, Ms. Lang. I'll see you sometime this week, little man." She stoops to hug Xavier before grabbing her bag and walking towards the door. I go with her going over the things they did today and checking if she needed anything extra for school or whatever. I have grown fond of Ashley. She comes from the average family. Her mother is an elementary teacher and her dad works as a banker. She has a younger brother who is in his second year of college studying to become a veterinarian. She uses the money from babysitting to pay off her car since her scholarships take care of her school expenses. She has a great head on her shoulders and she works well with my Xavier. I watch her drive off and I return to the house to start dinner and prepare for the week. I take out the things to make dinner and begin to prep. Xavier comes in and sits at the island and watches me. His expression says he has something on his little genius mind.

"Whatcha thinking about?" I ask chopping up my cilantro and onions.

"Mm, nothing." He lets out the most adorable sigh and I stop what I'm doing and take a seat next to him with my glass of water.

"Okay, that's not a nothing, sigh. What's going on?"

"I was thinking. Dad is married to Nessa and I wondered if you get married to the coffee man I will have two families. And you'd have a baby too." I did a spit take onto my floor when he dropped the baby bomb on me. I grab a paper towel and begin to clean up my mess. He didn't laugh at what's possibly my best faux pas ever which is evident of a serious concern for him.

"Baby, you arc thinking too far ahead. I just met Carter and we've only had coffee this morning. I may go on two dates with him this week, but that doesn't mean I'm going to marry him and have more kids. You have nothing to worry about."

"Oh, I'm not worried, mom. I just think it'll be great. Then you and dad can stop fighting so much." Every time Corey and I get together, we can't have a normal conversation without it escalating to the anger filled emotions that tend to spill out in our words. Although we try not to show it in front of our child, there are times that it does happen. Because of that, we limit our time around each other to five minutes. That's about how long it takes his wife to become concerned that I'm trying to take my husband back, or he hits on me. I nearly fell for it last month, I mean, he's still charming and fine, but I had to break his hold over me. I think that's why it was so easy for me to go out with Carter this morning.

"Your dad and I are fine. I know that the fighting bothers you and I promise that I will not allow my anger to take over my words anymore. Okay?"

"I just want you to be happy too, mom."

"As long as I have you, that's all the happiness I need, little man." I place a kiss on to his forehead before returning to the other side of the island and finish chopping my veggies and spices.

"So, will I get to meet him?" I'm super protective of my offspring. I won't allow just anyone around him. Even Ashley had to consent to a full background check. But he does bring up a good question. Would I let Carter into my circle?

"I'm not sure. It's possible." I take a swallow of my water wishing it was wine.

"I think I should meet the person who is dating my mom."

"We're not dating, son." I reiterate.

"Are you two going to dinner this week and going out on Saturday while I'm at dad's?"

"Yes, but..."

"That sounds like a date, mom." His little mind and smart mouth is right. We did go on a date of sorts and I agreed to see him again without hesitation or reserves. I don't respond but instead I take the chicken breast that I had defrosting overnight in the refrigerator out and wash them preparing to make his favorite meal, chicken flautas. I put them on to boil with a little seasoning and gather the other items I need to complete this meal. My kitchen is like my personal sanctuary. When I'm stressed I cook. When I'm thinking, I bake. This situation has me straddling the fence of the two so along with tonight's dinner, I'm going to add key-lime pie for dessert.

"Mom, you're making a pie too?" Xavier questions as he sees me take out my glass pie dish, graham crackers crumbs, and other items.

"Yeah, I'm in the mood for pie. Aren't you?"

"Sweet! I'm gonna make sure I eat all my food off my plate." He runs off to the living room and continues to play with his new Lego's. Meanwhile, I start prepping my tortillas and I put my side dishes on so that they can cook in conjunction with the main course. My phone rings and thanks to my friend, I have an Echo in my kitchen that is connected to my phone. I say answer aloud since I'm in the middle of shredding chicken.

"Hey, I assume you made it home?" his voice calls from the speaker. I freeze for a moment when I realize just how sexy he sounds.

"Oh, hey Carter," I manage to stammer out. "How are you this evening?"

"Oh, I just woke up from a nap. Had a coffee date this morning with the most beautiful woman I've ever laid eyes on." I blush at his comment before thinking of something snarky to say.

"Oh, this must've been after we had coffee. I looked a hot mess this morning." Xavier hears the conversation we have going on and sneaks in behind me.

"Hi!" he exclaims so innocent yet nosily.

"Hey, there little man. You must be Xavier," Carter replies his tone perking up and not so sensual.

"Yes I am. Are you the man that took my mommy out for coffee today?"

"Yeah, that's me. I hope it was okay."

"It was. She needs to get out more." I hear Carter laugh and a rush of embarrassment floods my face.

"And on that note, goodbye Xavier. Go clean up your toys." I demand. "Sorry 'bout that," I say to Carter when I return to my call.

"No problem. I like the little guy. So, what are you doing?"

"I'm making dinner. What are you doing?"

"Reviewing some emails and getting some contracts together for my clients." I roll and stick a toothpick in each of the flautas and prepare the oil for cooking while listening to him describe his day. "I really enjoyed this morning," he mentions amid our conversation.

"I have to admit it was nice. I hadn't enjoyed the company of another man in quite some time. So, where are you taking me for dinner Wednesday night?"

"I thought we'd go over to South Point and eat at the restaurant there. It's nice, cozy, away from wondering eyes so no one can go back and say they saw us together. What do you think?" I hesitate to answer for a minute because that place is costly. I should know, Jewel, myself and a few others went there to celebrate my twenty-seventh birthday two years ago.

"I hope I don't have to put out for this date," I say in a jokingly manner...he didn't catch it.

"I wouldn't expect you to sleep with me because I take you to a nice restaurant." His voice raises, and his anger shows up slightly.

"I was joking, Carter. I know you are not that kind of guy." He calms but I can tell that kind of joking isn't tolerated by him. *Oh, he's chivalrous.*

"So, what are you making over there. Sounds like you are cooking a holiday meal."

"Oh, I'm making my sons favorite, chicken flautas, with sides and a key-lime pie for dessert."

"All of that in one night?"

"Yeah. Sunday is our big dinner night."

"Man, I haven't had a home cooked meal in a while. I mean, I'm on the go so much, there's no need for me to put groceries in my house." I wonder if that is just a random fact he wants to share or if he's hinting around that he wants to come over. I'm about to go with the last thought when he interrupts. "Tiffany, I have to take this call. I just wanted to say hi and goodnight. I'll be in touch."

"Oh. Okay, well talk to you later." We disconnect our call and I notice I've prepared the whole meal. I call for Xavier to wash his hands and I plate up dinner setting it at the table. After saying thanks, he tears into his food and makes the most dramatic face when he takes his first bite.

"Mommy this is soo good," he proclaims. I just shake my head and say thank you, staring across the table thinking that one day, we will have a dinner guest.

IT'S 12:45 P.M. WHEN I PULL into work. I enter the casino and greet everyone as they speak to me while walking to the dressing room. I stop by the cage to see where I'll be stationed tonight so that I know what lip liner I should rock. My bar is covered by Casey so that means I'm back in the dollar slot section. I choose green glittered body lotion and do minimal make up but enough to make my eyes pop and my lips look juicy. I've made some pretty big tips with this combination. I let my hair free today in its natural state and this surprises Jewel when she comes in.

"Oh, my. Werk it hunty!" She snaps her fingers in an exaggerated fashion just to get her point across. "Yasss, my boo is ready," she adds.

"Girl, please. It's not that serious."

"Bitch, you are glowing. Did you get you some random dick this weekend?"

I laugh at her bluntness before answering. "No, bitch. I just had a good weekend with your godchild." I hand her a container with the flautas and sides and one with a slice of pie.

She takes them excitedly then she looks at me while I fluff out my curls. "Uh, no ma'am. You baked on a Sunday and it's not even a holiday? Who is it?"

I act like I have no idea what she's talking about and maintain my stance. "Jewel, there isn't anyone. I just felt like making a pie."

"Yeah, right. And Casey and I are just friends. Strictly friends with no eight inches of dick involved."

"Jewel, seriously… Wait eight?" I stop mid comment when my mind catches on to what she just said.

"Yes, and it's thick." She makes a circle with her fingers showing how thick he is, and we take a moment to thank God for a package like that before I turn back to the previous conversation.

"But, no. I'm not dating or even talking to anyone." She's not easy to keep things from. She's been my ride or die for the last twelve years. She was there when I met, married, had a baby for, and then divorced Corey. She has an IT degree and was working her way through college when she found this job. She freelances on the side for small businesses, helping them set up their security to protect their client's information. I remember when she told me one day the register system wasn't working and she, being the computer geek, had it fixed without calling the casino's IT team. It's also sad that she could get into the mainframe without much effort.

"I see. You just don't want to tell me. It's cool. Just remember I always find out." She blows herself a kiss in the mirror before going out to her section. Soon after, I walk out behind her and go start my shift.

As the afternoon progresses, the crowds begin to pick up. Most tourist tend to come in on Monday's, Thursday's, and the weekends trying to live out those infamous scenes in movies. The last hurrah men, the spring breakers, the group of older men looking for a reminder of the younger years, and my favorite, the divorce parties. Those ladies let loose and they have fun. They usually meet one of the last hurrah guys and leave the hotel tip-toeing with shades covering their eyes.

"Hey, Jewel, I haven't seen Tex in a few weeks. Is everything okay?" I ask because he at least leaves a message for her with the cage or Vic.

"I haven't received any messages, but he did say that he was going to be busy. I miss that old man," she sulks in her seat at the bar and I give her a rub on her shoulder. Casey sneaks in a kiss and suddenly she's back to herself.

"Okay, let's go flaunt our asses for these tips." She takes her tray and I follow behind her. We usually split the slot rows working on the opposite of each other. A group of men here from a convention have two rows occupied and they have been keeping us busy. Sure, we deal with catcalls, suggestive comments, and the occasional touching of our assets, but this bunch was a little more handsy than normal.

"Excuse me, pretty," a gentleman calls to me from his machine.

"Yes, sir. What can I get for you?" I manage to ask through a plastic smile. I place the handheld on the serving tray preparing to take his order when he grabs me closer to him, his hand firmly gripping my ass. This arrogant asshole isn't even drunk. He's been ordering sparkling water all evening.

"Well, for starters, you can get down on your knees and pleasure me while I sit here." He laughs at his comment thinking that it's funnier than degrading. A few of his friends join in the laughter and I roll my eyes pulling away from his grip.

"Sir, that comment will get you what you really don't want to happen. Did you need my service or not? I do have other people waiting." At this point I don't care if my attitude begins to show. One thing I can't stand is these young guys, no matter the skin color, who come in here and think that they can just harass us like we are cheap whores. By the way the cheap whores are working the street corner across the street.

"Oh, no, doll. I'm just kidding. Yeah, so bring my buddy another beer, and that one needs a refresher on his rum and coke." He pulls out a twenty and seductively rubs it against my breasts and down to my crotch before standing to stuff it into my shorts like I'm a stripper. "How about you and me hook up a little later? There's a lot more where that came from. I'm sure I have more money than you've ever seen and can buy you whatever you want." His breath is within inches of my ear and he manages to sneak in a free rub of my pussy before I push him off me. He goes to confront me, but a hand from behind him manages to stop his forward progression. I look and see Carter standing there. His eyes are dark and his face scowls from anger.

"I don't think the lady cares for you touching her in her private areas and I'm pretty sure that shove was her polite way to tell you to fuck off. When you felt the need to apply a band-aid to your embarrassed ego and retaliate, that's where I step in. As her attorney, I will advise you to remove yourself from the premises before I file a harassment claim against you that your great-grand kids won't be able to pay off your debts." The security team arrives to escort this scumbag and his entourage out. Jewel stands by for support and Vic is there to take pictures to post on the wall of shame. They will still deal with some legal issues stemming from this matter and I will have to make a statement, but the way Carter stepped up, well, that only increased his stock value with me.

"Are you okay?" he asks taking my hand in his. His eyes stare into mine and I turn away from his direct gaze. Jewel smiles when she sees my reaction and turns to walk away, not before speaking and fully letting me know she figured out the secret.

"Hi, Carter," she says giving him a friendly two second hug.

"Hey, Jewel. Do you mind if I speak to Tiffany alone for a moment? I need to advise her on a few legal things."

"Oh, sure. Legal things. Yeah, I gotcha." She smiles and winks at me as she walks away carrying both our trays and handhelds. I know I will find her at the station and will have to answer questions.

"Thank you for stepping in. You didn't have to do that," I say pushing a curly strand of hair behind my ear with my head bowed. He pulls it back into its place and allows his hand to linger for a quick second on the side of my face before removing it.

"Well, I saw how things were going and it was only right for me to do something." I glance at him and offer a smile and he returns the gesture.

"What are you doing here anyway?" I ask realizing he's on the casino floor.

"I actually wanted to see you. I had only arrived just before that guy touched you inappropriately."

"Yeah, what a fucking creep. I just want to take a hot bath and wash the thought of his breath and hands on me away."

"I bet. You can use the tub in my suite if you want," he offers.

"Carter, we are not at the bathing at each other's place level just yet."

"Oh, but we will get there? Is that what you're saying?" I laugh at his cute play on my words. He could be right. This guy before me makes me feel warm inside. Not the sexual way but feeling that empty void way. Our conversation on Sunday ranged from jobs, relationships, future plans, and a random question and answer about each other's likes and dislikes. I was comfortable which is something I hadn't been in a while. Not even when I was married, before Corey's dick slip, did I feel this way. I guess the marriage was doomed to fail after a while. All the signs were there I just never paid them any attention. My mind was always on Xavier.

"Let's take it slow and start with dinner first on Wednesday, okay?" He throws his head back and lets out a little grunt before looking back to me.

"Fine, I can wait. I have calls to make so I will go. If you need me for anything, Tiffany, call me. I'll be there." He places a small innocent peck on my cheek and puts that twenty-dollar bill from the jerk into the slot machine. "Here, let's see if you can take this bad thing and turn it good?" I press the button and hit on the first spin multiplying that twenty by ten. I cash out and give the slip to him to donate to his charity. This warms his heart and he smiles as he tucks the slip into his pocket. Suddenly, I'm looking forward to Wednesday.

Chapter

EIGHT

CARTER IS RELENTLESS IN HIS pursuit of me. He has done little things like send me flowers at work, anonymously of course, but Jewel knows who they came from. He had the car wash guys clean and detail my car on Tuesday and a lunch delivered for all the cocktail staff with a note attached saying we are appreciated and never should feel devalued. It's endearing if you ask me, but others tease, and it's only been two days since grope gate. Tonight is our first real date not to mention the first one I've been on since my freshman year in college. I'm a little nervous, to be honest. I asked for Wednesday and Saturday off from Vic so that I can have a day of preparation. Carter text me earlier to confirm the plans for tonight and wanting to send a car to pick me up. I understand he's being chivalrous and all, but the way I am about my privacy, especially around my child, I convinced him to meet at the casino parking garage instead. That way security's near and I mean for all I know, he could turn out to be a serial killer that's never been caught.

After spending the morning getting Xavier to school and

texting Ashley to confirm that she will be at the house by 6 p.m., I decide to go shopping for a dress to wear this evening. I have plenty of clothes, but I want something new for this occasion. I found a halter style body con with high collar neckline and mesh panel insert online and had the store to hold it for me to pick up a little later. Now that I have the dress, it's time to go get my hair and nails done. Even a little make-up.

My genetic make-up is one that is a bit confusing to most. I'm Creole, Native American, and Black, even though I identify as the latter. My family hails from New Orleans on my daddy's side and Oklahoma on my mother's. Most people mistake me for the traditional interracial race of black and white, but, I'm not. My daddy has that smooth sandy brown and wavy hair and green eyes like mine. My mother has smooth dark chocolate skin with cold black long hair that most women pay high dollar for nowadays. My hair has soft long natural curls and I usually wear it as such. My parents met when my dad went to his friend's wedding in Texas. My mother was one of the bridesmaids. He told me he was so scared to ask my mother to dance, because her stare could stop a man in his tracks if they came too close. But he did it anyway and the rest was history. They currently reside back home in New Orleans, which is where I was born.

When I have a special occasion, I go to the salon to get all dolled up instead of doing it myself. Jewel normally accompanies me, but today she's spending it with Casey. They made a turn in their relationship and have agreed to make it exclusive, not that they weren't behaving as such anyway. I guess it was to solidify their obvious relationship. After my wash, blow dry with heat protectant, and flat iron for a sleek look, I go to the nail salon for a French manicure and a quick tweeze of my eyebrows. The last stop is at the Ulta store on my way home for a few new makeup necessities. Corey is going to pick up Xavier today and bring him home after practice and meet Ashley here. I told all three of them to tell when he is at home in order for me to have peace of mind. Corey did his usual prying into my life and I completely closed the door on that subject. Ashley agreed to send me video detail of when Xavier arrives, and when I dropped the little prince off at school, he told me to just go have a good dinner and not worry about him. He'll never understand until he has kids of his own, but I appreciate him pushing me into the dating world.

I start my getting ready routine which consists of a relaxing bath with chamomile and a safe way to protect my straightened hair from frizzing. I lean back against my bath pillow and begin, the text message notification sounds. I grab it from the bathroom floor and see if it's Corey with a schedule change. That would be like him to ruin my date.

Carter: Hi. What are you doing?

To my surprise, Carter was the reason for my phone alert.

Me: Taking a bath. What are you doing?

I hit send and realize that telling him that I'm currently naked, may not be the best thing.

Carter: Well, I was looking at some emails and finalizing some things, so I can get ready for our date, but now you've given me something else to think about. (Smiley face emoji)

The embarrassment washes over me and I begin to sweat. I try my best to calm down and keep my curls at bay.

Me: Sorry. I shouldn't have said what I did. I'm looking forward to tonight. Are you?

Carter: Yes. It's been a hectic couple of days.

Especially when one of your clients is facing
yet another paternity suit. It's not the girls
who aren't loyal, if you ask me, but that's
what he pays me for. Good kid, just poor
decisions.

My heart skips when I tie the context clues together. Due to
confidentiality he can't discuss anything directly about his work
and I have the same NDA for my job since a lot of celebrities
frequent the establishment.

Me: Well, tonight, we will leave work at work
and enjoy a meal together. Maybe talk flowers
and beaches. Something away from your line
of work.

Carter: I'm sure we'll find something.

Me: Well, I'll see you soon. Bye.

Carter: See you soon.

We end the text conversation, I finish my bath and get
dressed. I leave Ashley a note about Xavier's bedtime chores, so
he doesn't sweet talk her into anything additional like staying up
later or putting away his dirties after his bath. I can tell he has
her wrapped around his little fingers, but she needs to stand by
the ground of the rules. I made dinner this morning using the
crock pot and put aside his portion, my portion for lunch tomorrow, and some for her should she choose to eat, which she
always does. That made clean up easy for me before I started my
date prep. I walk around the house a few times, checking the
doors and windows. Ashley arrives a little early which is no
surprise to me since she text me earlier and said she'd be here

around 5:30 pm. She enters the house using her passcode and catches me checking myself out in the mirror for the hundredth time.

"Wow, Ms. Lang. You're gorgeous. I love your hair like that. And that dress with the zipper up the back, wow. Your date is lucky to have you in his company." Her compliment nearly brings on the waterworks, but I keep them away.

"Thank you, Ashley. I'm so nervous about this evening."

"I can only imagine what it's like going back into the dating pool after a divorce, but you have nothing to worry about. You're the prize." Casting aside my no touch rule, I hug her and thank her for the kind words.

"So, all dolled up, are we?" Corey says as he enters the door. Xavier runs in behind him and hugs me at my waist.

"Wow, mommy. You look like a model. No, better than a model." I squat down to get eye level with my little prince and kiss him on his cheek since I'm wearing a red lip stick.

"Thank you, my baby. I made you some jambalaya and it's in the microwave." He takes off towards the kitchen stopping to wash his hands.

"So, do I get a kiss too?" Corey is always trying me and my nerves.

"Um, no. That is no longer my department," I say with a flippant attitude. I hand Ashley her check for the week including tonight, grab my clutch and kiss my little man bye while he stuffs his face with food. Ashley is sitting right beside him. Corey says bye to them as well and is on my heels.

"So, where are you going?" he questions.

"Not that it's any of your business, but on a date."

"Well our son is here with a stranger, what if something happens? So that does make it my business."

"Ashley, who you and I both vetted, has my number, Xavier knows my number, and you also have my number. If anything is needed that is emergent, I can be found." I hop into my car and start it up turning the AC on full blast given the time of year and the Vegas heat while he hangs onto the door.

"I'm just worried that this dude is trying to get into your panties, that's all."

"Well, unlike your wife, I have respect for myself and I don't just open my legs up to anyone." I close the door and take off toward the casino meeting spot.

I PULL INTO THE PARKING garage to meet him at the agreed location, the rooftop level. Not many people park there, and security is always up there checking for illicit activities. I'm not sure what vehicle he is in, but he does know mine. So, when a Mercedes AMG- E 63 S Sedan pulled in behind me, I knew it had to be him. I watch through the rear-view mirror as he steps out wearing a black tailor-made suit with the collar unbuttoned on his lilac shirt and matching pocket square. Suddenly I feel under-dressed. Nevertheless, I take a deep breath and go to open my door when he instead opens it for me. He extends his hand waiting for me to accept. With my clutch in my right hand, I place my left hand into his and he helps me get out of my car. The expression on his face is everything. He stares without words only allowing a smile to adorn his beautiful mouth. *Why am I thinking about his mouth?*

"Wow," he says. That's one word he manages to expel as his eyes continue to survey me.

"You don't look bad yourself," I respond adding a little chuckle hoping to break the tension between us.

"I'm sorry Tiffany. You're already gorgeous, but to see you like this...just...breathtaking." My cheeks fill with the fire of gratitude no doubt turning a pale shade of red. After I close my car door and lock it, he escorts me to the passenger side door of his car, opens it, and waits for me to strap in before closing it. He enters on the driver's side and we leave for the restaurant.

"YES, RESERVATION FOR JACKSON," CARTER says to the host as we enter the restaurant. Ever such the gentleman, when we arrive, the valet opens the door and Carter is waiting right there for me to step out. I kinda feel like all eyes are watching me, staring, wondering who I am on the arm of this man. He catches me surveying the crowd of onlookers and fidgeting with my hair knowing that I must feel self-conscious.

"You look amazing. That's why they are staring at you," he whispers in my ear then places a small kiss on my cheek. The host looks on and smiles before turning the attention back to Carter.

"Yes, Mr. Jackson. Your table is ready, and your server will escort you in a moment."

"Thank you," he replies.

"Carter. So glad to see you again." An older gentleman says as he shakes Carter's hand. I get the feeling that he's the owner or manager. "Oh. And who is this exquisite young lady? Is this your love interest?" I can tell the subject makes him a bit uncomfortable and a few ears perk up to hear his answer.

"Romero, I can never get anything by you," Carter replies. It's the safest answer he can give without a direct admittance or denial either. It also doesn't put either of us on the spot. They share a laugh and I smile joining in the pleasant moment. A young lady comes to escort us to our table while Carter and Romero have a conversation. As we approach our seating area, Carter doesn't miss a beat. He waits for me to take my seat in the cozy booth for two only to take his once I'm situated and after the conversation with the gentleman ends. Silence surrounds us as his phone keeps going off and he sends messages and email replies.

"He seems very nice," I say hoping to start a conversation and put the focus back on the evening. There is something about this that doesn't sit well with me. Kinda reminds me of how Corey would be so into his work and not into me during our marriage before the mistress.

"Huh? Oh, yeah. Romero is a great guy," he absent-mindlessly replies. His phone rings and he excuses, himself to answer. Our table is so secluded, that no one notices his absence. I sip on my water awaiting his return. If this is any indication how a relationship with him is going to be, I'm better off alone.

"Sorry about that, Tiffany. That was rude and extremely inconsiderate of me. It also was a matter I had to respond to. But you now have..." His words stop as he looks at yet another message that comes across his phone. He rolls his eyes and again excuses himself. A young man, who I can only imagine is our waiter, approaches the table.

"Hi, my name is Bo and I'll be your server this evening. Can I start you with a drink?"

"Bo, to be honest, I'm not sure if I'll be around for you to serve, so for now, just keep my water glass filled and the complimentary bread coming," My tone is laced with anger and sarcasm, but the way I feel right now, it's explanatory.

"Yes, ma'am. I'll be right back with the water pitcher." He smiles as he saunters away. I sit and observe the beautiful surroundings only to realize that I'm not enjoying myself. I can faintly hear Carter fuss or argue with someone on the other side of the wall from where we are sitting. I swallow down the last of my water while I gnaw on my bread, which is good, by the way.

"I can't believe I went all out for this date and I'm the only one present," I mumble. I pull a twenty-dollar bill from my clutch and place it on the table and go to leave when Carter reappears.

"Wait. Are you leaving?" he asks.

"Well, let's see. I put a twenty on the table for the wonderful waiter, Bo. I have my clutch in hand, and an Uber driver is just seven minutes away if I send for him now. So, yeah, I think I'm leaving." I slide toward the exit but seeing how I'm in a booth, and he has the advantage of already standing, he won't let me out. He grabs my clutch and places it on the table and interlocks his fingers into mine.

"Tiffany, I can't make an excuse for my actions. This is terribly inconsiderate of me but look. I turned my phone completely off and I'm all yours." He places his phone in my hands to verify that the evening now belongs to me. "So, please reconsider. If you still want to go, I'd understand." A few nosey posey's are onlooking and I don't want to make a scene, so I reluctantly agree to stay. He slides in right beside me, very close beside me and takes my hand once again.

"Carter, I told you my ex is an attorney. This just throws me right back into the same ol same ol. The only difference is that I'm not married to you, so there wouldn't be anything lost between us." I may be overreacting a bit.

"Tiffany, I'm so sorry. You deserve far more than what I showed here tonight, and I promise I'll make it up to you starting right now." A gentleman appears with 24 long stemmed, white, Ecuadorian roses.

"For me?" I ask.

"Well, I don't see anyone else sitting here with us. That was one of the phone calls I had to take. They were about to go to the wrong location plus they were supposed to have been delivered and sitting here before we arrived." I mentally tune him out while I smell each single rose. This was unexpected and wipes away my pettiness. "Am I forgiven?" he asks with a smile plastered on his face and sparkles in his eyes. I notice he has dimples in his cheeks and that melts parts of me he hasn't seen.

"Of course, and I'm sorry too." I go to place a kiss on his cheek when he turns his head and our lips meet instead. It was just a peck, but still it ignited something big.

"Thank you. Now let's eat. I'm starving. I waited all day to eat. I was so nervous and apprehensive," he says. He's clearly affected like I am about one little peck. He downs his glass of water in about five seconds and signals for Bo to return.

"Are you ready for a drink maybe an appetizer?" Bo asks as he makes a return.

"Yes, I'll have a whiskey sour make it a double and the Shrimp cocktail."

"Very well, and you ma'am?" I go to order when Carter interrupts.

"She can have whatever she wants," he says as he places a kiss on the back of my hand. Feeling school-girl goofy, I smile and refocus on the drink menu.

"I'll have a caramel apple-tini. and I'll share his shrimp cocktail." When you share or eat off of each other's plate, that means you are comfortable with that person either at the level of friendship or more than friends. I'm shooting my shot for the latter.

"Very well. I'll be back with your drinks and your appetizer." He leaves, and I can't help but pick one of the roses out of the box and hand to Carter.

"Thank you," I say handing him the rose after I place a kiss on it staining the petal with my red lip imprint.

"You're welcome. These flowers are only a tenth of the beauty I see in you."

"No, not the roses, although they are extremely beautiful, but for being persistent and asking me out. I feel if I said no, I would've missed out on something great."

"Thank you for saying yes. So, if I haven't told you in the last thirty minutes, you are fucking beautiful, Tiffany. All these eyes are on you because you light up the fucking room. I've seen you practically naked in your work outfit, but this looks even sexier. " I blush as our server comes back with our drinks. He held his glass up to mine and made a toast.

"To a clean slate." I love the way that sounds. I feel like with him I'm getting a new beginning.

"Clean slate," I say, and we clink glasses.

SOUTH POINT IS JUST MINUTES AWAY from the strip. It's located in the Valley and it has everything from fine dining experiences to a movie theater, casino, hotel, and even bowling. After dinner, he talked me into going as we were dressed. I tried to back out of it and he wouldn't hear of it. He said it was a date and we were going to have fun. He paid for the lane rental, shoes and of course the socks since I had on strappy sandals. We didn't place any bets, but we continued to laugh, dance, and act goofy until 11:30 p.m. The only reason we stopped is when I looked at my phone to check the time and I realized it was late.

"Wow, I guess I should be getting home. I have to take my son to school in the morning."

"Yeah, I have a client call in about three hours. Guess it's true about time flying and all," he says mirroring my words from the coffee date.

We turn in our rented shoes and he calls for his car from the valet and soon we are back at the meetup site. Always the gentleman, he opens my door and helps me out the car. We slow walk the short distance to the driver's side and I unlock the door placing my roses on the passenger side seat and start the car, so the cool air can keep them preserved. I see him standing there, watching me with this look of adoration in his grey eyes accented by the new moon's glow.

"Well, I had a really nice time with you," I say with my head bowed. I'm twirling my thumbs when his hand rests against my cheek and I take a deep breath when I feel its warmth. No words are spoken between us for what seems like an eternity. His thumb gently traces the outline of my cheek in a sensual, circular motion. Each time he's getting closer to my mouth until he finally passes the pad across my bottom lip. Without a word or warning, he crashes his lips onto mine. My heart beat increases, body shakes, and knees buckle a bit. I don't fight him. Instead I embrace this moment and wrap my arms around his neck welcoming this form of euphoria. He tongues me so hard that I know he can taste the mint I popped in my mouth on the way back to the parking garage. The ring from my cars Bluetooth breaks the kiss and I open the door to answer when I see its Ashley.

"Hi, Ms. Lang. Is it okay if I crash here tonight? It's a little late and I'm uncomfortable with driving home at this hour."

"Oh, yes, Ashley. Of course. You can take the guest room. I'll be there in a few minutes. Just set the alarm."

"Thank you. I already alerted my roommates, so they wouldn't panic."

"I'm sorry, dear. I guess I was having too much fun."

"No worries," she yawns. We disconnect and turn back to Carter who's standing there with his hands in his pocket. I already know what that means and the little glimpse I do take, tells me that's a real monster in those pants.

"Was that your sitter?" he asks, trying to avoid the tension.

"Oh, yeah. It was. I guess I need to get going. Again, thank you for a beautiful evening and the roses and the bowling. I had a lot of fun."

"I did too. Can't wait until Saturday."

"You'll see me again before then, silly."

"Oh yeah, Friday night's game. That's even better. I get to see you sooner." He reaches around and takes the door allowing me to get into the car. Once I'm buckled in, he closes it.

"See you Friday," I say. He leans into my open window and kisses me again and after a minute, we break for air.

"Friday," he says tapping the top of my car.

I roll the window up and drive off heading home for a quick shower.

Chapter

NINE

"**D**ID YOU HEAR ANYTHING I just said to you, Tiffany?" Jewel asks a bit annoyed. I have been in my own zone for the past five minutes and not exactly listening. I walked into the dressing area and when I opened my locker, there was a single red rose with a note attached. She didn't get a chance to see it, so she has no idea I'm knocking on loves door. After that passionate kiss we shared on the rooftop, under the moonlight, Wednesday night, he's all I've been thinking about. Well, during my non-mommy, off work time. He told me that he was flying back to his office Thursday and returning today for his game night, so this was a welcomed surprise.

"No, I'm sorry. I zoned out for a minute. What did you say?" I reply.

She rolls her eyes at me irritated that she has to start over. "Casey asked me to move in with him and I'm not sure how to handle that?" I take off my puppy-love goggles and put my bff hat back on.

"Jewel, that is a huge step for you. What about the lease on your place, should you decide to go for it? Or, he can move in with you," I suggest.

"I like his place better. It's bigger, the closet space is the perfect size, and the energy flows. I just don't know if we are moving too fast."

"You've only been dating off and on since last year, even though you recently labeled it as exclusive, you two haven't really dated anyone else. Well, except Micah, and that was just sex. I say go for it."

She looks at me oddly. "What the hell is wrong with you, Tiff? You are the non-voice of reason. Did you get laid Wednesday night?" She shoves me playfully and I shove her back.

"No. I didn't. But I had a great date with an even greater guy who bought me roses and took me bowling and..." My thoughts drift back to that kiss. I swear I can still feel his lips pressed against mine, taste his breath, his tongue.

"And?" she encourages me to finish my sentence.

"Nothing. We just shared a nice goodnight kiss," I utter modestly. I finish applying my glitter lotion to my arms and we head to the cage to get the setups for tonight's game. I see on the sheet that a few more setups have been added and that we are gaining Casey and another girl to work the evening.

"So, who is Jacqui?" I ask looking over the schedule.

"Oh, she's back? I thought we were beneath her," Jewel replies. "She used to work here about six months ago. She got into with the big boss, Dave, and told him that this was beneath her. I guess she came crawling back. You actually took her place."

"Oh. I see." I feel sorta conflicted about this person not knowing if she's gonna come in here with this top bitch attitude or not. I grab the setups, Jewel and Casey, who joined us finally, get the liquor and glasses, and we head over to the Tower.

THE GUESTS ALL ARRIVE, AND Carter is running late from a contract meeting. He messaged the hotel to advise them to let the guests in with no reservations. I thought he'd message me to tell me he was running late, but he didn't. I figure he is just keeping to the no pda rule while at work. Jewel and Casey are busy keeping the drinks and snacks refreshed while I make the bank deposit of the cash that's been converted to chips. I hear laughter at the door before it opens only to show Carter coming in and a young blonde, thin woman with more makeup on than MAC carries. She's cheaply draped all on his arm and that doesn't sit with me well. I take a deep breath and push down the lump in my throat.

"Hey, Jacqui, welcome back," Jewel announces aloud. I'm sure she saw the look and pain on my face and wanted to diffuse the situation. I glance toward the woman again and give her a once over before looking at myself in the reflection of one of the mirrors.

"Hmm, I thought they got rid of ratchet servers," Jacqui responds in a snobbish tone. I see Casey grab Jewel's arm and keep her near him which is a good thing. Because the Jewel I know, would've been on that bitch's ass faster than you can wipe with toilet paper.

"Mr. Jackson, so glad to see you. Here let me take your jacket," I say approaching him, making my presence known. He starts to remove it when he's helped by the bitch.

"Oh, no, darling. Let me get it." She seductively moves her hands across his chest until they meet the arms of his jacket and she slowly slides it off his body. He doesn't respond, in fact, he just stands there and allows it to happen leaving me to think that they have a history. He must see the hurt in my eyes when I walk to the little dining alcove where the poker setups are stationed at tonight. The tension in this room is palpable and I don't see it dissipating anytime soon. Carter comes to the table to get his chips and tries to make conversation with me.

"Hi, Tiff," he speaks. I peer up at him with a plastic look on my face before I speak.

"Good evening, Mr. Jackson. I have your buy-in ready. Just need to call the cage to get approval of funds." I place a call downstairs to get the approval code and Vic is confused why I'm even calling.

"Hey, Vic. I need approval for Carter Jackson."

"Why? You know he's cleared. It's his money he's playing with. What's going on?"

"Okay, thank you. I will tell him." I realize I'm going to have to explain my fake call to him later, but I needed a rouse.

"Okay, Mr. Jackson, here is your setup with your requested amount."

"Look, can we go in the massage room and talk?" he whispers so no one can hear.

I suck my teeth and press my lips before speaking. "No, I don't think so."

"Carter, do you want me to fix you your usual drink?" Jacqui says staring me down.

"Uh, no. I think Tiffany is going to do that for me. Right, Tiffany?"

He puts me in a corner and I have to oblige his request. I go over to the bar and fix his double Jack and Coke and take it to him as he joins his guests at the table. Even they can feel the energy in the room. "Here's your drink. Is there anything else?"

The first hand is dealt, and he catches a pair of aces on the first round.

"Yeah, stand right here for a minute." Jewel and Jacqui tend to the other guests and I'm stuck like I have glue at the bottom of my feet. The flop comes out and shows a king. The bets increase and

I'm mentally adding up the pot. It's up to five thousand already and we haven't even seen the others. The turn drops another ace and the odds are in his favor for a full house. Four of a kind is rare in poker and it'll put a few of the players out already. The bets keep raising and I calculate about twelve-five in the kitty. The dealer is about to lay down the river and as he does so, Carter's hand grazes and squeezes my thigh. The card is overturned and it's another ace. I just stare with a stone expression as does he. Others are thinking they have two pair or at best three of a kind.

"Well, gents, this first round busted y'all balls I'm sure but you can't beat two pair," the one gentleman says as he lays his cards down.

"Well, Bruce, I think you got ahead of yourself. I think three of a kind always beats two pair," Ray, his friend I met at the last party says. Others who didn't fold previously throw in their cards except Carter.

"I think we all know who is the lucky one here. Since my good luck charm is standing by me, I was bound to win." He throws down his two aces to pair with the other aces and rakes in all the chips on the table.

"Bullshit!" Gary says.

"She must have x-ray vision in those eyes and pass you signals or something. There's no way in hell you pulled that." They all laugh, and the dealer shows his hands before he sets up for the next deal.

"Tiffany, please, let me talk to you for a minute," Carter pleads.

I submit to his request and we walk to the alcove away from the guests. I can feel the sting of her eyes on me as we turn the corner. Before I can utter a word, I find myself lip-locked and pressed against the wall. We break from the passion that is holding us captive at the moment.

"I'm sorry I didn't call and I'm sorry for her behavior. I know how you wanted to keep the PDA hidden so I didn't think I should behave any differently," he says.

"Carter, I think a select few people should know what we have going on so that things won't be so fake when you're around. Starting with that bitch in there and Vic. Jewel knows and I'm sure Casey has caught on when he spotted you squeezing my thigh."

"I wanted to travel north and squeeze that ass, but I'm not sure we are at that stage yet." He moves his hands from my waist down to my ass and I move away slightly.

"You're right, we're not. But we will be." We lock in another kiss and I hear Jewel clear her throat.

"Okay Carter, baby. I'll let the others know," she says to make it seem like we are conducting business. I grab a bank bag and head back to the table with Carter to collect his chips. He stuffs two of the five hundred chips into my pocket and winks. I feel degraded somehow, but I know that is not his intention. The evening continues, and Carter comes out on top again. As we clean up, Jacqui tries her best to woo Carter, but he keeps his eyes on me. I'm busy laughing and joking with my friends helping them load up the bar cart.

"Carter, baby, let me go prepare your nightcap and your shower," she says rubbing her hand across his chest.

He politely pulls it away and backs away from her. "Oh honey, you don't have to worry about these people, they're nobodies. This new one..."

"Is someone I'm currently dating. Did you have anything to add to that?" Carter says interrupting her obvious planned insult. Her face freezes in distortion and she becomes visibly upset by his statement. He walks over to me and takes me into his arms placing soft pecks on my lips before landing the big one. Jewel turns to Jacqui and laughs in her face, causing the rest of us to erupt in laughter loudly and Jacqui storms out the door. I'm sure she's heading to tell Vic what she just heard and saw.

"I want so much more from you, but I'll wait until you're ready. I don't want to rush this," Carter says. This man is beyond a fling. I can tell by his actions, reactions, and cautious behavior.

"Thank you," I reply. All the chips are accounted for and I lock up the bank bags.

"Are you still going out with me tomorrow?" he asks while I continue to clean up.

"Of course! I wouldn't miss a 90's party for anything."

"Do we meet in our spot?" I think for a second and I realize that Xavier is with his father this weekend.

"No. Why don't you pick me up? Here's my address." I pull out my phone and text him my information. This, to me, is a big step toward commitment. It's only a matter of time before we declare that we are a couple, in public. I'm not sure how that will affect my job, not like I need it, but I like the independence it's given me, and I wouldn't trade it for anything.

"Great. I'll pick you up at 9:00 p.m."

"I was thinking you can have dinner with me first then we can leave to go to the party."

His eyes widen at my suggestion and is followed by a huge smile. "Oh, wow. She's letting you into the fortress, that's a major deal. Not even the mailman can get past her mailbox," Jewel adds.

"I'd like that. Do I need to bring anything?" he asks.

"Nope, just your appetite."

"Okay. See you at?"

"7:00 p.m. is fine."

"Okay. See you then."

"Come on. We need to get this back to the main floor," Casey reminds. I place a peck on his cheek knowing the mouth to mouth thing is leaving us a bit horny and then me and my friends leave.

"You know Jacqui probably told Vic, right?" Casey comments.

"Yeah," I reply.

"What are you going to say?" Jewel asks.

"I have no idea."

Chapter TEN

J ACQUI'S LITTLE PLAN TO RAT me out backfired when Vic said that he already knew Carter was interested in seeing me on a personal level. In fact, Carter asked him as if Vic was my father. It was a little joke, he said. That revelation was a load off my mind when Vic sat us all down once we made it back to the cage early this morning. After a few hours of sleep thanks to late night texting, I spend the day shopping at the grocery store, farmer's market, and panadería to get the freshest ingredients for tonight's dinner. I decided to do something simple like shrimp tacos.

I prep the shrimp by soaking it, so it can remove the fishy, dirty taste while I prepare the red cabbage, cilantro and red onions that go with it. I mix it all together before squeezing half a lime over it and adding balsamic vinegar and place it in the fridge.

While my shrimp purges and slaw marinates, I clean. My house is generally clean already, but when company comes, especially a handsome man that I'm kind of dating, I have to make sure it is extra clean. I condition my leather couches and change out my plug ins. Make sure that all the bathrooms have toilet paper and that they are super clean. Once I complete my chores, I go take a shower and put on my under garments before wrapping myself into my robe. I go drain the shrimp and then season it allowing it to sit for another thirty minutes. I take this time to check my polish and touch up any chips before applying my make-up. I lay on my bed playing candy crush trying to get my nerves calm. An incoming text alerts me and I read that Carter is on his way. I get dressed in my crop top and overalls and style my hair the way Aaliyah used to wear hers including the famous eye swoop. Throw on my big hoop earrings and my Timberland boots and I'm ready, except, I still have to cook.

I make my way to the kitchen and sauté the shrimp and prepare six corn tortillas. No sooner than I'm complete and the tacos are assembled, my doorbell rings. I answer my Ring alert and let him know that I'm on the way. I wash my hands and go answer the door.

"Hi," I answer nervously.

"Wow, you look like you just left the 90's. You do know that this is 2018, right?" I laugh at his approval of my outfit and show him inside. He didn't go all out in dress like I did, choosing to keep it somewhat professional. He's wearing a solid black tee under an electric blue blazer, with matching slacks.

"Well, this is my home. Make yourself comfortable. The dinner is ready and placed on the breakfast bar since it's just us two. I just need to clean my kitchen real quick." He takes my hand and escorts me to the kitchen.

"Have a seat, Tiffany. I will help you clean, but let's eat first. Here I bought some wine. I was always told to never go to a house without a gift."

"Thank you," I respond accepting the wine and adding it to my collection. He stands there waiting for my return and like a gentleman, he pulls out my chair and waits for me to be seated before taking his.

"I hope you're not allergic to anything I have prepared."

"Come on, I'm from Cali. I love shrimp tacos. Especially the baja type." This man knows food and that's a plus with me. He takes a bite and by the way his eyes roll, you'd think he had a mini orgasm. "Oh wow, Tiff. These are great. Perfect, actually." He takes another bite and chews allowing the juices to flow down his hand. I offer him a napkin to clean his hand, but he declines as he begins the third taco. I only prepared six and he's already gone through the first two. I remember how he said that he rarely gets a home cooked meal so I'm sure this is a welcomed change. I eat two of my tacos and I'm done. I offer my last to him and he takes it no questions asked.

"Those were amazing. I think I need to put in my request for them like once a week."

I laugh because he's probably not joking. Then I think for a minute and wonder if he's suggesting having dinner with me once a week over here.

"You want to have dinner with me every week? Here?"

His eyes light up at the suggestion and he smiles. "Yeah, if that's okay with you. If you can make shrimp tacos, you are a bonafide cook in my book. There's no way that I'm not eating dinner with you. If you want, you can cook a meal and we can have it at the hotel. I know how you are about your privacy. To be honest, I was surprised that you agreed to meet here."

"Well, my son is with his dad, so I didn't have that to worry about." He licks the juices from his fingers before wiping them with a paper towel.

"Will I ever meet your son?"

"I've been thinking about it. Do you want to meet him? Would that be something we do when we decide that this is a real relationship?"

"I thought this was a real relationship? I mean this will be our third date. There's no turning back now, plus Vic knows about us and he has no issues with it as long as it doesn't affect your job or my business relationship with the hotel." He brings up valid points and I take a minute to think about all he has laid before me before responding.

"Well, if all goes well, you can meet him tomorrow afternoon. I usually take him for ice cream when he comes back from his dads. You can meet us there if you want."

"Only if you're comfortable."

I grab his hand pulling him to me and giving him a kiss. "I'm sure. Just be prepared for the barrage of questions coming your way."

"I've never dated anyone with kids. Do I bring him a gift?"

"Are you trying to buy his affection?"

"No."

"Then, there's your answer. Get to know him first, then commence to bribery."

He chuckles while he stands and takes the plates to the kitchen. I follow behind him and grab my sponge so that I can clean my breakfast bar off and he hand washes the dishes. *SCORE!* A man that is this fine, knows a good meal when he eats it, and cleans? That's a win in my book. We put away the few dishes and I grab my keys, lipstick, and ID.

"Ready to go?" he questions.

"Yeah. Let's bounce." I follow him outside and notice he isn't driving the car he had at dinner. He's now in a Chevy Corvette ZR-1 straight from the 90's. He's going all out for the evening.

"Wow. My dad had one of these," I say admiring the vehicle. He opens the door for me and I get in and wait for him to enter on the other side and we leave for the venue.

WE ARRIVE AMONG A HOARD of paparazzi outside this plain Jane looking building. Usually this means that an uber celebrity is opening or starting a venture and to avoid unwanted attention, they do it under the radar, such as this. But apparently, they couldn't escape this pack of wolves.

"This must be one of your top clients for them to be out here like this?" I mention as he comes to a stop near the valet stand.

"Yeah, I hope nothing goes down. It would be disastrous." He strokes the sexy stubble on his chin as he surveys the surroundings. Two young men open our door and I step out and onto the sidewalk waiting for Carter to join me. He calls the other young man over to him and have a few words with them including hand movement emphasizing his point. I watch those entering and as the flashes from the light bulbs go off, I can make out a young man with blond hair and tattoos all over his neck. He's flanked by an entourage of what seems like thirty and I can faintly hear them yell "Brax" as he makes his way inside. My heart stops for a brief second only to be started back when Carter stands by me.

"You okay?" he asks in response to my startle.

"Oh, yeah. I'm good. I didn't know the level of clientele you had on your roster. I mean, I think I just saw Braxton Browne."

"You did."

"Is he yours?" He laughs loudly distracting the wolves for a brief second. Even Braxton looks this direction and waves at Carter and he returns the gesture.

"No. I need to be able to sleep unlike Mark, his attorney." The flashes go off again and they hound the next celeb. Carter takes me by my hand and escorts me in amidst the flashing bulbs, name calls, and autograph seekers. Once inside, the host takes us directly to the VIP section. The DJ is spinning the songs of the decade from all genres. I'm electrified with all the energy in the place. I catch myself singing along to the tunes and even dancing. Bottle service comes by with champagne and pours us each a glass.

"Let me do the toast," I plead.

"Sure, go ahead."

He holds his glass to mine and I look directly into his eyes. "To a night I won't forget." We tap the flutes together and take a sip.

"This is some good stuff," he says of our beverage.

"Yeah. That's top quality. So, who's your client?"

"I'll get him to come over and speak. He still owes me for the contract on this building anyway."

"Wow, pro bono work for the rich?"

"No. He was wrapping up a tour and then went home to rest for a few days. I took care of everything for him." I nod my head in understanding and take another sip when I hear the sounds of BBD's hit *Poison* start to play..

"Oh my god. You have to come dance with me," I say grabbing his hands and pulling him from his seat.

"Wait, I don't dance," he says. At least I think he said that. I snake my way through the crowd and find a spot where I begin to do some of the moves from the decade of honor along with the others in the crowd. Carter stands there and watches, smiling the entire time and trying to do some of those moves himself, confirming that he in fact, can't dance. I think it's endearing that he is at least trying. I try to be his tutor and show him a few moves that are simple and non-sweat breaking. He handles the wop pretty good and he keeps that as his signature move. The beat changes and *Let's Chill* by Guy fills the room with its iconic vibe.

"Oh, see this I can do," he says pulling me close to him and putting his arms around my waist. He even begins to mouth the words. In true old school fashion, I lay my head against his chest and we sway to the beat. This moment is surreal for me. Like, I'm here but I'm also looking at myself being here. *What is going on between us.* This is something that feels like, well you know. The song ends and as the music queues back up to the dance tracks, we make our way back to our seat.

"This is an amazing event. Thank you for inviting me," I express after I take a sip from my bottled water.

"I'm just glad you didn't say no."

"What if I did?"

"Then I would've left after the second song. I usually don't stay long at these events."

"Well, why didn't we leave? I don't want you to be uncomfortable."

"I was having fun watching you. How your eyes twinkle when you laugh or smile. Plus, I can tell you are really enjoying yourself. You must not get out often."

"No, not really. I hadn't been in the mood until recently."

"Oh? What happened recently?"

"I met you and you're challenging me to get out of my comfort zone." His smile is sexy as sin and my core melts. My lower valley tingles when I watch him lick his lips. He goes to speak when a familiar famous face interrupts.

"Hey, Kane. How are things?"

"Oh, they are good. Thanks for getting this set up for me. I have the takeover crew ready to assume responsibility tomorrow and they signed the NDA. I had the papers couriered to your hotel here in Vegas." My heart is skipping every other beat and I want to scream, but I won't. "Who's your date?" the celebrity asks.

"This is my date, Tiffany. Tiffany, I can tell you know who this is." He laughs, and I nervously stand to shake the hand of the man with the formally famous coif.

"I-it's a pleasure. I'm like a huge fan." He smiles and gives me a kiss on my cheek causing a near meltdown.

"The pleasure is mine. I like your outfit. You really dressed up for this event," he says. I can't speak. My words have left me. He laughs and then turns his attention back to Carter.

"Well, C, my man, I better get back to the event and to other endearing fans such as your friend here."

"Okay, Kane. Thanks for not stealing my girl."

"Oh, I wouldn't do that. You'd ruin me." And like that, he's gone. I sit back down and replay the conversation in my head.

"Uh, Carter? Did I just act like a teenager meeting her idol?"

"Um, yeah. It was pretty bad."

I rest my head in my hands and shake from side to side, appalled by my actions. I let my head fall back and sigh, I miraculously recover from embarrassment and turn back to my date. We sit back and watch the crowd not only grow but have dance offs including a mash-up of today's version of the running man and the real version. Before we know it, it's 1 a.m. and the party is still jumping. Carter even took off his blazer, (always the business man) and bust some moves from Vanilla Ice.

Kane sends us bottles all night and to say we are lit is an understatement. I did the fashionable thing and unhooked one of the overall straps revealing more of my midriff and the waist band on my boxers underneath. Since he wasn't into dancing, I found a guy on the floor who was willing to be my dance partner. Carter wasn't upset since it was a member of the hosts entourage. The next slow jam is played, and I thank my partner before returning back to my date.

I approach the table and see that he is ready to go. My hair is a sweaty, stringy mess and I'm still tipsy even after all the dancing.

"Are you ready to go?" he queries, placing his blazer around my shoulders.

"Yes. I think I will sleep well for the remainder of the day." He puts his hands on my shoulder and guides me out the door to the car waiting for us. We get in and he drives me home.

Upon our arrival he walks me to my door and we have the

awkward moment most people have on their first date. Should I or shouldn't I invite him in for a nightcap. After all, it is the third date.

"Tiffany, I had a fantastic time. I haven't been out like that in years and I'm older than you." I giggle because he sounds like I did at the beginning of the date.

"It was a memorable night. One I will never forget."

"Oh, and if you do, I have video and pictures. I think I'll show your son later."

"So, are you going to meet us for ice cream?"

"Yes, I'd love nothing more. I'll even have a scoop myself."

"Great. I was hoping you'd say yes." He tries to push my hair from my face, but the weight of its dampness causes it to stick to my skin instead. He tilts my face up to meet his as he comes in for a landing. He feels on my soaked body and when I allow him to graze my right breast, the passion is turned up. I'm pressed against my front door and our making out expands past first base. He begins to kiss and lick on my neck making my vj tremble with want. Heavy breathing follows, and I try to get my door open, so we can finish inside. Suddenly he puts the brakes on and I'm left confused. I sneak in a smell test for body and breath and outside the alcohol, I'm baffled as to why he stopped.

"What's wrong?" I breathe out.

"Nothing. I just think that maybe we should wait before we take this to the next level," he explains. That makes me want to drop my drawers right here right now.

"I get it and I want you even more for saying it." I laugh, and he joins in. "Thank you for being so caring and considerate." He kisses the back of my hand and I return his jacket to him.

"Goodnight or rather good morning, Tiffany."

"Goodnight, Carter. See you later." He gets back into his car and drives to the hotel. I go inside, jump in the shower, making sure to wash my hair before going to bed. Tomorrow, he meets my little prince and that will be the real test. Date four coming up.

Chapter ELEVEN

I ROLL OVER TO SEE the time on my alarm clock and notice it is 11a.m. I'm probably the only one in the universe that still has an actual, functioning, alarm clock since most people depend on their smartphones. I slow roll out of bed and go start my shower before checking my phone to see if Corey or Xavier has called. Instead, I see a picture message from Carter. He's lying in bed holding the camera up high. The caption reads:

Here's a picture of me so you can see me when you wake.

My heart smiles and butterflies flutter in my stomach. I can tell he's feeling something deep for me just by how attentive he is. Truth be told, I am too. It seems a bit sudden, for most, but when it's right, it's right. I reply with a simple 'good morning' before placing the phone down and jumping in the shower. When I get out, I'm greeted by my son who is laying in the bed watching his favorite program.

"Where's your father?" I ask since I'm in just my bath towel.

"He's in the kitchen," he says angrily. I know that something must've went down between them but instead of asking my son, I go to the antagonist himself.

"What the fuck is wrong with Xavier?" I ask storming into my kitchen.

"Well, good morning to you too. Did you have a good time on your little date last night?" he replies.

"What I did or didn't do on my date is none of your fucking business. What should be on your mind is why is my child in my bed sulking?"

"I told him that you shouldn't be dating anyone. He then said that if I hadn't left you, then you wouldn't have to date anyone. So, I yelled at him for that."

"He was telling you the truth and you got salty with a seven-year-old? Real mature, Corey. And what does it matter who I date?" My voice grows increasingly louder and his follows my lead.

"It matters if they're going to be around my son."

"Well, did you think about that when you fucked, impregnated, and then married your secretary? We're you thinking about our son then? We're you thinking about me then? No. Get the fuck out my house. Now!" He grabs his keys and storms out while I pace the floor back and forth trying to cool off. Xavier comes around the corner with tears streaming down his face and I'm hurt by the image I see before me. I go to him and embrace him allowing him to let it all out.

"Momma, is it my fault?" he asks through his pain.

"No. No baby. It's NEVER your fault, so don't you ever think that it is. Sometimes, two people fall out of love and they decide that they can't live with each other anymore. That's what happened with your dad and me. It had nothing to do with you. Okay?" He nods his head yes and I hug him again. When we separate, I wipe the tear tracks from his face with my thumb and grab a baby wipe from the counter to assist.

"Now, let me get dressed so we can go get our ice cream."

"Yes. I think I need three scoops today."

HIGH ROLLER | 113

"Well, I think you deserve three scoops. You had a great week in school too. So maybe you should get a triple sundae."

"Yes, with sprinkles and lots of whipped cream."

"Okay, it's a deal." I retreat back to my room and throw on some form fitting jeans, a tank top that shows just enough cleavage, and some scrappy gladiator style sandals. I have to appear good enough to meet a date but not suspicious for a seven-year-old to figure out. I pull my hair back into a ponytail before applying nude lip-gloss and just a touch of mascara.

"Mom come on. I feel my blood pressure going up," Xavier says in dramatic fashion of course.

"Ice cream has nothing to do with your blood pressure, little one." I laugh at his humorous attempt. It's adorable if you ask me, but my opinion may be biased. I do my usual check of the house routine with him hot on my heels before locking up and going to my fourth date...meet the kid.

ON THE DRIVE OVER HERE, I contemplated different scenarios on how the meeting was gonna go. From the mom, he's older than you, scene, to the I'm sorry Tiffany, I really don't like kids that much, scenario. Either way, I'm about to find out. As we pull into the parking lot, I notice Carter's car already parked. He seems anxious about today. He's sitting at a table his leg visibly bouncing and he's staring out the window absent-mindedly not noticing Xavier and I as we enter the shop. I notice that he has a big bag with tissue paper sticking out. I know that it's for Xavier since it has various Marvel characters displayed.

"Mom, the lady asked what you want," a little pint-sized voice announces, bringing me from my investigative works.

"Hmm, oh, I will have a single scoop of chocolate chip ice cream with caramel topping. No whip or cherry."

"Will there be anything else?" The young lady asks.

"No, that will be all." She announces the total and I go through my purse to grab my card.

"I got that. And can you add a single sundae made with vanilla ice cream and strawberry topping?"

"Yes sir," she replied. I glance at Carter and shake my head as he pays for the sweet treats.

"Thank you for paying for my ice cream, sir," Xavier says.

"Oh, it was my pleasure. I know your mother very well, and I thought it was a nice gesture."

"How do you know my mom?"

"Well, she works at the casino. That's how I met her." Carter takes the tray and Xavier follows as they continue their chat. I follow behind. Close, behind. We find a table and take a seat before Xavier continues his interrogation.

"Uh-huh, and are you the one that took my mom on three dates this week?" He shovels a big bite of his sundae into his mouth waiting on Carter's reply. Looking for my approval, which I give, Carter answers.

"Yes, I am. We had coffee, dinner, and went to a party. Was that okay with you?"

"Of course. I told my mom she should get out more." He takes another bite before continuing. "She really seems happy since last Sunday." He digs in again and I interrupt his whole spiel.

"Thanks, Xavier, but I'll answer the questions from now on," I reply. He shrugs at me and continues eating his dessert.

"Well, I think he and I are going to get along great," Carter smirks.

"So, what's your name?" Xavier asks.

"Carter Jackson, but you can call me Carter."

"No, he will call you Mr. Carter." I glare at them both with a stern face. They both turn away from my glare and take a bite.

"Is she always this mean?" Carter asks Xavier in a whisper tone that I can still hear.

"Yeah. It's best to just do what she says."

I laugh so hard that my ice cream falls out of my mouth and onto my shirt causing them to laugh too. "Okay, you two. You just met and you're already teaming up against me?"

"Mom, us men have to stick together." I shake my head in disbelief. Here I was worried that they wouldn't get along or Carter wouldn't date me because of my son. But instead, I see these two forming a bond over ice cream and male superiority. They continue to ask each other questions related to sports, comics, and school. Xavier is really comfortable in his presence and that makes me feel good about my decision to date him. They finish up, well, Xavier finally finishes. Carter and I have been finished for a while.

"I guess we should be getting back home. I have dinner to make and you have to get ready for school this week."

"Okay. Mr. C, wanna join us for dinner? My mom is a good cook." I'm shocked by his blunt offer for company and his disregard for not calling him Mr. Carter. We get up from the table and head outside to our cars.

"Oh, well, I wish I could, but I leave for New York in a few hours but I'll be back Thursday. Is that okay?" This surprises me because he didn't tell me of his travel plans. Not that he's obligated to tell me anything.

"Will you come to dinner then?"

"That's game night, cupcake. We won't be home," I inform him.

"Well. Maybe he can come to the game." He looks to Carter with wide eyes wanting an answer.

"I wish I was able to, little man, but, I have meetings through the evening when I get back," Carter explains.

"Oh, well. We can do something one weekend. My mom is taking me to Disneyland one day when she saves enough. You can go with us then." My son has diarrhea of the mouth telling all our business. I know for a fact he's comfortable with Carter and that makes me happy.

"Now, Xavier, I'm sure when Carter has some availability, he'll let me know. Then we can arrange a play date for you two."

"Mmkay. I can wait. See you later Mr. C." He holds out his hand and Carter shakes it. He climbs into his booster seat and straps in and I start the car, so the A/C can cool off the inside. I turn to face Carter who is standing there still holding that bag.

"On your way to a kids birthday party?" I inquire about the bag.

"Oh, yeah. I forgot to give this to him. Here, tell him not to open it until you get home. Please?"

"Carter, you don't have to buy him or me for that matter."

"I'm not buying anyone. I'm a nice guy and I like to buy things for others. Is that bad?"

"No, but some people like to use their money and power over others to get what they want. I've seen it plenty since I started working at the casino." He reaches his hand up to caress my face.

"I'm not one of those people. I truly like you and I wouldn't try to buy your affection or friendship. I know what those girls do up there after they clock out. Some of them make some good money since I represent the ones that are paying for it, others find themselves in a bad predicament because those guys are just jerks. I've represented some of those women in the past and I made sure those assholes paid for what they did. But that's not me."

"Just try not to make a fuss over me and my son, please." I turn to go get in my car when he gently pulls me back to him.

"I'm sorry. Can you please forgive me?"

"I'm not mad, I just want a clear understanding. That reminds me, are we in a relationship? I mean this is date four after all. I think that counts for something."

"I think it does too. How about we have one more date to make it official?"

"Okay. When? I need to make arrangements with Ashley or his father."

"Don't have the date yet. I just know there's a new club opening. Not one of my clients, but I was invited since this beautiful woman had fun at a certain 90's pop up party."

"Well, just keep me posted. I'd love to go."

"Good. I'd love to take you with me." He moves in closer and we are inches away from kissing when a reminder that my son is watching is made known.

"Mommy, are you going to kiss him? I don't think I should watch." I giggle at his keen observation and step back away from Carter.

"I guess we should leave," I say noticing how Xavier is making note of every move.

"Yeah, I think X-man has spoken."

"X-Man? You're nicknaming my kid now?" I ask in laughter. "I don't mind, to be honest. I think it's cute."

"Cute? I think its ingenious." We catch ourselves looking at each other for what seems like forever but only lasts about thirty seconds. "Is it bad that I want to kiss you right now?"

"No, because I feel the same. But my dad is watching so we can't." We both turn and see Xavier smiling big watching our every move.

"I better get back to the hotel and grab my things. I'll call you later, okay?"

"I'll be waiting." We depart with a hug, although that hug lasted more than a minute. I feel that this quick start to a relationship may soon be turning a corner.

XAVIER AND I PULL INTO the driveway of our home and I see a gift box on the doorstep. I immediately think of Carter, but that doesn't make much sense. Xavier gets out and heads to the package and I follow.

"It's for both of us, mom," he says as he reads the tag. I open the door and he carries it in since it is light in weight. I unbox it with caution and inside is a new set of LEGO blocks for his elaborate collection and a bottle of my favorite perfume. The note attached reads:

I'm sorry for my actions this morning. It's not right of me to impose my feelings onto either of you. Please forgive me. ~ Corey

I explain to Xavier that his dad sent this to apologize because he wasn't nice to either of us this morning. I went on to explain that Carter was going to be around a little more since we are kinda dating. He didn't have a problem with it. In fact, he expressed how he thought he was cool. I didn't mention the nickname Carter gave him.

"So, are you and Mr. C going to get married like dad and Vanessa did?" he asks.

"Son, we have to see if we really like each other first. Then we will date for a while. Who knows what will happen at that point. But you will be the first to know." I tap him on his nose and it makes him laugh. He hugs me only the way a child can hug their mom. Feelings of unconditional love and peace. This is something I know I will have forever.

Chapter

TWELVE

THE NEXT TWO WEEKS GO by fast since Carter is now back in LA handling business after his trip to New York. He managed to arrange for Xavier's favorite basketball player to come visit the team Thursday and co-coach their game. Corey wasn't thrilled and that made me happy. We didn't have a Friday night poker last week or tonight so Jewel and I took the early shift on the main floor yesterday to spend all day today shopping and getting ready for tonight's club opening.

Carter and I have been messaging like love sick teens while he travels. I understand the scope and depths of his job and he's been keeping tabs on me through Casey. He even invited them to the club with us tonight. That's why she's shopping with me today. She said I need to wear something that will make his dick jump out his pants. I kinda feel that it already does that by the glances he gives when he doesn't notice me looking at him, but she knows how to dress enticingly. I know just enough to accent. We hit a few lingerie shops, some party dress boutiques looking for the perfect body-con for me, and then the all-important shoe shopping.

Jewel and I have this love for shoes. While I'm more of a sandals and tennis shoes kind of girl, I have to admit there is nothing sexier than a kick-ass pair of heels. One that'll make the driest pussy get wet, as Jewel says. After my divorce, she bought me a pair of nude red bottoms and let's just say, a river was formed. The way they gently caressed my feet from the moment I first stepped into them made me feel like a new woman. We walk into the Palazzo on the strip and one sales assistant comes to retrieve our bags while another assistant guides us to the oblong shaped cushioned area. The ladies behind the register give us a scrutinizing look as if we didn't belong in there or possibly couldn't afford the merchandise. We request four pairs of shoes each and the gentlemen go running to retrieve them. While waiting, Jewel addresses the elephant in the room.

"So, are you gonna fuck him tonight or what?" I stare at her for a second, my eyes wide as that question came out of left field, even though it's been on my mind for the past two weeks.

"Why? Why would you ask me that?"

"Bitch. Like, you have been on four dates with him and you have had this pussy melting kiss laid on you and I'm sure your other lips are begging to be laid too. Why go through all of this for a fucking club opening?"

"I'm not doing this for just a club opening. This is our fifth official date. I think I should put in an effort to turn things up a notch."

"Fuck that. Set this shit on fire is what you need to do. Batteries are no replacement for a real dick, okay?" We let out a laugh that catches the attention from the other patrons in the store and a few stares from the ladies at the registers with a look of disgust on their faces. Jewel mean mugs them back and they turn away. I laugh hard but not as audible as previously.

"Anyway, I guess if things were to turn sexual, I wouldn't mind sleeping with him."

"Sleep- girl, Fuck. Okay, Fucking him. Say it with me. Fuuck-innnng. Tiff, you've been in a virtual lockout for nearly a year. Let that man reconstruct those walls, please. Just imagine what his mouth can do with your other lips." The associates return with our shoes and help us try them on. The one assisting me is kinda cute. Mediterranean tanned skin with black hair and gray eyes. His English isn't perfect, but his accent makes up for it. He helps me to my feet and over to the standing mirror, so I can check out the shoe.

"You like miss?" he asks. I take a few steps to check the support of the strap around my ankle and to get the feel since this will be a first-time wear with no break-in period.

"Yes, I like. Jewel will these go with that outfit for tonight?" I whisper shout. She sashays over to where I'm standing to inspect.

"Oh, yes hunty. Those will be perfect. Squat down and stand back up to check the balance of the heel." I drop it in my short shorts and pick it back up since Jewel and I like to dip low when we dance. The assistant grabs my hand for support and I'll be damned if he didn't wanna kiss me. He places his hand cautiously on my waist and smiles.

"Don't hurt yourself," he says.

"Thank you," I reply pulling away. I go back to where Jewel is sitting. The guy who's assisting her has worked his commission to its fullest. He's massaging Jewel's feet and she's loving it.

"Do you need help with taking off your shoes, miss?"

"Um, no. I'm good thank you for all your assistance. Can you take these and this pair up to the register?"

"Yes, miss." He looks sad that he can't massage my legs and feet like his coworker. I'm not sure they can even do that. I know it's not something you can pay for. I slide my thong sandals back on and walk to the checkout counter. Along the way, my phone rings. I expect it to be Jewel, but she's not far behind me. Instead the ID shows it's Carter.

"Hey, you," I answer.

"Hey, beautiful. Where are you? You didn't work today?"

"Uh, no. Jewel and I are shopping for tonight. Are you back in town?"

"Yeah. I'm about to crash then get up and get ready. I arranged for a driver for tonight for all of us. We can just meet here if you don't mind."

"Sure. That makes it easier. What time should we get there?"

"Are you, Jewel, and Casey going to eat before coming?"

"Um, not sure. We haven't thought that far in advance. I know Jewel and I will probably do a bite or two while we get dressed at my house. We will likely catch a car service to the hotel." The counter associate begins to ring up my purchases and announces my total a little loud and rudely might I add.

"That'll be one-thousand, five hundred, seven-four dollars, and twenty-eight cents and we don't have a lay-a-way policy," the sales lady says rather curtly.

"Where are you at?" he asks over hearing what I spent and her tone.

"At the Palazzo buying shoes." I say searching for my card to hand to her.

"Put her on the phone," he asks with a clipped tone. I pass the phone while I pull out my credit card. I hear his voice grow a tad loud amidst her yes and no sirs and tears well in her eyes as she hands me back my phone.

"What the hell did you say to her?"

"I just told her who I was, and what I do and how she needs to refrain from her tone with you or Jewel or I will call the owner personally." The young lady hands me my bags and doesn't even take my card for payment.

"We would like to thank you for your patronage and hope you will accept these as a gift from the owner," she says. Her demeanor certainly has changed since I first approached the counter.

"Oh, okay. Well, thank you. That's awfully nice of him. I'm sure my boyfriend will let him know. Oh, and her shoes were included too, right?" I point to Jewel's items at the register next to where I'm standing. She goes to that assistant, whispers something in her ear and pushes a few keys on the keyboard.

"Yes, ma'am. Hers too. We apologize for any inconvenience we may have caused." The other associate is looking around frantic and the manager comes out from the back and says something to the two ladies. They scurry away, and the manager offers her apologies as well. We accept and walk out.

"Carter, you called him, didn't you?"

"Well, I couldn't let that slide. See you tonight, Tiff." He hangs up and I can tell he was a bit upset about having to use his connection to resolve a customer service issue.

"What the shit was all of that?" Jewel asks as we head to my car.

"Well, Carter called to see where we were since we weren't at the casino, and he overheard how rude that lady was and lost his shit. He called the owner directly and the four pairs of shoes are ours for free. I'm pretty sure those ladies were fired."

"Damn! Your man got it like that?"

"I guess he does. He's going to use a car service tonight, so I said we will meet up at the hotel, if that's okay with you."

"Uh, yes! A driver means we are going to get fucked up!" We put our bags in the backseat and go back to my place for a little nap, nosh, and pregame later this evening.

CASEY AGREED TO MEET US at the hotel since he needed to do a quick inventory check for the weekend. I arrange for us to be picked up around 9:30 since I don't know where we are going, and I know that it will take about forty minutes for us to reach Carter's room. While getting dressed, we blast the sound system and put on some of the hottest songs from today and the 90s since I'm still feeling a little nostalgic. Jewel mixes our drinks as we take turns getting dressed. She helps me put on my garter and slaps me across my ass when she finishes hooking up the back.

"Woo. That ass is gonna get spanked tonight," she laughs mischievously.

"Girl, shut up." I throw my pillow at her and she laughs even more. I think her buzz is starting early. I receive notification our driver is outside. I step into my lace overlay skirt and zip it, making sure my garter is not showing before putting on my matching crop top. Both fit bodycon snug not leaving much room for dancing. My hair has some body waves from when I had it straightened last week so it has the right kind of sexy flair I want. I add a pair of diamond earring studs for the jewelry along with a simple bangle and I'm ready to go. Jewel, being the tawdry little tease that she is, wears a blue round neck sleeveless backless dress.

"You ready, girl?" I ask as she's finishing putting on her makeup.

"Yeah, let me grab my clutch." When we go, out she always leaves her things at my house and she picks them up later. Her clutch holds ID, one card, her fob for her car and house key. Oh, and the touch-up makeup. We actually carry the same thing plus our phones, of course. We both do one more check in the mirror and walk out to our ride.

THE RIDE OVER HAS ME second guessing if I want to go through with this evening. Jewel might have been playing around earlier, but some of those words stuck with me. I can feel the change in the dynamic and since I haven't seen him in two weeks. I know the tension will be there. Sure, we talk on the phone via skype, but it's not the same as in person.

We arrive at the hotel and thanks to some crafty planning, we go around the back entrance so that we are not seen to avoid unwanted conversation. We step off the elevator and I can hear him laughing with Casey as we approach the room. I take deep breaths as Jewel knocks and the door opens.

"Hey, you call for a couple of hot girls?" she says to Carter as he stands in front of us.

"Hey Casey, those girls we requested are here." Casey comes to the door with his wallet out pretending to pay for services.

"Okay, this joke has run its course," Jewel says as she pushes Casey back into the room and they begin to make out, leaving Carter and I alone to entertain ourselves.

"Tiffany, whoa. I didn't expect you to look this amazing," he says while holding my arms out searching me over from head to toe. I feel him drink in every inch down to the shoes on my feet then going back up again. I find a way to back out of this awkward situation.

"You too. I love the casual suit look, you know, with no tie."

"I'm gonna have a busy evening keeping the men away from you." He pulls me into his arms making me want to stay here forever. Our faces are within tongue distance of each other, yet we manage to stay apart for a brief conversation.

"I missed you these last two weeks. Thank you again for having James Durant stop by the basketball game," I say before I forget.

"You're welcome. You smell so good." He rubs his nose against mine before kissing me, making my legs feel rubbery. His hands make a path from my back down to my ass and squeezes. A clear signal that we have reached that next level point in our relationship. His lips softly trail along my jawline and nearly my neck before I pull away. Things are heating up a notch and I'm not sure if I'm ready. I walk to the bar and fix me a drink. I raise an empty glass to him checking if he wants one. He nods yes, and I begin to fix his usual. Casey and Jewel are making out heavily and I decide to break the tension.

"Ahem, so, where is this place, Carter?" I ask drawing attention. Jewel joins me at the bar and prepares her and Casey a drink while Carter comes to get his.

"Um, it's just outside the strip going west. They say it's like super sexy. Plush VIP sections, top shelf liquor, dark ambience, and one of the hottest DJ's. Although tonight I understand they have a celebrity DJ and a film crew."

"So, how did you get on the list? This sounds exclusive as fuck," Jewel inquires.

"A friend put us on as a favor to another friend I helped with a legal issue." He sits his glass down and signals for another as his room phone buzzes. Out of habit, I go to answer, but suddenly realize I'm not working tonight and I don't want to alert the staff of our presence. I pass the phone to Carter who shakes his head at my gesture. He says 'okay' to the person on the other end and hangs up.

"Well, the car is downstairs, so I guess we should be going." He dumps the remnants of the ice into the sink except for one cube. He places that into his mouth and chews on most of it using the remaining piece as a pawn in his seduction. He kisses me on the back of my neck and over to each side. The coolness of the water that drips trickles down my top and into my bra making my nipples hard. I inhale sharply when I feel his dick press into my back side and his left arm is holding me in place as his right-hand inches under my shirt. I lie my head back into the crook of his neck as he feels the fabric of my bra and just as he begins to go under the wire, the phone buzzes again. He breathes in and lets out a low grunt his head pressed against the back of mine. He answers and tells them we are walking down. I notice the other two are staring at us like they are watching a movie.

"Get a life," I say walking by them looking in the mirror to check my makeup.

"You're gonna give up that thong tonight, aren't you? And don't you tell me no, or I don't know, or that wimpy ass I'm not sure shit either. It's so obvious you want to ride his dick. Hell, Casey said that before I did," Jewel expresses. I decline to answer instead grab my little clutch and meet Carter who is patiently waiting by the door. The others follow behind and as they walk out, Carter whispers in my ear,

"Will you spend the night with me?"

"Let me think about it, okay?" I plea. This isn't a step to take lightly. This changes the relationship from a level two to a level three. If it's any good, it's a level four. He nods in agreement taking my hand and placing a kiss on the back. We close the door and join our friends who are waiting at the guest side entrance by the stretch SUV limo. I give him the side-eye glare and before I can say anything he offers up an explanation.

"It's part of the package. I had nothing to do with this," he says.

"Dang, Tiff, you ain't even fucked him and you already got him in check?" Jewel says. Casey laughs but I don't think Carter was impressed.

"No. I just told him not to spend money on me, that's all. I don't want that alpha male treatment shit." We climb into the limo and find even more bottles. One thing is for sure, we will be getting wasted tonight. I go to send a message to Corey only to find that he sent one earlier saying that he had to call Ashley to watch Xavier because his wife was having labor pains and they were at the hospital. I shoot Ashley a text to make sure they are okay. She replies that they are fine, the house is locked down with the security armed and she's going to be there as long as I need her. I thank her for being available and ensure her she will be well compensated. This provided some comfort, but it may not be a good idea for me to stay the night with Carter. I slip my phone back into my clutch and rejoin the others with conversation and drinks. Jewel opens the sun roof and in true Vegas fashion, she hangs out shouting and singing along with the songs on the radio, dancing and shaking her ass. Casey is getting an eye full of her naked puss, we all are actually. She comes back in and grabs a water to take a break from the libations.

Carter takes a call and plans for something work related, but I know that if I did stay, I wouldn't be there long since it seems he has a flight out in the morning. I tune out his business talk and play and joke around with Jewel and Casey. In fact, I even move to the side of the limo where they are seated, and we carry on until the vehicle comes to a stop.

"Are we here?" I ask Carter. He phones to the driver and confirms that we have reached our destination. Soon our doors are opened by the valet attendants and we all step out of the vehicle. We are ushered into an anonymous building hidden away from the main lanes of the street. Once inside, the things they described to Carter are confirmed. It's dark with black lights directing the path along the floor. Once they confirm you are on the guest list, you are then escorted to either general section or the VIP. Our attendant opened the door to the upper level section and when we step through, you can see the club scene unfold below us. People are partying, the music is thumping, and a good time is being had by all. They have women dancing in cages and on the stage flanking the DJ. The cool thing about the VIP sections is that you are completely closed off from the public, but they can see you thanks to the glass windows surrounding each section. It's kinda like the suites at a sporting event. The music is piped through speakers embedded into the ceiling, but you can also open the window for a more live experience. You use a touchscreen to order your beverages and anything else they offer, and your server arrives with those items. We collectively order a few things and while we wait, Jewel and I dance.

Chapter

THIRTEEN

FTER ABOUT AN HOUR IN the club, the alcohol is beginning to loosen me up and I become more amorous. Actually, when a song by Teyanna Taylor comes on, my inner freak comes out and Jewel and I begin a burlesque style dance with our respective dates receiving all of the attention. I separate his legs and straddle him simulating riding him to orgasm moving my hips to the music and acting out the lyrics of the song. I even get a bit sexual and lick him on his neck and suck on his ear giving him all indication that I want him. The look in his eyes is full of desire and it matches what I'm feeling inside. I sit here on top of him grinding against his obvious hard dick acknowledging a feeling I can't deny any longer because it's all on display here tonight.

"Carter, take me home," I whisper in his ear. He pulls out his phone and calls for the car service before excusing me from my position to talk with Casey.

"Hey, I'm going back to Carter's. If you want, y'all can crash at my house, if you don't want to drive out to Casey's. Ashley and Xavier are there." I explain to Jewel.

She looks at me for a moment with a wide smile on her face.

"What?" I ask.

"You're going to put it on him. I hope you're still protected. That man is dying to knock your ass up." We laugh but I check my calendar to make sure I haven't missed any appointments and to see where I am in my women's phase.

"I don't think so. Anxious to fuck, yes. Impregnate, no. I doubt if we have any relation beyond tonight outside the game nights."

"Why?" she asks.

"'Cause I won't be a prize to him anymore."

"Girl. Take your self-doubting ass on with that bullshit. For the last time, Corey fucked up, not mankind. And Carter, he wants more from you than your sweet pussy, trust me when I say that! I have the inside tip." Casey comes and scoops her up, carrying her back to the plush seating of the room leaving me to think about what she just said.

"Are you ready?" Carter asks extending his hand to capture mine. I see my friends and how they are so in love and realize that if I keep putting up roadblocks, I'll never have what they have.

"Yes, I'm ready. Let's go." He hands the server, who we see on our way out, two hundred dollars and thanks him for the evening. As we exit, we see the valet has the door open and we climb in going back to his room.

WE WALK INTO THE villa suite and he makes a call to guest services asking them to hold all calls. I put my clutch down and fix a glass of ice water. I'm in an unguarded position leaving him to surprise me kissing me with fire in his chest. I pull away only to have him grab me in his arms again. I try to struggle away from him, but his lips capture mine and slowly our tongues intertwine making me melt into a pile of sticky caramel. I pull back and push him away out of instinct.

"Fuck!" I say putting my hands over my mouth in shock as to what I just did. Not wanting him to think I don't want this, because I do.

"Did I do something wrong?" he asks.

"I... I didn't mean to push you. It was all reaction really," I stammer out my head bowed. He closes in on me once again, tilting my face towards his. Tracing its outline ever so softly with his fingers. Locking in on my green eyes that he loves, he parts my lips with his thumb. I swallow hard, feeling the hot tension building to a boiling point between us. I want to feel him in between my legs so bad, but this just isn't right. When I break from his trance, I realize that he has somehow moved us to the wall next to the bar. His hand is outstretched above my head and there isn't much room for me to escape.

"Carter, I don't think we should..." His lips crash into mine pausing my words. Soft, warm, and not filled with the fire of the first kiss but more effective. My hands instinctively wrap around his neck when the kiss turns up the desire within me. *Okay, I give,* I think to myself. He lifts me against the wall, placing my legs around his waist, leaning into me a bit to stabilize our position. His hands move slowly up my thigh under my skirt, discovering my garter. He pulls off my crop top shirt exposing my red push up bra and the tops of my breasts. We begin making out again when he looks at me with a deliciously wicked smile before standing me upright and looking deep in my eyes.

"You should go," he suggests

He walks away, and I don't know if it's because he doesn't like lingerie or maybe the thought of me in nothing but them. He fixes himself a drink while I'm left hot, horny, and dumbfounded.

"Did I do something wrong?" I ask trying to make sense of what just happened.

"It's not you, it's me. Honestly. It's what I want to do to you and I know it's not something you want. It's how you make me ache in ways I didn't think possible." He swallows his drink and pours himself another one. I'm not one to back away from a challenge, and I'm not going to start now. I shoot a quick message to Ashley letting her know that I will be out till early morning. She quickly responds with okay and I put away my phone. I pull my form fitting lace skirt off and let it hit the floor leaving on nothing but my red bottoms and underwear. He takes a seat on the couch and I walk to him. My heels click-clacking away on the marble floor. I take his drink from his hand and down it myself. Removing an ice cube from the glass, I suck the remnants of the drink off it and plop it back in the glass before handing it back to him.

I carefully position my right, open-toed Louboutin foot in between his legs with the tip carefully touching his semi-erect package. He squirms a bit and adjusts himself as he grabs my calf and begins to rub it. I pop his hands and wave the no-no finger at him. He takes the hint and sits all the way back. I take his glass and walk to the bar where I pour him a drink of my choice dropping a few long-stemmed cherries inside. I can feel his eyes firmly on my swaying hips and ass and this excites me.

"Why are you doing this, Tiff?" he asks as he takes a slow short drink of my special drink.

"What?" I respond innocently.

"Teasing me," he says looking through the rim of the glass.

"I'm enticing you in order to build up your desire to take me." I pick a cherry out of his drink and gently suck on the delectable fruit before taking it off its stem. His eyes grow a menacing dark gray and my core temperature rises. He puts the glass down and undoes his slacks where I easily make out his dick print.

"Tiffany are you good at following orders?" He asks as he takes his hardened cock into his hand but not exposing it from its bondage.

"Yes, sir," I say in my innocent girl voice. My response sparks something in him and he licks his lips in a salacious manner. I feel my breath catch wondering what that tongue could do to me.

"Stand before me," he commands. I straighten my position to be dead center of his view. He stands to his feet and my gaze remains straight forward. I can feel his energy as he walks around me slowly. Drinking in my spirit from head to toe, he stands behind me and my body gets goosebumps from the electric energy flowing between us.

"Hand me the glass," he orders. I start to walk to the side table, but he stops me.

"No. Bend over and hand me the glass." I slowly bend, exposing the bare cheeks on my backside since I'm wearing a thong. I'm sure giving him a beautiful eye full of my pussy lips balancing the tightrope. I retrieve the item and stand fully erect positioning the glass just over my shoulder to hand it to him. The condensation from the glass drips down and leaves its mark on my body. He takes his tongue and slowly licks the water droplet from its landing. I let out an audible gasp feeling the warmth of his tongue play along the blade of my shoulder. I close my eyes and allow my mind to relax so that my body can prepare for what's to come.

"Did I say close your eyes?" I turn my head towards the sound and when I open my eyes, I realize that he is standing right in front of me.

"No, Sir," I reply my eyes locked into the sexy storm brewing within his. Placing the glass onto the table, he takes the ice and outlines my lips.

"Lick them," he commands. I follow, and he continues to trace my body with the frozen water. He follows the contour of my tits paying attention to the areola, that even with the bra still covering them, my nipples still respond. He then trails on down south and places the ice right on my clit, applying slight pressure while watching my breaths become labored. I want him now. The thought of what will happen in a few moments time riddles my body and I become paralyzed with anticipation.

"I will leave you wetter than water when I'm done with you." He drops the ice onto the floor and replaces it with his fingers moving in and out at a slow, teasing, pace. A quick inhale of air with a quiet moan and he knows how I'm feeling. He removes his fingers and places them into his mouth seductively sucking on them. "I wanted to taste you from the moment we met," he whispers in my ear. I hear the sucking sound as he pulls his finger from his mouth and think, *fuck, I'm in trouble*. He stands in front of me and begins to undress with a smirk on his face.

His shirt is first and I recall the moment I spilled his drink on him the first game night and how he looked when he stepped out the shower. I remember wondering what those arms would feel like wrapped around me. His t-shirt followed, as did his shoes, socks, then finally pants. We never broke eye contact while he removed his clothing and I wasn't going to move until he directed me to do so. "Well, don't you want a peek?" he asks with a smile on his lips.

"No, sir. I can wait," I reply knowing that I want to see the whole thing balls included and not covered in cloth. He pulls his boxer briefs off and stands naked before me handling his junk in one hand directing my gaze with the other. When my eyes meet his dick, I realize size, based on race, is a myth. I quickly glance to him and he's confidently smirking. I stand and pretend I'm unaffected but, in my mind, I'm planning Kegel exercises and a trip to the sex store to purchase Ben-Wa balls.

He hoists me over his shoulders and enters the bedroom where he places my feet back on the floor and presses me hard against the wall holding my hands above my head. He pops open my bra taking one breast into his mouth. I writhe and wiggle trying to escape his restrain so I can interact, but he presses me harder.

"Carter," I call out as he moves from one breast to the next giving me immense pleasure. He pulls away for a second and wipes the saliva from his mouth before turning me facing the wall keeping my hands held high. Pressing his cock in-between my ass cheeks, but not in my ass, and slowly grinding against me is making me wetter than a flood. He pulls my hair around to the side exposing my neck where he begins to bite and suck along my shoulder line. My urges grow deeper and I wish he'd take me now, but he doesn't. He relaxes his hold and I reach up around his neck bringing his mouth closer to mine my fingers playing in his silky dark brown hair as his suction becomes unbreakable. I swear it feels like this was to be. His left hand moves up from my breast to the base of my neck where his fingers spread and lay gently applying slight pressure.

"Does this bother you?" he asks as he increases the pressure.

"No," I whisper laying my head back giving him more room to play.

"Will you tell me when to stop? I don't want to hurt you."

"Yes," My reply is simple, and he increases the pressure while inserting fingers from his right hand into my aching pussy. His grinding intensifies, and I feel myself about to come on those fingers giving me pleasure.

"Carter," I pant hoping he hears the plea in my tone. He does and soon I'm facing him with my legs using his waist to hold my position and his long, thick cock slams into me. He grunts with the first thrust and I gasp at both the size, insertion, and my walls being stretched for the first time in nearly a year.

"Fuck, Tiff. I forgot the condom," he says. We stop for a moment before he lets me down. On our second date, we talked about his former promiscuous ways, but he said he was always careful and gets tested twice a year. He even messaged me all his paperwork. I told him about my hiatus from sex and that I'm tested yearly just because. But I told him I wouldn't have unprotected sex with another person unless it was a new marriage. He walks to the bathroom and comes back with an unopened box of Durex XXL condoms. I still don't think it'll fit.

"You can examine them if you want," he says while handing me the box. I open it, pull out a new one and tear it open. I grab his already swollen erection, take the condom, and slowly slide it on carefully unrolling it to the end where he still has about two inches of unsheathed shaft. *I knew it.* He sits on the bed and beckons me to sit on top of him. I approach him and start on my knees first. I will need time to adjust to this big boy. I ease onto him little my little.

"Let me know when you can't take anymore," he says. I nod my head in agreement. I continue to try and fit all this man meat that I can.

"Okay, I can't go any further," I comment. He places his hands on my ass and maneuvers me in an up and down motion only stopping when I can't go further. Once I get comfortable, I maintain a steady pace allowing him the freedom to do more with his hands. He takes my hair and twists it around his hand pulling my head back taking a long lick from my breast to my lips.

"I'm gonna make you mine, forever," he says. He rolls me from my position and drops to his knees teasing me with kisses along my inner thighs. My legs are trembling with desire and my pussy is throbbing even more. He closes his lips around my swollen clit and suckles at it causing me to arch my back and my hands urge his head closer. That tongue I wanted earlier is now deep within me. He's alternating between flicking his tongue at the speed of a fan blade on high and sucking on my nub until he renders my body stiff and I come with month's worth of pent up sexual frustration that even B.O.B couldn't relieve. As I lay here shaking in my aftermath, he excuses himself and goes to the bathroom where I can hear him do a quick gargle before exiting out the other door that leads to the living area of the suite. Now, I start to feel odd until I see him come back with that bucket of ice and the bottled water from the mini bar.

"Thought I left?" he asks looking at my expression.

"Well, I did feel weird," I reply.

"No, I want you to cool down. So, I brought the ice," He takes my shoes off, rolls down my thigh high stockings removing them. Taking a cube, he rubs it over my feet and massages them with his hands before placing my toes in his mouth one by one using his tongue to go in between each digit. This feels oddly erotic and my body responds to this level of foreplay. Not even in my years of marriage have I experienced what I have with Carter tonight. He takes another cube and runs it up my thighs following his trail with his tongue giving me a live demonstration of cold and hot. He circles my clit with the ice and leaves it there for a few minutes until it is numb. He takes that same piece of ice and places it in his mouth. When he stands I stare at him and can't believe he's still fully erect. I just knew he would have gone soft by now.

"On your knees, Tiff," he commands. I look at him with a hint of concern and he makes a small correction. "On the bed, please," I turn around and get in doggie style position pulling my hair to one-side. He pulls me back a little and slowly inserts his dick inside me. My mouth drops open as his penetration brings me elation unfathomable. He grunts as he pulls out and re-enters me.

"Fuck, Tiff," his speed increases and I find myself grinding back against him realizing those moves were driving him crazy. I reach between my legs and grab his balls and begin to massage them and he drives deeper within me. I mentally discover that in this position I can take all of him. I do mean all ten inches.

"Carter," I moan aloud. He pulls my hair as he digs deeper slapping me across my ass each time I buck back.

"Stay with me," he whispers in my ear. "Just for the night," his plea is sexy and full of want which is something I never thought Carter needed.

"Yes," I reply. He pauses in his motion only to collapse against my back before rolling onto the bed wiping the sweat from my face before grabbing the room phone.

"Yes, this is Carter. Can you send up some champagne and a

fruit platter? Just tell them to put it in the fridge and the champagne on ice, uncorked. Thanks." He disconnects the call and turns his attention back to me.

"Are you okay?" I ask. His face is not the jovial person I'm used to seeing. Full of arrogance, confident, and a lawyer in every sense of the word. This man before me, isn't those things at all. He's calm, with peace on his face, but confused at the same time.

"No. I don't think I am. It's you."

"What do you mean, it's me? Did I do something wrong?"

"No. You did everything right. You resisted me and made demands of me. I had to fight just to get dinner with you. We had a great time at the pop-up show, and tonight was great. Meeting your son was even better. I feel a connection with you I never had with another woman. I think you are a ghost and when I wake up, this will all be a dream." He touches my face and I place my hand on top of his letting him know I'm real.

"I'm not going anywhere unless you want me to. Except in the morning I have to go home to my son."

"I'll take you. Just don't leave without me. Okay?"

"Okay." I reply. He kisses me and rolls me onto my back where we make love all night into the twilight hours of dawn.

Chapter

FOURTEEN

"**H**EY, SLEEPY HEAD." I GROAN and mumble turning back over pulling the covers above my head. I'm exhausted. Carter had me all over this room feasting and pounding on my pussy like it was a new invention. During our down time, I asked if he ever slept with a black woman before. He looked at me with a bit of cross in his eyes and I had to tell him that I worry what people might say or think about our relationship. He admitted to sleeping with two other women like me. His first girlfriend in high school and his first almost fiancée in college. He said they were buxom beauties but didn't have my green eyes, shapely hips, and their lips weren't as full.

"Come, on. Wake up. We have to go pick up your son."

"Pick him up? Why?" I thought I was just going home.

"I have a day of fun planned for us and I need to make up for his grumpy ass mom not coming home last night."

"Oh, I came plenty last night, thank you, and you should know." I feel the sting of his hand across my already sore cheeks followed by a pillow shot to the head.

"Keep on and I'm gonna make you come again tonight. Now get up!" I kick like a child throwing a tantrum then reluctantly do as requested. I see that he is already bright-eyed, bushy-tailed, and dressed in jeans, tennis shoes, and a Mario Bros. tee. I search for my under things and I remember my top and skirt are in the living room. I run through the shower, use the guest toothbrush in the bathroom to freshen my mouth, and throw on last nights' ensemble.

"I went to the gift shop and got you a tee shirt in case you didn't want to wear your shirt from last night."

"Good idea." I swap shirts and grab the travel deodorant from the bathroom and apply. I put on some lip gloss and a little bit of mascara. I pull my hair back into a ponytail and slip on my shoes and we head out the door.

"Going home late, Ms. Lang?" The bellhop asks when he sees me step off the elevator of the main entrance.

"Uh, yeah. I overstayed my welcome with Mr. Jackson and he is kind enough to see me home." Carter places his hand on the middle of my back and keeps it firmly in place. This is going to be an issue with him if I don't acknowledge our relationship, but he has to understand that not only is this my job, but I don't want people up in my personal business.

"Well, that is nice of him. You have a nice day. I will see you tonight, right?"

"No. My son is going to a friend's party, so I will be with him. You have a great shift." I see the valet standing by the car with the door open. He shuttles me in before taking the driver seat and pulling off.

"So, you can't tell anyone about us?" he says as he pulls his sunglasses off his face and looks at me with a slight scowl. This is not the conversation I want to have right now.

"Carter, you are a high-profile client and I can't be involved with you in the manner that we are, and you know that."

"Victor already knows and besides, you don't have to work

there. You can work for me and my firm. You're beyond qualified to keep the accounting department inline. That way no one can say anything."

"Yeah, right. I'll be known as the black bitch that is hated immediately just for getting a created position and even more hated when they find out I'm fucking the boss. I can't do that either, Carter. I'm sorry."

"So, this is just what, fucking, with no emotions? If so, then I'm out. I'm already sorting out how I feel about you and those aren't feelings I can easily get over." His phone rings breaking our conversation.

"Carter speaking. Hey, man how are you doing? Yeah, I'm on my way there now. Got a stop to make real quick but should be there in about an hour. I have to check with Jimmy. Okay, I appreciate you doing this for me. Yes, I will take care of those things. Okay. See you soon." He hangs up and puts his shades back on. I want to reach out and touch him, but he still has a sense of anger about him. He's asked me before about leaving the casino and taking a job at his company, so we don't have to hide our relationship. I have to think about my son, too. I turn to face him, and he's focused intently on driving. I turn back to looking at the scenery outside and think about the situation at hand. I really need to talk to Jewel. I shoot her a text to arrange a get together.

I see we're approaching my neighborhood, so I pull myself together and put my thoughts on Xavier. I know he's gonna have questions. For a seven-year-old, he is a tough prosecutor. I check my appearance and hair making sure that I don't look like the night I had and put my compact back in its place.

"You don't need a mirror to see how beautiful you are. I can tell you every day, if you want," he says. Staring at me with those beautiful gray eyes.

"Carter, you are a strong, smart, fine as hell, man, who can have any woman and all the pussy he wants and not have to be bothered with a divorced single-mother and her smart, mouthy child. Why?

Why not the life of an entertainment lawyer who handles all avenues of clients? I'm not a charity case. I have my degree, but I like working at the casino. Hopefully one day I'll make it upstairs, so I can utilize my education. I don't like being treated like I need someone. My husband did that to me for years. Making me stay home to take care of the house and our child while he moved up the ladder at his job eventually making partner. I don't need you to rescue me Carter because I'm not drowning or in trouble."

"I don't treat you like a charity case. I just show you affection. If it means coming to your house with breakfast on a Sunday morning, or taking you to secret concerts, it's not out of charity. It's because I want to be with you. I know what I can have, but I want what I can't have and that's you, apparently. I want all of you. I want your Sunday through Saturday, twenty-four hours, from sun up to sun down, you. And please don't think I'm trying to do you like your ex did, I'm not stupid. I offered you my company position to help us both out. I wouldn't treat you any different than I do my employees now, except you will be the one I come home to every night. You don't want to tell anyone, that's fine. I'll keep it quiet, but not for long. You just need to decide what you want from me." The car comes to a stop. He shuts the engine off and steps out to open my door answering a call in the process.

"Mommy!" I hear the angelic voice of my baby call to me as he runs towards the car.

"Hi, lovebug. How are you?" I tickle him, and he laughs showing his missing tooth.

"Are we still going to my friends party?"

"Baby, I don't know. Mr. Carter has secret plans for us today that I didn't know about. We don't have to go if you don't want to." He thinks for a minute then asks me a question.

"Mommy, do you like Mr. Carter?" I know that I do like him I'm not sure if this is a conversation I'm ready to have with my son.

"Well, baby. I'm not sure. How do you feel about him?"

"I like him. He's cool and fun and he knows all the athletes."

"Yeah, but that's his job. Do you think he's okay outside those things?"

"Yeah. He said that he likes me, and I said sure you do. I'm a cool kid." My son has no filter and an innocence I wish I still had. I rub his head in a playful manner and urge him to go back in the house, so we can get ready to leave. Carter completes his phone call and joins me at my side.

"Business keeps you going, doesn't it?" I ask when I see the sign of frustration on his face.

"Well, that's the price I pay for doing what I do. It's one reason and one downfall as to why I'm expanding."

"How so?"

"I do extensive background checks on everyone I hire. From the cleaning staff, to my law associates and partners. When something comes back that I won't tolerate, then I have to start over."

"Why are you expanding? You have your own company with A-list type celebrities." He casually places his hand on my face, stroking my cheek with the pad of his thumb and locked into my eyes.

"Because I have other things I want in my life. That means moving things around, so I can always make time for them." I begin to sweat and start fanning myself. *This guy is serious.* I swallow hard as he leans towards me and I turn away from his advance.

"I need to go get ready. I won't be long." I scamper off to my room where I close and lock my door before sinking onto the floor.

"What am I going to do?" I say aloud thinking no one heard me.

"Do about what, mommy?" My perfect little ears comes from my bathroom spraying his little bottle of cologne that Carter bought him.

"Oh, I think I dropped some money that I was going to put in our vacation piggy bank."

"That's okay. I'm sure we have plenty with the money Mr. Carter gives you at work."

144 | ML PRESTON

"Have you been going through my purse again?" I ask him.

"No, mommy. That's wrong even if I want a piece of candy. I know not to do *that* again. But, Mr. Carter said that you help him at work and he gives you a big paycheck. I figure that it must be enough for our trip to Disneyland."

"You told him about our plans to go to Disneyland?"

"I can't lie to my new friend mommy. He won't like me if I do that." A knock at the door interrupts our talk and I answer.

"Sorry, Ms. Lang, but your guest said to hurry along please. There is a time limit on today's events."

"Okay. Tell him I'll be out in five minutes or less. Can you please make sure Xavier has his backup shoes and a change of clothes? Oh, and text me your Pay ID again so I can pay you, since I don't have cash and really hate using checks."

"No need, Ms. Lang. The gentleman paid me, very handsomely might I add. Plus, he has me on staff for the week whether you need me or not. He's so sweet." My expression must reflect what I'm feeling as she quickly retreats, and Xavier follows. I begin to take off the clothes I have on and switch outfits. I don't even realize that Carter has made his way to my room. I walk out of my closet buttoning my jeans and slipping on my cami only to walk dead into him.

"Slow down, you almost took me out." My reaction takes over and I punch him in his shoulder.

"Where do you get off paying my sitter? I told you I don't need your money or rescuing."

"So, I can't be a nice guy? Why does everything always seem like charity to you if someone is just being nice? What are you trying to prove to yourself? If I hand you a napkin, will you think I was stopping you from getting your own?" I hate when he's right.

"I'm sorry. You are a genuine person who has feelings for me and because I'm still fearful about failing and being on my own..."

"But you don't have to be. I'm here with you and I want to be. You will never be alone if I have anything to do with it. Plus, you have amazing friends, co-workers, and a soon-to-be boss that can't seem to keep his hands off you." He pulls me closer and I laugh and his corniness.

"Boy, you are a silly duck." He nuzzles my neck and I feel more relaxed.

"Ahem." The sound of a throat clearing takes me out of my moment and I look towards the door and not happy with who I see.

"Corey, what are you doing here?"

"Tiffany, nice to see you too. I came to see if Xavier wanted to go get some new toys."

"I told him no, because I was going somewhere with my new friend, and he just walked in here." Xavier chimes in from the other side of the door. The men do a stare off and suddenly, I'm glad Carter is here.

"Oh, Corey, this is Carter. Carter, this is my-ex Corey, Xavier's dad." They shake hands and I love the match up. Carter is about four inches taller and his shoulders are broader thanks to his workout regimen. My inner happiness meter is coming to life because I know the question he's going to ask next.

"Nice to meet you, Carter. So, what do you do?" Corey always felt that he was superior to all others, even in college.

"I have my own business," Carter replies with great unspoken confidence.

"Oh, small business man. I like that. Well if you need an attorney, I can help with those pesky business forms." The handshaking doesn't stop, and I grab a pair of no-show socks and slip them on while watching the showdown.

"Thanks, but I don't think I need an attorney." Carter laughs at the suggestion.

"Well, frivolous lawsuits are on the rise with new businesses."

"I know. I defend people from such things."

"Oh, you're an attorney. I made partner at my firm within two years. Are you a partner?" The dick measuring contest is about to get real.

"I have my own firm. I'm an entertainment lawyer. I have a large clientele list that I keep out of legal troubles." The expression on Corey's face let's me know that Carter hit the target, but of course he has to save face.

"Oh. Well, in that case you are a decent attorney. How did you meet Tiffany?" He quickly changes the subject.

"I met her on her job at the casino. Saw those sexy green eyes and I couldn't help myself."

"Oh, so you two are serious?"

"Depends on what you mean by serious?" I know that has Corey's interest piqued, but I'm ready to go.

"Hey, baby. I think we should probably get going. Xavier is really excited about whatever you have planned. Sorry, Corey. We do have plans for today. Maybe next weekend you can go toy shopping."

"Oh, okay. So, where are you headed?"

"I don't know. It's a surprise. Carter planned it all by himself. He's spontaneous like that." Xavier comes in sporting a pair of little Ray-Bans and I know where those came from. I glare towards him and he shrugs his shoulders in an innocent manner.

"Let's go people." Xavier demands and tries to snap his fingers like I do when I rush him along. Carter picks him up and they run outside to his car. Corey grabs my arm to pull me to the side while walking out.

"So, you're serious about this guy?" I don't feel like I have to defend anything that I do to him.

"Were you serious about the girl you left your family for?" I walk through the house checking the windows, doors, and turning all electronics off.

"She's my wife now," he exclaims. I check the fish and drop them a few flakes while I answer his question.

"Well, he's my boyfriend, I think. Besides, what's your point?" I set the thermostat and turn on the hallway light. Ashley gathers her things and heads outside to join Carter and Xavier when she hears the conversation volume increase.

"The point is that is our son. I don't want him around another man."

"Well, I didn't want him around another woman, but hey, he calls her other mom."

"Is he going to be calling him dad?"

"No. I don't know. Why do you care?"

"I don't. I do care about our son."

"Well, trust me when I say that he is in very capable hands." I open the door and show him out while I set my alarm. I see Carter and Xavier are waiting for me at the now replaced limo SUV and not the car we arrived in. I know it's not a battle easily won so I climb in and Xavier immediately hugs me.

"Thank you, mommy, for not making me go with dad today. I like hanging with Mr. Carter."

"Now, X-man, remember I told you to call me Mr. C or Carter, but not Mr. Carter."

"I know but my mommy gets mad when I don't say Mr. Carter." This kid has no loyalty to me and will rat me out to the cops if given the chance.

"Well, I'll talk to her. Hey, you remember that tablet I had, and you liked?"

"Yeah?" Carter pulls out a new tablet complete with headphones and hands it to him. There is a little case that has his name engraved and a logo of his favorite basketball team. I don't say anything, I just know that I have one less thing to buy for his birthday.

"So, showering my little prince with gifts. What do you think you are doing?"

"Scoring brownie points with the MILF? Oh, never mind. I'm already doing that."

I roll my eyes and let out a little laugh. "So, where are we going?"

"Well, if you peek over to your left, you will see." I glance out the window and I see a private plane.

"Oh, you're doing a tour of a plane. He loves planes. That's super sweet."

"Well, not exactly. Come on." The car stops, and we are walked up the stairs to the private jet.

"Good morning, Mr. Jackson. The pilot is making the final checks and we will be ready for take-off. We should arrive in about an hour."

"Thank you, Gwen. Please make sure that Xavier has the VR goggles for the system I had installed, and he may want breakfast. Check with him before we take off. Tiff, did you want anything to eat? I know you must be starving." He wiggles his eyebrows and I laugh.

"Coffee. I will have a coffee, smart-ass. Thank you." I check to make sure my child is buckled in his seat before returning to mine and getting comfortable. After takeoff, I recline back to grab a nap while Carter whips out his laptop and begins working.

Chapter
FIFTEEN

"**H**EY, BEAUTIFUL." A VOICE STIRS me from my much-needed but short nap, but it is not the voice I expect to hear those words.

"Hey, kiddo. Why did you say that?"

"Can a son just give his mom a compliment?" I pinch his nose for his little smart sound bite and Carter laughs.

"Come on. We've landed. The car is waiting, and this little guy needs to be blindfolded with his mother's permission." I stare at him awkwardly because he's asking me to blindfold my child, and I don't know where we are. He throws me an innocent smirk with matching eyes and I give in.

"Come here, Xai. Let's put on your blindfold so that Carter can take you to this huge surprise he has planned.

"Are you sure you don't know mommy?"

"I certainly don't, and he won't even tell me. Probably thinks I'll tell you." I tie his silk blindfold over his little eyes and grab his hand and we start to descend the stairs.

"You know, I have a blindfold for you too," Carter whispers in my ear when I pass by him. I look back and he gives me a wink. I shake my head and gaze at the limousine that is waiting for us at the end of the red carpet.

"Carter, what is all of this?"

"It's a surprise for Xavier, my new best friend. Now, hurry." I search for clues and I can't see anything to tell me where we are. I think about using my phone but before I grab my purse, Carter cleverly reveals that he has my phone in a lockbox.

"How do I know you are not planning on kidnapping us and killing us or something?"

"Really, Tiff? Don't be paranoid. Trust me, in about ten minutes, you will know and then two minutes after that, he will know and you both will be...happy." I help my baby get into the car and buckle him in. I put his headphones on to his kid-friendly playlist and make sure the volume is up just a little. He begins singing along at his non-inside voice giving me the time I need to talk to Mr. C.

"Why?"

"Why what?"

"Why are you doing this?"

"I feel like we had this conversation earlier when I laid out all my intentions. But if you feel that you need a more definitive answer, okay, I'll give it to you." He leans in to my ear placing his hand on my thigh, his fingers cautiously near my vagina. "I'm going to make you mine at any cost. In the bedroom I'll make you beg me to stop, and outside I'll treat you like you deserve to be treated."

"Did you bother to ask me what I wanted? That's right, you're a guy used to getting what he wants." I place my hand squarely on his junk before moving to his knee.

"You don't see us in a relationship? I mean, you called me your boyfriend to your ex, after all. Now, I know it was probably something you were doing to let him know that you moved on, but I think it was you asserting my position in your life and the life of your child. Was I wrong?" Again, with the right shit. I think about the last few weeks that we've gone out on dates plus the time spent getting to know each other on poker nights and how this came to be a relationship. He's dropped by a few of Xavier's basketball games which is big to him since his dad hasn't been there. Not to mention the time he's spent doing other things like volunteering at a PTA night with me, and this big secret today.

"I hadn't realized that I put you in this position without discussing if this is what you want," I say.

"If I didn't, you wouldn't have been able to place me here and I wouldn't be able to see your green eyes light up when we arrived here." He lets down the window and I see that he has flown us to Disneyland. I'm filled with shock and my heart rate increases.

"Damn you, Carter." I swing at his arm but miss when the tears begin to roll. He must've anticipated this reaction as he pulls a handkerchief from his car pocket. He places a kiss on my forehead. I hurry to clear my face, so Xavier can't see. He moves over to the other seat and removes my baby's headphones.

"Okay, buddy. We are here. Now, before we get out the car, you have to promise me no peeking, alright?"

"That's fine. I can't see anything anyway." Carter steps out the car and takes my son's hand and I follow behind. When the limo pulls away, the stars of *The Princess and the Frog* appear.

"Okay, on the count of three, blindfold off. 1, 2, 3!" The expression on Xavier's face is one that I will never forget. No matter how our relationship ends, this moment will last forever. Xavier jumped up and down and screamed only the way an excited child can. Clearly the hero of the day, Carter officially captured my heart in this moment.

"Thank you, Mr. Carter," Xavier says as he hugs him hard.

"You're welcome, little buddy. I think the Princess has something for you." The character of Tiana walks to him and hands him a crown fit for a Prince. She places a kiss on his cheek and he's smitten. He grabs her hand as we walk through the private admissions area where a carriage is waiting for us.

"Cool! This is the best day ever. It's not even my birthday!" Xavier exclaims as he uses the stairs to climb into the ride. Before we get in, I stop Carter in his track.

"You, sir, have some explaining to do. I know you have an ulterior motive."

"I do."

"What is it?" He begins to speak but backs away.

"I'll tell you when the time is right." He assists me with climbing into the carriage making sure to get a hand full of my left ass cheek before climbing into the carriage himself. As we go through the roads of the park, stopping at every ride, and pigging out on all the park food, the bond these two create is magical. In fact, by the time we land back in Vegas, they are both asleep with Xavier in his lap and his arms lovingly wrapped around him. I don't want to wake them, but after I snap a picture for my personal keepsake, I gently kiss my baby on his cheek and rub his head to wake him. He pushes me away, so I move to the bigger baby. I plant a kiss on his lips and he opens his eyes as I pull away. Our lips don't part ways, in fact we kiss again, again, and again. His mood is not full of the fire from last night. It's softer, loving, not controlling. When I think about it, he's been acting like this all day. The sound of a little boy's giggle breaks the moment and I feel my cheeks turning red.

"I knew you liked him mommy," his laugh is infectious, and it melts my heart.

"Well, let's get in the car and get you guys home, and you in bed. You have a game tomorrow, right?"

"Right. Are you going to be there?" he asks Carter.

"I plan on it."

"Good. I want to tell all my friends about what my new best friend did today." We exit the plane and climb into the waiting car and head back to my house.

"Hear that. I'm his new best friend. What am I to you?" Carter asks.

"Hmm, I hope that you're my new bestie and will stay the night with me for our first sleepover."

"That, I can do." He lets out a deep sigh as if that was what he wanted to hear.

TODAY WE HAD A GREAT time. Carter stayed over last night, as agreed, but not in my bed, like I hoped. Instead, he slept in my home office on the futon out of respect for my child. This man keeps winning me over. Even when I snuck into the room late at night and tried to seduce him, he turned me away. My feelings were hurt, but he made up for it by having breakfast and coffee delivered. Took me a moment to forgive him. Especially when it took my special toys two hours to bring me the release he could've done in one. They spent the day outside on the court practicing before we went to Xavier's game. As usual, Corey wasn't there, citing issues with one of his clients. Xavier told him, it was okay, and that Carter was filling in for him. I figure that had to sting when he heard that. Corey tried to ask me if Carter was taking his father position. I told him no and that they have their own great bond.

"Dinner is ready." I call out towards the living room.

"Okay," I hear echoing back. I take the pitcher of homemade lemonade to the table and my two gamers appear and sit down.

"Uh, no. Xavier, please tell our guest what the rules are."

"Oh, snap. We have to wash our hands first, so all the germs of the video game won't invade our tummy. I know it's not real, but it makes mommy feel good." This kid is growing too fast for my liking. After my implemented three-minute hand washing, they return to the table where I have the plates served and glasses filled. Carter begins to take a bite and Xavier stops him.

"OMG, Mr. C. Mommy is not going to let you come over if you keep messing up. We have to give thanks."

"Oh, say our prayers? Okay."

"No, we just give thanks. Mommy doesn't want to offend others' beliefs, so we just say thank you."

"Thank you for this food," Carter says. Xavier does the cutest face palm and I giggle a bit.

"Xai, it's okay. He's a guest. You will have to teach him how to say thank you like we say thank you. But there was nothing wrong with what he said. In fact, it was perfect." He takes a bite of the mashed potatoes and flashes me a wink. We all begin to dig into our plates and no conversation is being held. Suddenly, Xavier had an important question to ask.

"So, mommy, why can't Mr. C sleep in your room? He's your friend, right?" I choke on my drink as my child has truly caught me off guard.

"Are you okay, Tiff?" Carter asks while holding back his on laughter.

I swallow what's left of my drink and waive him off.

"I'm good. Why should he sleep in the room with me?"

"First of all, he's your friend and you kissed him. That makes him your boyfriend. I thought girlfriends and boyfriends sleep in each other's room and watch tv."

"My, you know a lot of stuff. However, some people do but not everyone does. I think that we shouldn't sleep in the same room and Mr. C agrees. It's really the right thing to do when a person has a child."

"Oh. I just don't want you sad because your friend isn't with you."

"How sweet, but I'm not sad. We are good friends." He accepts my crappy answer and we finish our meal. I get up to take plates to the kitchen, but Carter stops me and relieves me of my waitress duties.

"I'll rinse these and load them you go get him ready for bed."

"Thank you, Carter." I take Xavier to his room to get him ready for bath and bed. After tucking him in, I head back to the living room where I find Carter grabbing his things and hanging up the phone with his driver.

"Oh, you're leaving?"

"Well, tomorrow is Monday. I have some contracts to review plus I have to go out of the country."

"What do you mean out of the country? Why didn't you tell me sooner?" I feel a panic in my voice when I ask. I'm so used to him being here and me working every Friday night that this throws off my schedule. Okay, it's making my heart confused. I mean, I'm cool with this being a newly formed relationship, but still.

"I have a client starting a world tour overseas in Tokyo. I have to oversee the contracts and make sure everything is okay. He will arrive by Thursday and the kickoff is Friday. I'll be back by Saturday."

"That's six days without you."

"You never see me until Friday anyway unless I sneak onto the casino floor."

"But…"

"But what, Tiff? You won't give me a solid answer about where I fit in your life even though I have made a firm stand for what I want with you. I'm not going to put everything in my life on hold while you figure out what you want." I have been stutter stepping when he questions our relationship, and I did claim him earlier. I just don't want to be hurt again. Corey destroyed my thought of love and for the last year, I wasn't looking for another relationship. This has me confused.

"Nothing. Will you call me?" That's not the answer he was hoping for, but he accepted it anyway.

"With the time difference, I don't know how that will work."

"What's the difference 5, 6 hours?"

He chuckles a bit. "No, babe. Try 17. So, when you are getting up at 8 a.m. to get little man ready for school, it is already 1 a.m. the next day. But, since I tend to stay up late, I can call you."

"You better call me." I place my arms around his waist and my hands firmly on his ass and he does the same.

"Are you gonna spank me when I get back if I don't?"

"Maybe." We kiss and things warm up when his driver pulls in.

"I guess I better go. Damn you make it hard for me to leave." He begins to tongue kiss my neck and I moan in response.

"Then don't go. Stay the night. My dad gave you permission." He lets out a deep, throaty growl as our foreheads rest against each other.

"I can't. I really have to get business squared away."

"When do you actually leave for Tokyo?"

"Tomorrow morning. Yeah, the flight is out at 8:35 a.m. so, I will have to be at the airport by 6:00 a.m."

"I really wish I knew. Maybe things…"

"Things were just fine. Tiffany, this has been a wonderful week-end. I spent time with you and X-man. This was…" He pauses for a moment and I inspect his eyes for his unfinished thought. He looks back towards his driver before turning back to me.

"I gotta go. I'll call you in the morning." He places a peck on my cheek and heads to his car. I watch him get in and he doesn't look back at me. When I close my door, my stomach knots up and I become sad. This man is fastly becoming my everything and I'm afraid to let him know. I turn to my friend for a little comfort.

"Hello, chocolate chip ice cream," I mutter aloud. I grab a spoon and the chocolate syrup and head to my room where I can sulk in peace.

Chapter

SIXTEEN

"**M**OM, MR. C IS ON YOUR phone. He said he's about to board the plane."

"Okay, tell him to have a great time and I'll talk to him later." I yell from my shower. I decided last night that I wouldn't take his call this morning. I need the distance to make my feelings clear.

"He said okay and to make sure to check the account." If he put money in my bank account I'm going to scream. I shut off the water and run to grab my phone and check my bank balance. It is just as it was yesterday. I'm puzzled by the statement my son made so I ask him for clarity.

"Xavier, are you sure he said check my account?" I throw on my clothes and put my hair up in a ponytail and we get in the car, so I can take him to school.

"Yes. Ma'am."

"Did he say what account?"

"No, ma'am. He just said, tell her I will call her later and to check for the account." I still have no idea of what this kid is talking about. I just shake it off pulling into the circular drive at the school.

"Okay, Scooby. Have a great day. Ashley will pick you up."

"Mom, don't call me Scooby. Call me X-Man like Mr. C."

"You really like him, don't you?"

"Yeah. Can I tell you something?"

"Sure."

"I like him better than dad. I mean, I love my dad, but his job keeps us apart."

"Well, being a lawyer is very demanding. I'm sure he loves you very much."

"I love him too, mom. But, Mr. C, it's different. He does the things that dad should do."

"Does that make you sad?"

"No, I like it. I feel guilty, though."

"Well, don't feel bad, son. If that is how you feel, you should never let it make you feel bad. Okay." The other cars blow their horn and I know I need to move forward. My son gets out the car not before giving me my special raspberry kiss. This kid is my life and there is nothing I wouldn't do for him. I pull off and head to work.

"So, RUMOR HAS IT THAT Mr. Jackson had him a good ol' time Friday night. Some green-eyed babe with a body shaped like a Coke bottle was seen leaving his room Saturday morning and with him. Wonder who that was?" Jewel says. I look at her and her smile is as wide as the strip outside. "So, you two finally hooked up. Took y'all long enough. That man was feeling you from day one, even though it was a rough start. I watched him all night just staring at you. So, how was it?"

"Oh, no. I'm not going to do that. I never share details about things that personal."

"But you are admitting it happened, right?"

"I'm neither confirming nor denying anything." I grab my apron and start off to the floor when Vic calls me to the cash office.

"What's up, Vic?"

"Hey, doll. Mr. Jackson left a hefty amount of cash for you in his bank account. He said for you to set up a game for next Friday. Said that you all discussed the details before he left." Check the account that's what he meant.

"Oh, sure. I will need a key pass for his villa suite."

"No problem. He has you on his list of approved guests, so a key is yours. What do you do for this man in these games? He's never asked for anyone to setup personally before."

"He says that I bring him good luck." I take the key and go to his suite. When I open the door, it's obvious that it has been cleaned. I look around and a flood of memories come to me. They vary from the first night we met, to last Friday. I clear my head and walk over to the bar to grab the banker's bag and his list of preferred and alternative drinks. As per my usual routine, I check for missing barware, do a glass count, and make sure the ice buckets are empty and cleaned. I notice that one of them is missing so I go on a hunt till I remember where it is. I open the door to the room where he captivated my body and soul. When I spot the missing ice bucket I grab it with the memory of him playing with my nipples using the ice that was contained within.

"That must be some thought you are having, girl." Jewel says as she walks in with the bagged snacks to restock his bar. I couldn't answer her because it was just as she described. I gather the container and head back to the bar area.

"So, still not gonna tell me?"

"Nope."

"Come on, Tiffy. I need this for the spank bank later."

"Eew, you can use your own fantasies for that. I don't want my friend getting off on my experiences." She laughs, and I soon follow. I gather my list for the liquor store, the bank bag, and leave a note for the night staff before leaving to go work the casino floor.

The flickering lights, bells and whistles of jackpots being won prove to be the distraction I need. Serving drinks to the eager gamblers and blowing on the die to those who also think I'm a good luck charm makes the evening go by fast. I count the tips I've acquired, and it gives me just enough to put in for the walk-in closet that I've been saving for since I no longer need to go to Disneyland. I go to the cash office to turn in my chips only to find that Victor is by himself.

"You need a hand with the countdowns?" I ask.

"I've got to audit these table counts, and Marilyn went home sick. I called Jacqui, but she's not answering her phone or the page." Jacqui usually disappears when she's at a table with a customer who won't let her go.

"I can help. I'm pretty fast at counting." Vic doesn't know that I have my degree and I have a few months of cash office experience when I worked at a bank as an intern.

"Sure, come on. I need any help I can get." I put my chips in my locker outside the office and grab a pair of latex gloves. I sit down, and he tries to explain the process, but I start the countdown immediately. Instead of saying anything, he stands there watching. I finish one cash box in under five minutes. He loads it on the cash cart and goes back to his table. I catch him looking at me as I continue to work at lightning speed. I have to admit, this makes me feel like I'm doing something worthwhile and that I may need to rethink Carter's offer.

"Okay, these ten are complete. Do you need me to enter them into the books?" He shakes the mouse to make the computer wake up and shows me how to input them to their customized program.

I take my tally sheets and begin to upload the information. When I finish, Victor has a Bahama Mama waiting for me.

"I have never seen anyone work like you just did. Why didn't you tell me that you knew how to do this?"

"To be honest, I just wanted a job when I came here. I was starting my life over, newly divorced with a kid. I get plenty in my agreement from my ex, but I just wanted to do something for me. Just to be able to prove that I can do something for myself. I hadn't done any accounting work since my son was born, so I stayed away from anything related. Tonight, was just what I needed."

"Well, you can have a job back here if you want?"

"No, I'm good. I was offered a position at a law firm and I think I'm going to take it. I have to make sure that the money is right and that I don't have to move."

"So, is this your two-week notice?"

"This is my hold on, let me check this opportunity out first, notice." He smiles, and I grab my drink and finish it before heading home.

"What's up Tiff? You don't bake like this unless something is seriously bothering you," Jewel says as she enters my kitchen. I came home at 11:00 last night and tossed and turned until I surrendered to my thoughts. I've been up since 2:00 a.m. baking cupcakes, cookies, cakes, and now a variety of pies. I will save a few for my son when he returns from his dad's and maybe take some to work and share, but the majority will go to the homeless shelters in my area.

"I just have a lot to think about and consider before Carter gets back."

"Like?" she says as she runs her finger inside the bowl scraping the icing.

"He offered me a job."

"Keeping his bed warm?" I whack her across the knuckles with my wooden spoon.

"No. That's rude. At his firm." I continue to mix my ingredients.

"Yeah, but isn't his firm in Los Angeles?"

"Yeah. That's what I need to discuss with him among other things."

"So, what will you be doing?"

"I'll be using my degree finally. Help keep an eye on his firms accounts and make sure there is no funny business going on."

"That sounds like a sweet opportunity. I'd think that you wouldn't have to go to Cali for that. Maybe he can set you up with a remote office."

"Well, he'll be back this weekend, so I can talk to him more then. In the meantime, taste this." I shovel a spoon full of filling for my key lime pie into her mouth and the way her eyes roll into the back of her head lets me know that the pie is just right. I think she's having a moment to herself with the sounds that are emitting. I fill the graham cracker shells with the filling and set them in the fridge to set. Since that's the last pie, I begin cleaning up. Jewel helps and starts putting all the ingredients away. When we finish, I pull out a bottle from the wine fridge, uncork it, and pour us a couple of glasses while we have a seat on the couch. Xavier is spending this week with his dad, so I don't have after school duties and will take advantage of my me time.

"So, remember when Casey asked me to move in with him? I think I'm gonna do it." The out of the blue comment by my friend caused me to choke on my pinot grigio. The most shocking fact is she has to be serious since she would've never mentioned it if she weren't.

"Really? Well, that's good, right?" I'm not sure of her thoughts so I eliminate the need to be funny but also feel her out as far as what she thinks she wants.

"It is good, actually. I love his condo overlooking the lake out in Henderson. It's a wonderful place."

"But?" I interject feeling that turn in the conversation.

"But, I don't know if I'm ready to make that move. I like my job and with it comes a lot of flirting. I'm also giving up my non-committing status which means I can't see Micah when he's in town. Even though we are strictly casual with no strings, when I slept with him a few weeks back it made me think about him differently too. I can't believe I'm catching feelings for people. Ick!" She's right. The look in her eyes says she's falling for someone. I think she likes what is happening with Carter and I and that makes her think about Casey, but on the other hand, her and Micah have fun together and the flirting is shared, not one-sided. Then again, Casey always treats her with respect, except at the club when he was ten seconds from fucking her in that VIP section.

"Well, if you're looking for my opinion, I don't have one."

"Why not?" she whines.

"Because if I say or suggest something and it doesn't work, you will blame me. I'm not trying to have that kind of drama in my life."

"But, Tiff, I need you. I don't know how to figure this out." She lays her head in my lap and softly rubs my legs. She's just as bad as my child when it comes to buttering me up.

"No," I exclaim.

"Fine. I guess I will have to use my blackmail card I was saving for a rainy day." Now, over the years, we have both made some bad choices and have the photographs to prove it. For her to go into that pandora box just to get my opinion on a love matter causes me to recant my previous answer.

"Fine, Jewel. I think your future is with Casey. Micah is fun, good looking, and I can only assume he dicks you down right, but there were boundaries set up with him from the beginning and if he wanted more, he'd tell you." She thinks for a beat before sighing heavily and plopping down into my lap, once again.

"Yeah, you're right. Casey is great. When we have sex..."

"Stop. TMI territory. I don't want to know."

"I wasn't going to give you details. I was just going to say he makes sure I come before he does. Whereas Micah isn't as caring." I need us to talk about our boundaries again. Jewel is always over-sharing.

"There's your answer. Now move, I have to go box the cookies up so Corey can come by and get them." No sooner than I say that, my door opens and in comes my little man and his dad.

"Mom, I'm here for the cookies. I couldn't wait till Friday." He digs in and snags a couple while I box the others for him to take to school.

"So, you made your dad drive all the way over here to get these."

"That and dad said he needed to talk to you about Mr. C." I close my eyes, so no one can see them roll and then open them to find my ex taking a few cookies off the platter.

"Tiff, can we go out on the patio and talk?"

"Jewel, can you watch the cookie monster here and finish boxing these up, please?"

"Of course. Are you going to tell your ex-man how good your new man is?" She plops a cookie in her mouth while looking at Corey in his eyes. There is no loss of love between these two. I signal Corey to come on and we head out back.

"Vanessa and I are separating. She says I spend too much time at the office and obsessing over you and this guy you're dating."

"I'm sorry. If you're looking for sympathy, I'm fresh out."

"No, I'm not looking for that. I was hoping that maybe we can try to rekindle our relationship." I tilt my head to the side to look at him. I'm trying to figure out how he can even remotely wrap his mind around the idea that I'd want him back.

"So, you mean to tell me that you are wanting to come back to me, after you cheated on me with her, got married, have a baby on the way, and since you are obsessing that a new man is in my life, she now wants to leave your ass and I'm supposed to be like, okay?"

"No, I should've never did those things to you and I want my family back. I want you me and Xavier together again, in this, our forever home."

"Let me just stop your fantasy right there, Corey. This is my and our child's forever home. You are not a part of this. You have a wife who wants your undivided attention on her. Your obsession that I have finally moved on is insane. I don't think you want any of what you just spouted off to me. I think you are jealous of Carter. I'm sure Xavier tells you about all the things they talk about and the things he's done for him, and that's eating you up. You think that you are being pushed out of his life, but you aren't. Xavier loves you and you are his dad, but he has, we have someone else in our lives too. And that you just have to deal with. Go home, Corey. Apologize to your wife and let her know that she's important to you." He rolls his head backwards and sighs aloud before looking back to me.

"I just don't want to be replaced. Before this guy came along, Xavier shared everything with me. Now he tells me that it's okay if I miss the game or don't buy him something and that he went on a private plane to Disneyland. I feel like I'm missing out." Part of me understands his pain, the other part of me is like 'too bad, so sad'.

"Corey, I think you and Vanessa need to sit down and talk this out. You need to hear her out and she needs to understand that your son is just as, if not more than, important to you than she is and that it is not some feeble attempt to get me back. That will never happen. Ever! I don't care if this relationship with Carter lasts forever or not, I will not backtrack. I love that I have even opened myself up to moving forward and not hung up on my past. The relationship, not you. I was holding on to something that had died years ago even though we've only been apart for one." He grabs my hands and holds them out in front of his mouth placing a soft kiss on the back of each of them.

"Thank you, Tiffany. You're strong, beautiful, smart, and I was a fool to fuck it up. But you hold no hate toward me and you raise our son beautifully. I'm sorry I fucked it up."

"I'm sorry you fucked it up too. I loved you. I still do, but not in a romantic way. I say we vow to be better friends."

"The kind with benefits?" he jokes. At least I think he is.

"Um, no. This pussy is currently controlled by another person."

"I bet he's not as good as me."

"You're right. He's better." I turn and walk back inside the house leaving him to stroke his own ego. I make sure all the treats are packed and even take a key lime pie and box it up especially for Vanessa with a sincere note attached. I give the message to Xavier and tell him not to share with his dad and give it only to her. Jewel spots what I did and no sooner than they leave, she pounces on me for information.

"So, what was in the note? Did you tell her how her hubby is over here trying to get that good pussy?" I laugh out loud because my friend is amazing with no filter. Thirty minutes ago, she realized she was in love with Casey and now she's back to her usual crass and crude ass.

"No. I finally let my past go and I simply told her that she had nothing to worry about from me."

"So, this means you are..."

"I'm going full throttle with Carter. I can't stop thinking about him. He's so involved with me and Xavier and our day to day. He sends him a message everyday making sure he's doing his homework, if he's practicing his free throws like James Durant suggested, through me, of course. I wanted to wait and see where this was going before I gave him his number. All of this after a few weeks. I know it seems kind of fast, but what if instead of me needing to move on from Corey and the past, he was the one that needed to find a reason to change? What if we were meant to find each other?"

"It's possible. I mean no one knows when it will happen or who it will be with. Like you and I both know I'm fine being me, but I feel even better when I'm with Casey. At first it was cool just flirting but then when he asked me out, I said yes immediately, without thinking. So, who knows. You and Carter could be made for each other and Corey was a stop along the way. Then again, Corey probably altered the path when he cheated on you." She makes a valid point. She never committed solid to one guy, not even for a date. She would suggest things to do and they'd do them. But the Corey thing, well that's scary. Here I thought we'd be together forever, but things changed. I wallowed in self-pity for months only allowing Jewel and my shadow see me in pieces. I wouldn't even let my parents see me disheveled when they came out to visit last year. Now, I seem to be picking up those shattered pieces, storing the memories where they are supposed to be and making new ones. I grab my phone and shoot Carter a text.

Me: Hey you. Or rather, Kon'nichiwa.

According to the time table link he sent me, it should be just about 9:00 a.m. in Tokyo. I'm hoping I catch him before he starts working. Ten minutes go by and I don't get a response. I chunk it up to schedule and finish cleaning my kitchen. Jewel joins me making it easier to complete. She boxes up some goodies for her to take home to go with her ice cream and we say our goodnights.

"See you at work tomorrow," she says as she walks to her car.

"Okay, see you then. Text me and let em know you've made it home. You know the routine." She waves at me as she takes off. I grab my phone to check for missed messages but still, nothing. He must be really busy, I think to myself. I channel surf with no landing plan as my body and brain wind down from all my exhaustion. I manage to pull myself out of my bed, shower and return to its warm covers. I'm sure I'll have my normal wake up message in the morning.

Chapter

SEVENTEEN

"**M**OM, I'M HOME," MY LITTLE angels voice calls out when he enters my bedroom. Corey sent a message earlier saying he'd see him in the door, but he wouldn't be coming in because he had a company dinner to get ready for. I'm doing my normal mid-week chores of spot house cleaning which includes a couple of loads of laundry leaving me not in the mood for socializing. I hadn't spoken to Carter but once since he left last Monday. Even then it was fast paced, and I felt brushed off. No morning messages, no emails, no calls, just nothing. I even tried to use Face Time to maybe do a little virtual peep show, but he never answered. He was scheduled to be back in town last Saturday, but I haven't seen him yet. I asked Vic if he had heard from him since he has a game set up for this Friday. At least that was the excuse I used to find out my intel. Vic said he hadn't notified the hotel of any changes.

"Hey, cupcake. Mommy is in her room." He comes around the corner and runs to hug me. I put the vacuum in its upright position and shut it off before embracing my baby.

"Hey, did you have a good time with your dad?" Due to my change of shifts on Monday and Tuesday, and Ashley's, Corey agreed to keep our son an extra two days.

"Yeah, I did. And Vanessa said thank you for the pie, by the way. I forgot to tell you the other day."

"That's okay. I'm sure with school and basketball, you were busy, and it slipped your mind."

"She also gave me this note to give you. Am I like the designated mailman? She told me the same thing you said which was not to let dad see it." I take the note from him and put it in my nightstand to read later.

"Go put your things away and your dirty clothes in the laundry room so I can wash them."

"Vanessa already washed and folded them for me. I'll just go put them in my drawers. Can I go swimming later today?"

"Sure. I had the pool guy come clean the pool the other day so it's ready to go. Ashley will be coming by today too."

"Why? Is Mr. C back?" Xavier's innocent question reminds me of Carter's prolonged absence.

"I don't know dear. I still haven't heard from him. I just thought we'd have a nice dinner here and hang out by the pool. Ashley is coming over to get some work in for her graduation requirements."

"Are we going to her graduation?"

"If she invites us we will go."

"Cool! I've never been to a big graduation. I mean I was at my own kindergarten graduation. It was a long time ago." This kid thinks he's old. It's only been two years. I shuttle him off to put his things away and finish cleaning. An alert on my phone makes me think that finally Carter has replied. My stomach fills with butterflies but they soon vanish when it is just a banking alert. I shower and find me a simple outfit to put on after I check on the food in the kitchen.

I try to get in touch with Carter a few times and still no

response. I find myself near a panic state and almost take that leap into calling hospitals and jails, which considering some of his clientele, wouldn't be a shocker, or even contacting his offices in LA. Instead I text Jewel for support. She informs me that she and Casey are on their way to Reno for a mini-vacay and that I'm just overreacting. Maybe she's right. I wish her safe travels and tell her I expect details when she comes back.

Another two hours pass and I'm no longer worried, I'm pissed. It's been four days since he should've had his fine ass here. I shake the thoughts from my head and go to the kitchen. Since the food is ready, I turn the heat low to keep the dishes warm while we go swimming. Ashley has made it to the house and has agreed to go swimming with Xavier in the pool. Frustrated with my mind being preoccupied with shit I shouldn't even be thinking about, I decide to join them. I put on my one-piece barely there suit and my sunscreen and lay out in my lounger while watching them play Marco polo and volleyball. They even have races and either my son is a good, strong swimmer, or Ashley let him win. I vote for the latter.

"Hey, Mr. C. you're back," Xavier shouts from the pool. I whip my head around and find his six-three frame, and pepper sprinkled with a little salt scruff on his strong chiseled jawline. His grey eyes twinkle with the sun's reflection off the pool and his smile is big and bright when Xavier comes to give him a hug and some fist bumping.

"Hey, X-Man. How are you?"

"Good. Mom's pissed, though. I hope you have a nice present for her." Like I said, my son would sell me out. He wasn't lying. I'm quite pissed.

"Well, I think I have something that will make her smile." I can't help thinking that he's talking about that sausage in his pants. I smile, without him knowing, of course, but still I'm pissed. Xavier runs and does a cannonball into the pool and finishes playing with Ashley. Carter comes and stands above me, blocking the sun. I know that I'm a black woman, with creole and native American bloodlines, but I still like laying out in the sun. It's good vitamin D. Right now, I need the other variety of the D.

"Aren't you going to hug me, say hello, something?" he says. I roll over onto my back showing the sexy design of my monokini. It has a small crochet strip connecting the top bikini piece to the bottom but from the back it looks like a standard two-piece design. My breasts barely stay covered and his attention is all on me. I catch a glimpse of the flowers and small box he is carrying and signal with my eyes to put the items on the table. He catches on and I go back to enjoying the sun. He pushes my legs over slightly and sits on the end of my lounger taking my feet into his hands and begins to rub them. For a moment, I forget that I'm mad at him for his lack of communication. When my mind brings me back to reality, I snatch my foot from his hands and sit up to confront him.

"No calls, no texts, no emails, and you were late getting back to Vegas. Based on the information you gave me, you were supposed to be back in Vegas last Saturday, Carter. If you don't want this relationship anymore, let me know now. I've been on the pain train and I'm not going back." Carter looks out at the pool and sees Ashley and Xavier looking on as my voice escalates. He nods his head towards that direction and I turn to see Ashley helping Xavier out of the pool. I hold my head in embarrassment as they scurry into the house. Another mommy temper I'm going to have to explain.

"I had a detour into LA to get some things in order. Sorry I didn't let you know. I wasn't aware you had plans or anything like that."

"If you had bothered to respond to my messages or emails, missed calls or any form of communication I was trying to convey, you would've known. I knew you just wanted a fuck buddy all along. You're thirty-five years old, never married with no serious relationship on record."

"Fuck buddy? Really? Is that what you think?"

"I mean you splurge, spoil, connect with my kid only to get the pussy and I was a fool to believe you wanted more, or that you were even the one I wanted." He throws his hands up in an exasperated manner and storms off. I give chase because no one walks away from me.

"Excuse me, don't you fucking walk away from me, Carter Jackson," I exclaim as he gets closer to the house. He stops and turns to face me. I can tell he's upset thanks to the clinching of his jaw that make the veins in his neck pop. I've only seen that once before, well twice. When he was yelling at someone on the phone when I first met him two months ago and, well, when we had sex and he was coming.

"What the fuck do you want me to do, Tiffany? I've apologized, I've explained why I was late and you just want to not even try to listen or be reasonable and you are trying to accuse me of being with someone else. I don't have to defend what I do to you or anyone for that matter. And as far as fucking you goes, if I wanted just that, I would've had it the first night. I connected with Xavier after we fucked, so that should be a clear signal that it's not your body." He turned and continued his storm out grabbing the small box he placed on the table earlier, but this time with less anger since we had to cross through the house in front of Xavier. I follow him outside to his car and as he prepares to get in he stops and turns to me.

"I get it, he hurt you and you're scared but I'm not him. I'm not your ex." My words can't find their exit. Just last week, I was telling Jewel that I wanted to go full steam ahead with Carter and here I am caught in my own damn feelings. "If you want to be in a relationship and can stop holding your past over your present and possible future, you know where to find me." He gets into his car and slams the door shut. The car starts and I'm left standing there with the proverbial egg on my face. He just called me out on my insecurities and I can't even be mad about it. I watch him turn down the street and hear his Porsche accelerate. How did I let it get this fucking bad this fast? He just got here.

"Fuck," I yell out. I turn to go back into the house and I see little hazel eyes looking out the window of the door. I truly fucked this up on all fronts. I open the door and Xavier is standing there with his head bowed and tears pooling.

"Hey, cupcake, what's wrong?" I ask knowing the answer and this site in front of me has me tearing.

"Mr. C isn't coming back, is he?" His voice crackles as he forces the question out.

"I don't know, son. I may have been mean to him and didn't have reason to. I'm sorry. I really messed this up." The tears begin to fall, and he runs to his room. I had no idea he had great feelings for him. I clean my face, throw on my sweats and a t-shirt, and go to the kitchen to fix plates for dinner.

"Ashley, will you be joining us?" I ask. My voice fluctuating like a teenage boy approaching puberty as I fight back my tears.

"Yes, and if you don't mind, I'd like to stay over. I don't have classes in the morning and if I stay, I can knock out all my remaining hours."

"Su- sure," I say pausing to clear my throat. I prepare her a plate and place them all on the table.

"Xai, dinner is on the table," I call out to him. He comes sulking to the table wearing his specially made crown from Carter. I don't put up a fuss because I know it'd be a losing battle at this point. I say this evenings thanks and we begin to eat, or at least attempt to eat. We make very little small talk, from Ashley thanking me for the meal and telling me how delicious it is to Xavier saying how this was his favorite. Those two have no problem cleaning their plate but for me, I keep stabbing at each item and shaking it off before moving on to something else. I keep hearing Carter's words strike against my eardrum and travel to my heart. Why did I act so callous with him? I think to myself while continuing to play with my food.

"Mom, can I have a cookie? I cleaned my plate," Xavier asks pulling me from my mental pity party.

"Oh, of course. Put your plate in the sink." He and Ashley get up from the table and I take my food and wrap it before placing it in the refrigerator. I go to my room and lie across my bed allowing my pain to overtake me until my phone interrupts. I hope that it's Carter, but it's Jewel asking if I heard from him yet. I gave her the short version of the events and soon my phone rings. I reluctantly answer knowing there is a yelling banshee on the opposite end.

"What the absolute fuck, Tiffany? Why did you go off the insecure edge like that?"

"I don't know, Jewel. I just sat here and kept thinking. I called a few times and they went to voicemail, he didn't return my texts, we had no communication during the time he was gone except for once. Then he tells me that he had business in LA, so he went there first before returning to Vegas. That just sounds foul to me."

"Tiffany, he's an entertainment lawyer! Fuck, girl. He's gonna be gone at times because he has a good list of A-Z list celebrities. It's his fucking job! Get the damn stick out your ass and relax. I'm sure if he wanted or even had other pussy, he wouldn't even had bothered to show up at your house. That's some foul shit, and he doesn't travel that way." I sit in silence listening to her words now mirroring Carter's but in a different way. She continues to talk, and I continue to sulk in my own pity.

"Do you hear me Tiffany?" I come back to the conversation and pretend that I understood what she said."

"Yes, I hear you," I reply.

"So, you do know where he is?"

"Uh, no. I don't. He just said that if I was serious, I'd know where to find him. But the thing is, I don't know. "

"Well, think about all the times you've had conversations. Did he mention a place he likes to go think?" I think back over the late-night texts and phone calls when we were acting like teenagers. We spouted off random likes and dislikes ranging from movies, to music, to ways we relax when we are stressed. Mine involves yoga or sitting in silence by my pool, his was...

"Oh, shit," I exclaim. "I think I know where he is."

"Then go. Call me later. If you don't call, then I'll know you're either tired or busy having your legs in the air."

"Shut up. Bye." I press end on my phone and get dressed in some jeans, a tank top, and booties. I grab my jacket and head out the door.

"Hey, Ashley, I'm leaving for a bit, but I'll definitely be back. Please be sure to lock up the house." I shout out rushing through the halls.

"Mom, where are you going?" Xavier asks catching me walking out the door.

"To apologize, hopefully." I place a kiss on his cheek and head to Carter's thinking spot.

Chapter

EIGHTEEN

I WALK INTO THE BAR among clouds of smoke from various vices. The lighting is dim, not club dark, but just enough where you can make out faces as you walk around. I get a lot of invitations to come here and a few people approach me wanting to buy me a drink, but I gracefully decline. I look around to see if I can spot him since I didn't see his car outside and I just about give up my search until I see the silhouette of him coming from the men's room and take up residence at the bar. This must be his seat since there was already a glass sitting there along with some aviator lensed shades. I can tell he is slow sipping when I walk up beside him signaling the barkeep for a refill for him and one for me. Taking the seat beside him, he glances over and sees me before turning back to his drink. The bartender replaces the empty glass with a full one and sits my drink in front of me.

"That'll be eighteen-dollars, miss," he says as he places a napkin beside my drink.

"Run a tab," I say handing him my card. I get another side-eye glance from Carter as he takes a slow pull from his drink. It feels like forever is passing between us since neither of us has uttered a word. The only time you'd hear a word from Carter is when his phone rang, and he answered or from me when I changed up my beverage. The bartender occasionally looks to us for conversation, but we never pick up on the hint.

"So, you found me," after fifteen minutes, according to the clock, words pour from his lips with a bit of happy and a lot of I'm still fucking pissed at you.

"Yeah, I did." My comeback wasn't that much better. I turn to face him even though I'm only viewing the side profile. "I owe you the chance to explain. I - uh- reacted poorly and I'm so sorry, Carter. See the thing is, when I was with Corey, I never paid attention to the signs 'cause I was wrapped up in Xavier. He called me out on those things while we were going through our divorce. That day in the court house conference room was hell. From that moment forward, I made a vow with myself to never allow communication to be an issue should I find myself in that situation. I also vowed to never be in a relationship, but that vow didn't last long." I turn back to my forward-facing position and tend to my peach margarita.

I look around and notice the bar begins to pick up with patrons and some of them are even dancing to the music playing overhead. A group of people are playing pool in the back and you can hear the enthusiasm from the shots made or missed. Another crowd is watching the game on television, shouting at the refs like they can actually hear them. Then there are those hanging at the bar, eating bar food, drinking and having conversations with the ones next to or around them or the barkeep. Carter just sits, not talking, just slow sipping. I notice the little box he had at the house earlier is sitting on the bar in front of him and he's staring at it intently.

Since there aren't any additional words being shared, I call for the tab to be closed and prepare to leave.

"Why are you leaving?" he asks.

"Well, you haven't said anything, so I figured that you didn't want me around." I fight back the tears threatening not wanting him to see me fall apart. It's my fault, anyway. I allowed my past to fuck up my present and possibly ruin my future with this man. He ushers me to sit back down.

"I've been sitting here for the last two hours trying to figure out if I was the one to fuck this up. I didn't call like I promised. No text, no emails. But then I thought, with the time difference and all of the meetings and things I had to attend, it wasn't something I could control and that you have to understand, that's my job. That's what I do for a living. I stay busy and I travel, a lot. I have no intentions of fucking around on you. I'm not Corey, Tiffany. Not in the least bit. I wouldn't dare hurt you. The song changes by the hand of the barmaid who had been ear hustling. I mean you can only wipe down a bar so many times when no one is sitting there. He pulls me to the floor with a slight smile on his face.

As the song plays, we dance close. Pelvis to pelvis, close. His hands are firmly around my waist and his arms feel like they miss me laying within them. His chin rests comfortably on top of my head when I lean against his chest. My cheek feels the rumble of his strong heartbeat and I take a deep breath relaxing. After the song completes, *Ain't No Way* by Queen Aretha herself begins to play. I close my eyes and allow her to speak the words of someone loving another when they have a wall up. It fits our situation perfectly, except he's Aretha and I'm the person she's singing to.

"This song is us," he mutters into my hair. I look up at him knowing that we have found our biorhythm. If I can think of something and he can say the same thing, there's no doubt that we are connected. "Why are you looking at me like that?" He asks with a chuckle.

"I was just thinking the exact same thing, except you're Aretha." He smiles taking my face into both of his hands and kissing me softly.

"How I missed kissing these lips," he says as our embrace breaks. He presses his forehead to mine as we remain connected and continue to sway to the music. "Being in Tokyo was hell. I'm sorry I didn't call and explain the situation. I didn't want to bore you or upset you. I thought that surprising you would be enough. I didn't think you'd worry so." Tamia's *Stuck with Me* begins to play and she's putting my feelings out there on display. I notice how Carter makes me feel complete even though we've only been seeing each other for a little more than a month. Perhaps closer to two. I take my hands and place them on the side of his face as he stares into my soul. He has no emotions and his gaze is intent. I lick my lips in preparation for his crashing into mine. Short, wet, and sweet kisses filled with passion render my knees weak, but I manage to stay on my feet.

"I fucked up, Tiffany. I broke a rule I had in place," he whispers as his forehead is back against mine. This causes concern with me because what I fear the most may be revealed.

"What did you do?" I question while looking at him with concern. I know he said he'd never hurt me, but I still have the right to be concerned.

"I said I wouldn't fall for anyone. That I'd maintain a single life and date occasionally. But you changed that rule and now I'm making changes in my life to make sure you and Xavier are in it." His words are a different kind of heavy. Did I just win the heart of LA's most eligible bachelor?

"What do you mean?" the words are out of my mouth before I even have a chance to think of what I was saying. A major brain to mouth miscommunication.

"I mean, I'm falling for you, hard. Like I think I may even be in..." I press my finger against his lips not allowing him to finish that sentence. It's something about that word that makes me all emotional especially if I feel the same. At least I think I feel the same. I'm pretty sure I do. I said I'd go full throttle with him once he returned and he's here now. I take him by his hand and walk over to the bar, so he can retrieve his things.

"I didn't see your car outside," I say posing the obvious question.

"I used the Lyft service."

"You wouldn't mind driving my car, would you?"

"Depends on where we are going." I think long and hard before answering.

"Home."

WE ARRIVE BACK TO MY house finding Ashley asleep on the sofa and Xavier next to her on the floor surrounded by Lego's. The scene is so cute, I snag a picture before waking Ashley and helping her to the guest room. Carter picks up Xavier and puts him in his bed. I watch from outside as he pulls the covers up over him making sure he is snug. Thankfully he had on his jammies. If I had to wake him up, he'd never go back to sleep.

"Wow, he's a heavy sleeper like his mom," Carter says as he meets me by the door. I grab his hand and take him to the family room where we can talk without waking the little King.

"I know he's a lot like me. That's what's so scary. I know I'm obstinate and quick-witted, and quick-mouthed." He rushes in and kisses me knocking me back a few inches but making up for it by grabbing me into his arms.

"I can't stay over, Tiffany. I keep thinking about you in that swimsuit earlier and trust me I want to use it to tie you up to the bed, but I should get back to the villa." His hands grip my ass cheek hard sending my libido into overdrive. I want to mount him right here, right now, but I respect his wishes.

"What's your work schedule like tomorrow?" I ask.

"I have a phone conference tomorrow morning and some documents I'm expecting to receive at the hotel by messenger. Other than that, nothing since the guys are coming in for poker night Friday. Why? What do you have in mind?"

"Well, I was thinking, I'm off tomorrow since I have to work Friday night. So maybe you can come by for breakfast if it's not too late or maybe lunch." I seductively run my hands over his hard chest paying close attention to his nipples as they respond to my touch. *I wonder what else is responding*, I think to myself. I take a chance allowing my fingers to travel down his midline to the button securing his jeans before moving on to the package itself. He lets out a loud hiss as we stare into each other's eyes and I continue to tease.

His phone buzzes and he answers stopping all plays on the field.

"Yeah, Carter. Okay, be right out." I know there is no chance we can pick up where we left off.

"I guess your ride is here."

"Yeah and not a moment too soon. You are extremely sexy, and tantalizing, and damn near had me breaking my rule."

"You're sweet, Carter. I never thought I'd meet a man considerate of my son's feelings the way you are. I feel bad that I was trying to tempt you to stay." We walk to the door and I see him out. I stand in the door way with my body resting along the jamb looking at him longingly as he enters the car.

"I'll be here around 9:00 a.m. and I'll bring breakfast, okay."

"I'll be waiting." He gets in the car and they drive off heading back to his hotel villa. I finish cleaning up the toys and kitchen before heading to bed thinking about him. The look in his eyes as my hand gracefully caressed his dick through his jeans was of a deep, dark, desire. He remained motionless but highly aroused awakening that same want within me. Before long, I find my nipples responding to my thoughts. I figure this is the best time to jump in the shower and put my removable shower head to use.

"MOMMY, WHO IS PICKING ME up from practice today?" Xavier asks as he comes into my room while I finish getting dressed. "Why are you putting on makeup just to drop me off?" He adds to his laundry list of questions. I have to come up with something quick.

"Uh, I have a business meeting this morning. I want to look presentable and not like I just rolled out of bed."

"Oh. Did you make your bed up?" Geez this kid is quite inquisitive today.

"I was up a little early this morning. What is with all the questions?"

"You always told me that if I want to know something, just ask. I'm just doing what you told me. Did you apologize to Mr. C last night?" Just like me. The only thing that lets me know he is any part of his father is his facial recognition features, minus the eyes, those are mine too.

"We met, talked, and I apologized." I put the last clip in my hair and I'm ready to go. "Now, go grab your backpack and your gym bag so we can go, nosey."

"Okay," he says jetting out of my room to his own to get his things. I meet him at the front door and we walk out to the car together. I help buckle him in, when he calls me.

"Mom?"

"Yes, baby."

"I had a dream that Mr. C put me in my bed last night, is that weird?"

"Well, maybe you were missing him so much that when you were put in your bed, you thought it was him."

"Yeah, I knew it was you though, because I could smell your

perfume." I smile while watching his expression in my review and I go to take him to school. Along the way, I think about the direction my relationship with Carter is taking and wonder if I should talk to Xavier about it. I was just about to say something when my thoughts took another turn. Carter mentioned that he had business to address in LA and I get a feeling that it had nothing to do with his firm. I know he has the game tomorrow night and I still haven't told him if I'd work for him. Maybe I need to get some of these questions answered before I make any decisions. This affects not only me but my son too. Seems like breakfast will have a topic of discussion and not as much of making up sex like I thought. I pull into the circular drive of the school and drop off my little cupcake.

"Okay, dear. I'll see you later tonight. Have a good practice. Oh, and your dad is picking you up today."

"Okay mom. I love you."

"Love you too." He closes the door and I head home for my breakfast date.

Chapter
NINETEEN

I PULL BACK INTO MY drive to find Carter resting on the hood of his car talking on the phone. He has a basket of what I can only imagine are breakfast items sitting next to him and he has a duffle bag as well. I park and go to exit when he meets me and opens the door for me. I step out of my car and he plants a kiss on my cheek as he continues the conversation.

"Yes. That is correct. Can you make sure those get delivered to me tonight? No, it has to be tonight. Tomorrow I will make sure they are signed and get them back to you. Okay, Leah. See you soon. Bye." My mind is wondering who Leah is, but I know it's just an associate of his. He puts his phone back into the case before giving me a proper kiss.

"Good morning," he whispers in my ear as he uses his mouth to nuzzle against my neck. Suddenly, I love becoming a morning person.

"Good morning. How'd you sleep?"

"Well, I didn't really. Thoughts of you played with my mind

while I tried to go over some contracts and things, keeping me up most of the night. What about you?" His lips teasingly trail under my chin down to just where my cleavage shows then back up.

"Mmm, well after a long shower, I slept like a baby."

"How long of a shower are we talking?"

"The water ran cold and I was still in there for about thirty more minutes."

"Looks like I got some work to do." He picks me up and cradles me in his arms. I smile wide as he is doing this with no effort. We walk to the door when I remember he left the breakfast on his car hood.

"Um, did you forget something?" He nods his head and when I think he's going to put me down and run back to retrieve the morning goodness, he instead carries me over to his car, grabs the basket and bag, before proceeding back to the door. I relieve his hands of the items since I'm a handful on my own. I punch in my code to unlock the door and he opens it with me still in his loving arms.

"You know the next time I carry you like this you'll be my wife." His words take the breath from my lungs and I'm in a daze.

"Excuse me, what?" I ask as my feet find ground. I place the breakfast items on the kitchen table and his personal bag in the living room cleverly escaping his clutches.

"The next time I'm carrying you over any threshold, you WILL be my bride."

"Carter, you're crazy. I'm not getting married again." The words leave my mouth before I get a chance to think about them or their consequences. His look turns stone and we are back to where we were yesterday evening.

"Oh, see, I thought we were in a relationship with naturally progressing steps. Such as, dating, falling in love, becoming engaged, marriage, and a family. But I guess..." He speaks so fast, not speedy auctioneer fast, but his words are so natural and come easily that my mind pauses when he speaks about love.

"Wait, wait, wait. What? Falling in love? Are you in love with me, Carter?" He runs his hand over his scruff in a precarious manner and I realize he too suffers from brain to mouth malfunction. "Carter, did you hear me?" I ask walking toward him in at a slow pace.

"Look, it's the only way I can describe how I feel around you. At first, I knew it was lust. The way you looked in your uniform, how embarrassed you were wiping a spilled Jack and Coke off me, made me rock fucking hard and I hadn't been that way in a while. You were so preoccupied with what you were doing, you didn't know you had those beautiful breasts in my face. So yeah, lust was definitely first. But something changed. I'd be lying if I didn't say that my first goal was to bed you, when Walter had asked me to introduce you, I just remember thinking, this is my girlfriend, Tiffany. See my brain overpowered my libido. You left me intrigued and mesmerized. As the days turned into weeks and within the short two months of knowing you, I kept wanting more. While I was in Tokyo, I figured out what it was that I was missing." We're standing face to face and he grazes my cheek with his thumb. I swallow hard as this moment captures me. I feel a change in the dynamic and I know that this is a major revelation."

"What's the 'more'?" I ask while dangling in suspense. He searches me over with his gaze before picking me up and wrapping my legs around his waist.

"The more is you. All of you. You're the more that my body craves, wants, and needs. Why my mind wonders in the middle of the night and I can't sleep. Why my heart knows peace when we're together, even if everything else is in a state of chaos. I know it's you that I want." I smile to fight away the tears of sentiment threatening my eyes that he loves so much.

"You got all that from a wipe down?" I jokingly ask. He laughs and his eyes twinkle. I know he's in love with me.

"Carter."

"Yes, baby," he responds. I struggle with what I want to say, with my emotions. I bite my lip thinking about my next word choice. He places me on the kitchen counter while keeping my legs in their place.

"I-uh. I believe..." His phone rings and I'm thankful. It's hard for me to say how I feel about him. I know I want to go forward in this relationship, but I don't know if I'm where he is, and I don't want to hurt him or worse, lead him on. His call ends and he has a look of concern on his face.

"Is everything okay?" I ask.

He rubs his chin again while his eyebrows raise in a questionable manner. "I think I may have showed my hand too soon." His words are easy to decode, and I understand he wishes he didn't tell me how he felt.

"I've seen you play, and I know you always come out on top," I remind him. He lays his head in between my breasts. Not in a sexual manner but one of needing comfort. I kiss the top of his head repeatedly reminding myself that I still haven't said anything to him. He looks up to me and I see the love he has for me in his eyes. I lean down a bit to kiss him. That one peck turned into another, and then into a full-fledged tongue fest. His hands wrap around my waist, slide up my back under my shirt, and unhook my bra freeing those in bondage. I let out a slight moan as his scruff playfully teases my breasts while he lays kisses and licks onto them.

Not one to waste any time, he swiftly carries me to my room where we crash onto the bed. Switching up positions of authority until we are both naked and I find myself under his sexual prowess. My nails find a place in his back and with each thrust they dig and I arch my back. This isn't like the first time where I was wondering if I'd be able to walk.

No, this is the right time. It feels right. Our bodies are connecting as one and his groans and grunts are matching mine. He takes a break to position me on top and sit up, so we are face to face. My hair is slickened from the sweat, so is his. Yet, I continue to grab and play in it circulating my hips. He takes long sensual licks of my neck, tasting each bead of sweat that I produce. My head falls back enjoying this pleasure.

He moves to my breasts and suckles on my nipples hard. Slowly circling them with his tongue. My rhythm increases as he engulfs them. He takes his left hand and runs his fingers through my hair grabbing a hand full and softly pulls on it while his other hand finds a home at the base of my neck. He counter-thrusts his hips as I grind deeper and harder. His hand applies soft pressure as he frees his other from gripping my hair and sustaining my head in a retracted position. My eyes meet his and we stare, neither of us giving concession to each other as shockwaves pulsate throughout our bodies.

"F-f-uck!" he exclaims as his body tightens and he grabs me into a tight hold. I wish my reaction was as simple as his. My explosion came with skin ripping, shoulder biting, tears streaming force and the words, "oh god" shortly following. Wrapped in his arms, he pulls me down and we lay there trying to catch our breaths and stop the tears from flowing. I've heard of people having orgasms so powerful that they cry. I didn't believe it since it never happened with me. That's another myth shattered by Carter. He releases his hold on me and turns to his side. Taking his hand, he wipes my face and smile.

"Why are you crying? Oh no, did I hurt you?" His sudden conscious of what we were doing, while we were doing it, is charming.

"No, no, baby. You didn't hurt me at all," I say taking a deep breath and letting it out. "I think these are from pure joy. I had an out of body experience with that one. I'd actually like to go again."

He looks at me with shock. "Uh, no, Tiff. I'm tired. My body is actually hurting from that one. But we got all afternoon. Let's take a nap or at least eat breakfast."

"Mmm, okay. You nap while I..." I slide under the sheet and take his dick into my mouth. It didn't have any problem with standing back at attention.

"Tiffffffffff," he drags out my name as his hands find my head once again. I circle my tongue around the head of his penis before taking him whole once again. I continue in this manner, allowing the saliva to drip from my mouth onto his cock and using my hand to assist. I ease my swollen pussy onto him and slowly roll my hips. His hands grip my hips and move along with my rotating and bouncing moves. His neck cranes back and his face is under the pillow. All I can see is his sexy Adam's apple. I lean forward to lick it granting him the moment to flip me onto my back. He lifts my legs and positions himself on his knees wrapping my legs around his neck. He grips my thighs and slams into me. I call out loudly and am thankful I don't have neighbors.

"I told you to let me rest, but did you? No." He thrusts again, and my nails find the skin of his thigh. I dig deep and I'm loving this. "So, now you have to deal with me fucking you hard." He drives into me harder this time.

"More," I say encouraging him to continue the drive. He delivers, and my world is forever turned upside down. See, with Corey, he remained vanilla. In fact, the most I've seen him do outside of traditional is when I busted him with his now wife. With him it was always missionary and always in a bed with the lights off. We barely showered together. Carter is different and exciting and is awakening things deep within me. I'm not afraid to ask for...

"More," I cry out. My body is in a tingling frenzy as another orgasm threatens. He sees it in my eyes and pulls me into an upright position with my legs still firmly wrapped around his neck while moving himself to a sitting position. Oh, the things this man can do. I may feel like a pretzel, but it's worth it. He drives deeper, and I come crashing down. My mouth agape with no audible sound. I fall back and my body shakes. He prolongs this orgasm by stroking my clit with his finger until he finally comes. The veins in his neck pop out and his skin glows red. He falls onto the bed gasping for air. I try to remove my legs, but he latches onto them. Laying there stroking on them until his breathing has calmed. He places gentle kisses on my feet moving up my legs avoiding the hot zones. Soon we are laying face to face.

"Damn, I could get real used to this vision every morning for breakfast," he said.

"Mmm, me too," I reply.

"You know, you aren't obligated to tell me you love me." I take a deep breath and slowly let it escape my nostrils. I kiss him softly, gently, non-aggressive, non-inviting. I nudge my way under his chin resting on his chest lazily drawing imaginary circles. Why am I being so pent up? Jewel saw it from day one how my mind kept going back to him. Why can't I admit that I do love him? There's no time table on when things like this happen. I have to let go of my past. I close my eyes and allow only the sound of his breathing and heartbeat fill the space between my ears. I mentally go through every block I have with this relationship and I let it go. I close the door on the infidelity from my marriage and realize that Carter is nothing like him. Furthermore, my son adores him and calls him his new best friend.

"Carter?"

"Mmhmm," he replies his hand rubbing on my naked ass.

"I love you."

His hand motion stops. "Really? With no feeling of obligation implied or otherwise?"

I look up at him and he's smiling from ear to ear. "Do you always have to lawyer up?"

"It's a habit. I'm quite good at it. Ask my clients." We laugh.

"Yes, silly. I'm sure. I'm sure I'm ready for this new relationship, I'm sure I like having you around, I'm sure my son adores you and shares my same feelings. Yes, I love you."

"I knew you did." He lays back with both arms under his head with an essence of arrogance and smugness abound. I take a pillow and swing it directly to his face. That stirs him and soon he's chasing me naked through the house. I run outside and cannonball into the pool. He soon follows. I continue to evade him until he corners me as I try to climb out. Laughter and heavy breathing is all you hear.

"Let's go grab the now brunch that you brought over and eat out here by the pool."

"That sounds good. I'll grab my bag and throw my sweats on. After we eat, we can shower, and I'll help you clean your room and refresh your bed. Then I'm going to fuck you senseless, but not here. Back at the villa. You can stay overnight, even bring Xavier and I'll get him his own room, just say you'll be there."

"I can't. Ashley isn't available, and Corey isn't able to get Xavier until tomorrow since I work. I have to be here, at home." I think it's the insta-family he's craving. That makes me want to know more, but I decline since I'm suddenly aware how cold I'm becoming.

"I think we need to go grab that shower because I'm freezing," I say climbing out the pool. I go to my little storage chest on the side and grab two oversized bath towels. I wrap myself in one and hold the other up as an offer for him to come get it. I watch as he swims a short lap to the other side and emerges from the water like a commercial. At least it is in my mind. It's like he's moving in slow motion, the water is clinging to his body, and despite the coolness of the water, his dick wasn't shriveled much. My eyes are trapped in their gaze of this gorgeous specimen now standing before me. He takes the towel and has this slight smile on his face.

"What are you staring at? No, why are you staring at me like that?"

"Oh, I'm having a flashback," I manage to put that sentence together with hardly any thought since my brain seemingly has partnered with my eyes in the visible assessment of Carter Jackson. I know he has an amazing body, maybe it's the lack of show that has me captured. I take control of my bodies movement since my brain is occupied with other thoughts, and head back into the house to the kitchen.

I take out the food items from the temperature-controlled bag and begin to plate them up. The items are still warm and only need minimum heating. He has French toast, eggs, bacon, sausage, and an assortment of fruit and pastries. I take the first plate from the microwave, I pass it to him and pour him a glass of juice and pop a pod into the coffee maker for his cup of joe.

We haven't spoken a word since returning into the house, but I have caught him looking at me. Smiles pass along his lips as he watches me put everything away while my plate heats in the microwave. I pass him his coffee and place the sugar bowl and creamer in front of him.

"Thank you," he says.

"Did you need something to go with your food like ketchup, or some other condiment? I ask when I notice he hasn't touched his food. I pop in another pod, so I can have some coffee. I know I definitely need it.

"No. I'm just waiting on you." I smile taking my plate out of the microwave and set it next to him. He pours me a glass of juice while I finish sweetening my coffee and adding the creamer. I sit down, and he grabs my hand giving thanks. *He remembers*, I think to myself. I bite my lip trying to keep the blushing away. He finishes, and we begin to eat. The first bite of the French toast is like butter melting in a hot skillet.

"Mmm, this is great. Where'd you get this? I have to take Xavier."

"Norm's, I think. I asked one of the guys at the hotel and he recommended the place. I called and placed the order and picked it up on my way here this morning. I will say that this is very good." He stabs at his toast and takes another bite.

"Yeah, I agree. Think I'll take Xavier there on Sunday. Will you join us?" The room falls silent and he doesn't answer. I finish chewing my food and put my fork down turning to face him.

"What? Are you going back out of town?" I know that he in fact is a busy lawyer and will more than likely have another tour to kick off or movie set to travel to.

"I am, but not for work." Okay, loop officially thrown and now I'm intrigued.

"Oh. Where are you going?"

"To see my parents in Tennessee." I think now's the time we should get to know more about each other's background.

"Oh, so you're from Tennessee?"

"My dad's side is. My mom was born in California. I stayed out there after I graduated from college and started my work with a prominent law firm. From there it's all history."

"So, why the trip home? Is everyone alright?"

"Yeah. They are good. I just have a box of stuff to pick up and I haven't seen them for a while. I mean we talk at least once a week. When my mom's gets a project idea in her head, everything is subject to being tossed out."

"Sounds like my parents. Notice that is plural. They both are headstrong people who always have to get what they want. That's how they ended up together. My dad had to have my mom and he was persistent, kinda like you and how you were trying to get me to go out with you." He smiles at the comparison. Most people know that a girl looks for someone like her dad when searching for a mate. We continue our stroll down family lane and sprinkle in cleaning along the way.

After placing fresh sheets on the bed, we lay across and continue our talks. I learned he didn't get married to his fiancé because her dad never approved of their relationship. He tells me how his mom was hurt by the racial reason her dad gave and he vowed to never fall in love again to keep her happy. Makes me wonder if he'll tell them about me.

"Until I met you, that is. Then all vows were rendered null and void." He stares at the ceiling with a small showing of pain as he thinks about that time in his life. I don't want him to get down, so I get our conversation back to normal and off memory lane.

"Hey, why don't you follow me into the bathroom?" I stand and pull him to his feet and he lazily gets up. I go into the bathroom and start the shower. While the water warms, I grab my bathrobe and one of the ones I got from the hotel as a gift from a guest.

"Here, you can put this on when you get out." I take two more large bath towels and sit them on the counter. When I turn to face him, he is at full staff and veins are poppin'. He walks my direction and I think he's going for some sexy as hell, romantic type move. Instead, he grabs his phone and connects it to the Bluetooth speaker I have for at home spa day. The song, *Losin' Control* by Russ begins to play, and he pulls me in for a slow, albeit naked, dance. His choice of song fits me and him perfectly. Too perfect. Tears begin to flow when I realize this song is everything about me. The wetness hits his chest and he hugs me tighter and all of my pain comes out. He guides me to the shower where we continue to dance to the music under the rainfall.

His kisses are sensual and make me wet. I want to speak but his tongue is in the way. I lift myself up and straddle him. He supports me grabbing my cheeks and I slowly lower onto him. You'd think that with the pounding my pussy took today, I wouldn't want to feel him inside me again, but I do. We move in slow rhythm while I slowly ride up and down. The look in his eyes is of love. I think about how he looked at me at the 90s party and of course the club opening and how even then his look was amorous. Maybe he's been falling for me, I think to myself as our slow grind continues. The shower serves as the perfect backdrop to this moment. It's steamy, hot, wet and romantic. It's also soundproof which is a feature I had added when I first moved in after watching some movies that featured shower sex.

"I love you, Carter," I say as my hip motions increase. I cover his mouth with mine and can feel when he comes. He grips my hips so tight that I know I will have a bruise in the shape of fingers. He positions us against the wall as he continues to erupt hard. He rests his head on my chest while I continue to move pushing my orgasm over its edge. I let out a loud 'oh my god' as my legs grip tighter and my hands pull his hair.

"I love you too, Tiffany." He grabs my soap to lather me up and I turn to do the same before we rinse, dry off and take a much-needed nap.

Chapter

TWENTY

I WOKE THIS MORNING FEELING refreshed and brand new. To say I was feeling myself would be an understatement. Breakfast will never be the same, even if we tried to recreate it. After our nap, we said our goodbyes and he went back to his villa at the hotel. I fixed dinner for Xavier and was even nice to Corey when he dropped Xavier off. Corey knew what happened based on the wattage of my smile, but thankfully my son just thought I had a good day off. Don't think Corey didn't try me, because he did, but I deflected all his negative energy or attempts to go down memory lane. I walk into the casino with my head held high and the energy to match. He messaged me earlier to tell me that he missed his conference call this morning because he was so tired from his breakfast meeting yesterday. We talked on the phone for an hour before he had to go meet with a few clients. I go into the dressing room and hear laughter and chatter but when I walk by, it all stops. Glaring eyes watch me go to my locker and true to Carter's form, a single rose with a card attached.

"Hmm, I guess you must not be that good of a fuck if you only get one rose," Jacqui says. You'd think that after ratting me out to Vic failed, she'd leave me alone. But no, the bitch had to come for me and had her little flunkies deep under her spell. I guess they will have to get it too.

"Hmm, did you ever get any roses? From what I was told, the best your sorry pussy got was a cheap feel up, your mouth game was subpar, and well, to put it mildly, you were passed around more than cards on a poker table. He only kept you around because you talked about how you needed money to fix your botched plastic surgery."

"I never slept with Carter Jackson,"

"Yeah, I know. That's why I know you never got any flowers from him or any of his dick. So never mind what he puts in my locker, worry about why yours is empty." I close my locker and walk off running into Jewel on the way out.

"Damn, slow down, girl," she says capturing my attention.

"Oh, shit. Sorry. My mind was somewhere else."

"What's wrong?"

"That fucking has been and her group of loyal ass kissers tried to come for me. You know I don't like getting upset." I run down the whole scenario to fill her in on my attitude. Instead of her going in there and literally ripping hair out of heads, she gives me a hug.

"You are the biggest winner in all of this. You have what she always wanted and now will never get. Even though I love the sorry pussy line, I think you did well by leaving it as is." Just then the lot of them come walking out smirking as they walk past. Jewel sticks her foot out and trips Jacqui who is up front causing a domino effect. I laugh and follow Jewel into the dressing room.

"What? Oh, you thought I was just gonna let her ass get away with that shit?" I love her. This is why we're best friends.

W<small>E WALK ONTO THE CASINO</small> floor and head over to the cage to get the things for tonight's game. Since I run set up and stock for Carter, Casey doesn't have to bring the liquor up just the glasses. Snacks are already in the room along with the bowls and the dealer has new cards ready for the shoe. The energy of the cage is a little flat when we walk in. No tears or nothing like that, just different.

"Hey, Vic. I'm here to get the setups for tonight." He wheels me the chips, the bank bag, and change drawer with the approval credit lines for each guest. I go over the list to see if there is anyone new and continue to check off items on my list.

"So, uh, I guess you two are pretty bummed about tonight," Vic says looking at Jewel and I.

"Why? Is the casino closing?" Jewel asks perplexed by Vic's question.

"No. Well, didn't Carter tell you?"

"No, I think he kept Tiffany busy yesterday morning, but business was not involved." I punch her in her arm for that comment. I still prefer some level of discreteness.

"Oh, maybe I shouldn't say. That's really Carter's business." Vic walks away and leaves us standing there confused. "Any ways, I think you should get on up to the villa. See you at cash out." We head over to the Villa and are surprised when Carter is already present. I check the time on my phone to make sure we didn't lag to long on the main floor. We arrive at the normal time which is an hour before game start. Carter usually shows up thirty minutes after.

"Hey ladies, come on in. Casey and I are creating a signature drink for tonight," he says as we enter.

"Signature drink? Wow, you're in an extra saucy mood. That must've been some breakfast yesterday," Jewel says. Casey smirks as he pours four glasses of the new concoction.

"Mmm, breakfast. Well, that is the most important meal of the day," he utters while placing his arms around my waist and nibbling on my ear. I giggle in response to his nuzzle.

"Oh, gawd. Get a room," Jewel exclaims.

"That's funny, I thought this was my room." Carter's rebuttal is funny and it

actually, silences my friend.

"So, what's this noise Vic is talking about?" she asks since we have his attention.

"Yeah, he seemed a bit sad and asked if you told me something," I add. He looks to Casey and he shrugs his shoulders in a way that could be interpreted as, that's your choice.

"I wanted to wait until later tonight to tell you, but even when the guys get here, you'd still find out, so I guess I should tell y'all now. Tonight is the last poker night I will have here at the Villa." Jewel and I look at each other in shock.

"You knew about this?" Jewel says as she looks at Casey for an answer. Carter walks away and to his room and comes back with a file folder.

"Well, Carter confided in me about a few things related to business and this is one of them. I told him that based on his plans, it's a good choice."

"One of them? I thought you were just going to visit your parents, not return to LA all together," I say a bit confused.

"I'm not moving back to LA. In fact, that's another change I'm making."

"Wait, Carter. You told me that it'll take a lot for you not to come in here monthly for a weekend of fun with your buddies so that you can relax and be unseen and not on call. Now you're going back to that?" Jewel and Casey have known Carter longer than I have, so for her to sound as concerned as she does, makes me wonder what he has up his sleeve.

"Here, ladies. This should put your mind at rest." He opens the folder and inside are two contracts. One with my name and one with Jewel's official government, Ebonee Amaka Davidson. She earned the moniker Jewel of the Nile, shortened to Jewel, when others found out her name means Ebony Queen in Egyptian. I skimmed over the contract making it down to the nuts and bolts of said contract.

My eyes open wide when I see the details. He's offering me a six-figure salary for being head accountant at his firm, which isn't bloated because of our relations, it's actually base for the top tier in that group. I'd be responsible for expense reports for the firm, royalty audits, fraud, breach of contract, and other items as applicable from a financial perspective.

Jewel will be head of IT. She will make sure that the security is set up on all the computers, laptops, tablets, watch for hackers and set up surveillance. It's really a cake job since she and two others will be working together, but she's the head. I can see the tears in her eyes as she reads over what he's offering, and I know it's what she wants. I don't have to ask if she's happy, this look says it all. She closes the folder and hugs Carter.

"This is...wow, Carter. I'll give you an answer tomorrow after I look it over." She rushes to the bathroom no doubt to freshen her makeup and Casey follows.

"What about you? What do you think?" he asks, while sipping on his drink.

"You were serious about me working for you?"

"Yeah. I knew anyone who can count a large cash pot with her eyes only, pays attention to details when it comes to money and I need that in my business. My clients need that." I nod in agreement. I continue to scour over the paper in front of me.

"This is a lot to take in," I rebut. "If you're not going back to LA, what about your offices?" He smiles and goes to speak, but a knock at the door interrupts and he goes to answer.

"Hey, Carter. Did we catch you and Tiffany being naughty?" Dwight says as he and the others enter. I gather my composure and put the folder away.

"Now, do you think if I had him occupied, he would've answered the door? Or even be awake?" They all laugh at my joke but not Carter. Jewel and Casey return to the gathering and I start taking cash and handing out chips. The dealer shows up and starts some test shuffles while Casey is making the drinks. Carter and his friends engage in small talk, Jewel being over there to serve as the woman's view. I lock up the cash box and excuse myself to his room and close the door behind me.

I take a seat on his bed and lay my head in my cupped hands. That is a beautiful contract he sprung on me. I don't know if I can do the job. The door creeks open catching my attention. Jewel comes in and sits beside me and lays her head on my shoulder.

"What's up?" I ask while twiddling my thumbs.

"That's quite the load he dropped on us," she replies letting out a deep breath.

"Yeah, It's a game changer for sure. I need to really think this out," I reply.

"Me too.

Casey said that I should take it. The money and benefits alone are excellent. More than I was making at the other place. A lot more."

"Just think, we could leave the casino life behind us. Go into the office environment, but I know it wouldn't be clinical. It'd be fun."

"I know. What's stopping you from saying yes?" She questions.

"What's stopping you?" I rebut. We both stare at the wall in silence, neither of us having a response. I hear a loud rumble from the other room and nudge Jewel, so we can go back to our appointed duties for the night. We walk into the room and hear laughter as the games have begun.

"Hey, babe. Where were you? I've been losing all my hands. I need my good luck charm." He grabs my hand pulling me close and softly rubs on my thighs. A king comes out on the river and he pulls three of a kind. With the make of the cards on the table the probability of a straight or higher is slim.

"Ayyee," he exclaims as he is declared the winner. He stands up and kisses me before returning to the game. I take his glass and go refill his drink.

"So, Carter, you finally settling down," his friend Dwayne says. I wait to hear his response, but Jewel and Chase start a conversation that also keeps me intrigued.

"Chase, what are you talking about?" My attention is fully on Jewel and her conversation.

"I'm talking about making this permanent." He gets down on one knee and pulls a ring box out of his pocket. Opening it, he reveals a 2-carat princess cut ring flanked by baguettes. It is simply stunning, and my best friend is about to become engaged. Carter sees me with my hands over my face and stops the game. The guys join us around the bar.

"Ebonee Amaka Davidson, I've loved you for a while, now. We dated off and on, but I knew that I had to have you forever. So, I waited till you were ready. Now, I want to make you Mrs. McIntyre. Will you marry me?" Her eyes fill with tears and a smile replaces her usually crass mouth. She's speechless thanks to her hyperventilating.

"Well, damnit Jewel, say something, shit," I exclaim. The laughter gives her the breath she needs.

"Yes. Yes, I will fucking marry you Casey Aaron McIntyre." Tears stream from his eyes as he picks up his bride to be and swings her around as they embrace. The room claps and mysteriously champagne is opened. I look to find Carter smiling and passing around flutes. Now I know that isn't standard bar ware and that explains why he was here early. I make my way over to him where he is having a conversation with one of his poker pals.

"You knew about this didn't you?"

"Maybe. I also may have helped him get the ring at cost and not retail pricing."

"Sneaky." He laughs as Vic, Tamara, and Ericka join us for a mini celebration. Jewel and Casey re-join the party from the room where they made phone calls to their parents to share the news. Tamara, Ericka, and I gush over the ring while the guys offer advice to Casey. If I had to choose who my best friend should marry, Casey is my number one choice. Before I started working here, I always heard about him and how he made her feel. Tonight, he took a step towards her happy ever after. The one we used to talk about when we were in college.

"So, Tiffany. Will you ever jump the broom again?" Tamara asks. All eyes look at me and I think the guys tune an ear too.

"No. It'll take a lot for me to get married again."

"So, you'd be happy just being with a man and not married? What about Carter?" She whispers the last part.

"I don't know. I mean, I like being with him and my son loves him, but marriage, that's a huge step and we're too new at this." They both give me a side eye with scoffing included.

"What?" I ask.

"Okay, you've done fairy tale land before, but Carter is the real Prince Charming. I mean, this guy is opening a business here in Vegas, for you. He's moving things around in his life, for you. That golden paved pussy of yours has this man completely in love with you. You're making that man turn in his playa card. And trust me, that ain't easy." Jewel looks at her sparkling new jewelry to drive her point home. I think I need to have a talk with Carter about our relationship.

I decide to change the entire scene and get things back to normal.

"So, are you guys playing poker or not? Cause I got a large amount of cash that I'm responsible for and I will turn it in with no refunds or payouts given." Carter and his crew scuttle to their seats not wanting to lose the money they dropped on this game.

"Wow, she has a mean streak," Damien says to Carter, jokingly of course.

"No, she's about her business and that's why she's going to be in charge of the accounting department."

"Oh, it's that good?" The guys laugh but Carter doesn't seem to think it's funny. He leans in on his elbows and surveys the table.

"What's that good?" He questions. A few eyes turn away while Jewel and Tamara look at me with that *oh shit* look. Casey tries to diffuse the situation by refreshing Carter's drink, but he waves him off and Casey retreats.

"I'm just joking, you know?" Damien says trying to back pedal his way out this pond.

"No, I don't know. Enlighten me." Carter places his cards on the table, before leaning back in his chair, his hands pressed together.

"I meant the attention she gives."

"See, no you didn't. I've known you too long Damien, so I know how your mind thinks, and I've allowed it to roll off my back and never tried to put you in a position to explain your womanizing ways. You, thinking that this is all "guy" talk or whatever, but today it stops. Not because you personally attached one of those quips to Tiffany, but because I'm sick of hearing the bullshit fall from your lips. It's rude, crass, disrespectful, and we spend hours in litigation trying to protect women from shit like that. So, if you want to continue to work for Jackson Law, you will clean up your shit immediately. That goes for any of you here at this table and those back in LA."

Carter stands up and walks to the bar to take the drink once offered to him. He swallows in one gulp and then signals for another. The room is so quiet, you can hear the dings of the elevators from the hall. Tamara and Casey begin to clean up and Jewel starts putting the snacks away. I walk over to Carter and place my hand on his. He looks at me with heat in his eyes and I now know what he looks like when pissed.

"I'll stay over," I whisper in his ear. He smiles and kisses me on the cheek.

"Games over. Everyone go home. Tiffany will refund each of you in full and I'll cover the cost for tonight." The dealer collects the cards that were previously dealt, and Jewel gathers the poker chips and arranges them for me. I hand each of the gentlemen back their checks or cash that was left for a deposit and they leave, words unspoken.

"I guess I better get this cash back to the cage," Vic says breaking the tension in the room.

"Vic, sorry about tonight. Please charge the cost of the setup to my room and my accountant will ensure the bill is paid in full and a little extra for the troubles.

"Sure thing, Carter. Girls, I'll see you when you clock out." Vic takes the setups and heads back to the cage. Casey and Tamara aren't too far behind with the bar.

"I guess I'll go see if they need help with anything," Jewel says as she grabs her tip bag. Carter stops her and hands her a few folded hundreds.

"For the wedding. Congratulations." He places a kiss on her cheek and she gushes.

"Thank you, Carter. It's been a pleasure being your hostess. I'll get back to you on your proposal tomorrow. Just curious, if Tiffany says no, not only will she be making the dumbest mistake ever, but would my position still be available?" Carter laughs but takes her hand before answering.

"Yes, you can still work for me, even if she says no. The Vegas office will open regardless of my choice of staff."

"Okay, then. That's good to know." She places a kiss on my lips on her way out catching me by surprise as usual.

"Gotta love my friend," I say as she leaves, wiping my mouth. Carter takes my hand and leads us to the couch where we sit. He turns to the side and swings his leg carefully over my head and urging me to lay back onto him.

"Sorry I lost my shit," he says softly stroking my arm. I can still feel his heart racing a bit as he calms down.

"It's okay. I just wonder about the atmosphere of your office."

"Those guys will be fine. They've seen me at my worst." I don't say anything. I just sit there and take in the events of the evening. I realize there are a few things that I want to cover.

"Carter?"

"Yes, babe." I turn on my side, so I can get a better view of his face and he looks to me, locking his gaze with mine.

"Are you moving back to LA?" He contemplates for a moment before answering.

"It really depends on you, to be honest."

"How? Why?" He inhales deeply and sits up from his reclining position. I turn to meet him face to face.

"I've been looking at some property, mainly online, to have a house built. The thing is, I want it to be your home too. Yours and Xavier. I know that you don't want to get married again, at least not now, but what if we lived together? See, I want you. I don't even look at other women since we've met. You're exactly what I've been looking for my whole life."

"But, I have a kid. You're rich and single and hot. You hang with celebrities and know fashion designers and shit."

"That's my profession. That doesn't mean that's what makes me happy. You make me happy. You put me and others in our place when we let our egos get out of control. You are raising Xavier with values and a strong foundation. Those are a few things that I love about you."

"But why move here? Why not keep your place in LA?"

"Would you and Xavier move to LA?"

"No. I mean, I would, but his dad is here, and I can't do that to him."

"Exactly and I wouldn't want you to do that. So, what about

moving in with me?" I want to say no, but my reasons are invalid. He's done nothing but taken a genuine interest in me, my life, my child and kinda already stepped into that role of protector. The sex, well, it's a great bonus. Minus the miscommunication issue and my insane need to hold on to my hurt of a failed marriage, there is nothing wrong with us making this union official and moving in together. He's even normalizing my work life by making me head of his accounting team, should I accept.

"I don't know, Carter. Today was a big news day. You've dropped bombs on me directly and indirectly since I walked into the doors today."

"I know about the job offer, but what was indirect?"

"Oh, Vic assumed we knew that tonight was the last poker night, but we didn't. Then you helped Casey plan to propose to Jewel. It's just a lot to take in and I need some time to sort all of this out individually." He lowers his head and bobs it in an agreeing manner. I don't want him to think or even feel that I'm trying to let him down or say no. I'm just a give me a minute kinda woman. These changes, all of them, will have a ripple effect based on my decision and I need to make sure that it's the right one. My phone rings and it's Jewel.

"Hey, girl," I answer.

"Hey, Vic said we can go home just come down and clock out. We will get full pay of course since this was a private event. I'm going to wait for you in the dressing room."

"Okay, I'm coming down." I disconnect, and I grab my badge and keys. "Hey, Carter. I'll be back. I'm going to go clock out and change. Will you still be up?"

"Yeah. I have to do a little work and check in for my flight in the morning." He takes my face into his hands and gives me a sweet kiss on my forehead that I wasn't expecting. I un-pucker my lips and walk out the already opened door.

"Back in a few. Did you want me to bring you anything from the restaurant?" I ask trying to get his spirits back up.

"Nah, I'm good."

"Okay." I turn to head to the elevator and here the door close behind me. I think about how I could've worded my response better. I guess I will just have to show him when I get back.

Chapter

TWENTY-ONE

I WAKE UP ALONE IN his bed. His flight left at 7:00 this morning and he said he wasn't going to wake me. He did leave me a note stating that he was going to call me later and to make sure I tell Xavier that he will be back next week. I crawl out of bed and put my clothes on. I tried every seduction move I knew but he didn't take the bait. Instead, he worked while I watched a movie. When he did get in the bed, I held him close stroking his arms, his head, his chest until we were sleep. I brush my teeth and leave to go grab Xavier from his dad's. I pull into his drive and see them outside tossing a football. This is the picture I had always hoped to come home to, but this isn't my home and as of last night, no longer my fairytale.

"Hey, you two," I say getting out of the car. They are both in sweats and a tank t-shirt. I can't help but notice Corey has bulked up a little since we were together, and it does look attractive.

"Here mom, catch." Xavier tosses the ball to me and I receive it. "Now toss it to dad," Xavier requests. I throw it over to Corey who then tosses it back to Xavier. We do a roundabout with the ball for a few minutes. When Xavier passes it to me, Corey sees an opportunity to tackle me to the ground. He joins in and jumps onto his dad's back trying to get him off me. We're laughing and having fun until Corey and I lock gaze. There was a time when that look had me naked in three minutes, but those feelings are gone. His feelings for me are becoming evident on my hip so I gently push him off.

"Well, now that we had a little fun, Xavier, go get your things so we can go."

"Okay mommy." He runs into the house giving me a chance to speak with Corey.

"Hey, Corey, I need to run something by you."

"What's up?" he replies as he dusts the grass off his sweats. My eyes wander to his dick and yeah, I felt that. I shake my head and continue.

"I may be leaving the casino."

"Good. You didn't need to be there anyway. Did you get another job?"

"Sort of. Carter is opening a division of his law firm here and wants me to take on the head of accounting position." His eyes widen at my news and he makes a face that gives me the indication he's not pleased.

"So, he's just going to hire you with no experience because he's fucking you? Come on Tiff, you're smarter than that." I tried to have a nice, no attitude conversation with him, but he just blew that all to hell.

"So, you and Vanessa got married because she takes diction so well?"

"No, I was wrong, I'm sorry. I'm just worried that..."

"That he what, Corey? That he will take care of me? Give me the life you promised but failed to deliver? Care for your son as if he was his own and push you out the way? You shouldn't have to worry about those things. They aren't going to happen. He's taking care of me and my needs and he does love our son, but he respects your position in his life. In fact, he's moving here so he doesn't interfere with you and Xavier. He's not a monster, Corey. He's a great guy."

"He's moving here? That's a good gesture. Maybe I should get to know him better."

"I think you should. He asked me and Xavier to move in with him after he completes the build of his new home."

"Are you going to? What about our home?"

"That's just it, Corey. That home was our home. But you aren't there anymore. Maybe we can sell it and put the money in a trust fund for Xavier for college."

"Have you told Xavier?"

"I plan on talking to him today. I really needed to talk to you first and let you know. After all, these changes affect you as well." He thinks for a minute. You can tell he's thinking because he makes no eye contact and he appears to be having a mental conversation with himself.

"Well, I think it's great." I didn't expect Corey to say those words. I expected a fight.

"Really? I thought for sure we'd be having a battle of words by now."

"No. It's time for you to find your happiness Tiff, and I think Carter is the one for you. I see how happy you are when he's around or even when you speak his name. Yes, even the way Xavier talks about him. But most importantly, I love that he's making sure my son and I remain together. That's aces in my book." In all my shock, I give him a hug and make him drop the football. Our hug lasts a little longer than it should out of emotions. I'm finally letting go of it all. I wipe the threatening tear as we separate. Xavier and Vanessa come outside, and I open the door, so he can put his things inside the car.

"Hi, Vanessa," I speak as she approaches. She waves back as she waddles towards me and I give her a hug. "How are you feeling?" I ask.

"Like a houseboat. I'm so big. This little girl needs to come on." The reveal of their baby is news to me and I scream out of pure excitement.

"A girl! Wow, I didn't know. How awesome. Congratulations you two!" I rub the belly and the baby kicks. I'm not sure if that's a good thing or I don't like this lady thing.

"She's very active these days," Vanessa explains.

"Well, Xai, I think we should get going. Did you eat breakfast?"

"A little. I knew you were coming so I know we are going to our spot. Will Carter be there?" That felt like a burn to me, but I will have to talk to him about the best way to bring Carter up around his dad.

"Uh, no honey. He went to go visit his parents in Tennessee. It will just be us today."

"Oh, so he's out of town?" Corey asks.

"Yeah. He has to go help with a cleanup project. Xavier, tell your dad and Vanessa bye." Xavier gives them a hug and gets into the car strapping his seatbelt on. "Well, you two, I will be in touch this week. Remember to call Ashley if something comes up or the baby wants out." Corey laughs and waives as Xavier and I head to the diner for breakfast.

WE ARRIVE AT OUR HANG out and place our usual order. While we wait for the food to be delivered, I decide to take this opportunity to talk to my son about some potential big changes.

"Xavier, I need to talk to you about a few things. Is that okay?" He takes a big sip of his chocolate milk and looks at me with his big hazel eyes.

"Sure, mom. What's up?" I thought about this conversation ever since that silk black presentation folder hit the marble bar yesterday evening. I take a deep breath and think about the words I'm about to say.

"Son, A few things came up yesterday at work and I really need your opinion to help me make a decision. Are you okay with that?"

"Sure. Is it work related?"

"Well, one of the situations is. See, Mr. Carter is opening his new offices here in Vegas and he wants me and auntie Jewel to work for him. So, we won't be at the casino anymore." I hold his hand in a touching way and he looks at me crazy.

"So, what's the problem?" I'm tickled by his honest response and it's the perfect answer.

"I guess there is no problem, I just wanted to let you know. See what you thought."

"About you getting a new job working with your boyfriend? I think that's cool. When do you start?"

"Hmm. I guess in two weeks. I do have to tell them at the casino that I won't be working there anymore." The server brings our food and we tear into our bacon burgers and fries. After a few bites, I decide to move on to the bigger concern.

"How's your food?"

"It's good," he replies with his mouth full.

"Look, there's one other thing I need to talk to you about. Carter is moving to Vegas." His eyes light up and grow wide when I tell him that. He begins to bounce up and down in his chair.

"Really? Is he going to move in with us?" Well, shit. He takes the fun out of everything.

"No, he's having a house built."

"Oh, well, that's cool. We can go over to his house and visit and stay over, right?"

"He actually wants us to move in with him. Now, I know you love our home and we can stay there forever if you want to. I just want to make sure that I'm open and honest with you and that you know..."

"Cool! We can be a family like I wished for." He interrupts my long explanation with his enthusiasm taking me completely by surprise.

"What do you mean, wished for? You're okay with this?"

"Well, I was outside one night with Ashley and I saw a falling star. Ashley told me that I should make a wish, and I did. I said that it wouldn't work, but it did." I sit there with a shocked expression on my face. I always said my child was wise beyond his years and I was worried that the changes may be too much for him. I should've known better.

"Okay. Then it's settled. I'll turn in my two weeks' notice at work tomorrow. I'll also talk to Carter about us moving in together. I love that you are okay with it, but I make the final decision."

"Yes ma'am. I know. Are you going to marry him?" I did a real live spit take into my child's plate. Thankfully his burger was in his hand and the fries are in a separate container. I take a few moments to calm him down and make sure he understands that it isn't necessary for us to move in with Carter.

"Xavier, I know you are excited about your dad and Vanessa and the new baby, but it's not a competition. I don't have to marry Carter or have a baby like they did to be happy or for us to even be a family. Carter loves you and we don't live together now. So, if we move in with him, that doesn't mean we will get married or even have a baby. That just means that we want to be together and live as a family."

"So, I don't get to call him dad or other dad?"

"No. Stick with Mr. C, son." My phone rings that awkward ring letting me know that it's a video call. I answer blindly thinking it's Jewel since she normally calls around this time. To my surprise, it's Carter.

"Hey, babe. I wanted to let you know I made it home."

"Hi, my love. Glad you made it safely. How was your flight?"

"I can think of other things I wish I was doing at 5 am? Like stealing sweet kisses from your pu-, hey X-man," he recovers when I stop him from finishing that sentence in front of my child.

"Hey, Mr. C. Mom said that you are opening a new business here and that she's gonna work for you." When will I learn to not tell him anything that I don't want repeated.

"That's enough Xavier. Go finish your meal." I take my phone from him and continue my conversation.

"Ugh, that kid will tell everything," I say. Carter laughs, and it instantly makes me smile.

"So, you decided to come work for me?" he asks enthusiastically.

"I'm turning in my two weeks tomorrow."

"Wow. That makes me so happy. I was hoping I didn't have to hire someone. I'm already having to staff up this new location. This will help a lot with my Vegas based clients. The acceptance letter is in the folder I gave you. You can sign it and I'll get it on Friday when I come back." He's forever in lawyer role. I just nod my head in agreement. Xavier is finished with his meal and I really have lost my appetite. I take my food to go and we hop into the car. I put my phone in the cradle, so I can continue my talk with him.

"So, how are your parents? Were they happy to see you?"

"Yeah they were. This is my mom Emma and my dad Vincent." He turns the camera around and his parents are waving at me. His mom is a small framed lady and definitely shorter than her son and husband. She has sandy blonde hair that is graying at the roots and sparkling blue eyes. His dad is a little shorter than Carter, but his olive skin tone and those grey eyes match his son's. His hair is greyer than his mom's but he still is a handsome man.

"Hi, Tiffany. It is nice to meet you. Our son has told us so many wonderful things about you," his dad says as his mom shakes her head in agreement.

"Yes. Yes, he has. Too bad you couldn't come with him on this trip. We'd love to meet you and your son in person." I smile all the while thinking that Carter told his parents that I have a kid. Usually that is something a man tries to hide when speaking to his parents.

"Maybe next time," I reply unknowingly of my words since my head is still caught in the fact that Carter is spilling all the tea about our relationship to his parents.

"Okay, dear. I will hold you to it. I will let Carter take back his phone now. Talk to you soon." His mom gives the phone back to Carter and he switches from video call to regular phone conversation.

"So, you got off the plane and told your parents about me first thing?"

"No. They've been knowing about you. For about a month now, actually. I did want to bring you and Xavier out with me, but my folks have some legal things for me to go over and sign. So, I decided we can do it later."

"I'm sure we wouldn't mind," I answer as I pull into our driveway. I look at the door and there is a package waiting in my little self-constructed shelf.

"Mommy, can I go get the package and open the door?" Xavier asks.

"Sure, cupcake." I hand him the house key and he jets out the car. He opens the door and sets his things down before coming back to the car where I am still on the phone with Carter.

"Oh, that was fast," Carter replies as he hears the door close. I examine the envelope and it is rather thick. I know I wasn't expecting anything like this or at all. The senders name is unfamiliar and is in the form of initials.

"Yeah, he bought me this thick ass envelope. I have no idea who it is from."

"What's the name? Is it a company you know?"

"CAJ Enterprises. No, I'm not familiar. It feels like just a bunch of papers."

"Then open it. I know about this company. It's an investment group. They probably want to present you with retirement opportunities since you recently started working at the casino." I don't think twice about it and open the package. It is a thick stack of papers, but it's not for retirement options.

"Ca-Carter, this is...this is from you. Are these the papers for your house that you're building?"

"Wow, mom. Look at how big the pool is," Xavier says while peeking over my shoulders looking at the colorful renderings.

"Yeah. After you went to sleep last night, I thought that if I had the papers of the house I'm building, sent to you, it may help influence your decision. Look at the kitchen area." I look over the prints and he has my dream kitchen. He included two double ovens, since I love to bake and a big breakfast island for us to enjoy a close setting in the morning or other gatherings. I shut off the car and walk into the house with all these renderings and use my table to piece them together. This is going to be a monstrous house. My house is plenty big now, but this.

"Look mommy, a basketball court with my name," Xavier spots the rendering that is all about him.

"Carter, you are sparing no expense," I say.

"Well, actually, this will be done at cost for me since I have a few friends in the construction business and I have money saved for this. I always wanted a big house." I continue to ooh and ahh over these drawings and I'm mesmerized.

"Was this house designed with us living together as a family or did you always have this in mind for your home?"

"I always had this in mind. I added Xavier's name to the courts last night. But to answer your unspoken question, this is my house with or without you."

"Really? What do you need with two double ovens?"

"I throw company events every year. A bigger house means I no longer have to rent out space. I'll have my own."

"When do you break ground?"

"Uh, I think next week. The schedule is back at my office. I'll have my secretary to send you an email."

"Oh, you don't have to do that."

"No. You are my girlfriend and I want to be completely open, honest, and transparent with you."

"Boy, you are a tough, non-negotiating person."

"No, I just like to show my cards. I have nothing to hide. You should know this."

"Oh, is that a nudge to poker?"

I put all the renderings back into the envelope and look into the freezer to find something for dinner. He obviously hears my ramblings.

"What are you doing? Rearranging your kitchen?"

"I'm looking for these chicken breasts for dinner."

"Mmm. I already know it's going to be good. What are you making?"

"Just some chicken alfredo with broccoli and bacon."

"Oh, god, Tiffany. Please tell me you're going to cook like that at our new house."

"Of course, I am."

"Oh, wait. So, you decided to move in with me?"

"Well, it takes about six months or so to build the house. I figure two things. It will take a minute for me to get this house decluttered and packed. I already explained to Corey what was going on and he said that if I chose to move in with you, we would sell the house. I then talked to Xavier and of course he was all for it. So, I figured, why not. I mean we have time." It's quiet for a minute and I figure he's taking all of this in or changing his mind about the insta-family.

"I love you," he utters tenderly.

"I love you too. It's time I started acting like it. When will you be back?"

"Not soon enough. Friday, then I have to fly out to LA to close on the sale of my property and then grab the keys to the new office in Vegas."

"Let me ask you a question? Do you ever rest?"

"I will once I get this office open. I plan on taking less caseloads and splitting my clientele. I need all the time I can get to spend with you and I want to be there for Xavier."

"Will you train me on your billing system?"

"Yes, I will have Donna in LA help get you familiarized with the system. Then I will have a few people you can train to work under you. That way we can spend time together and go on vacation. We can take Xavier and go snorkeling in the tropics. Maybe you can wear that swim suit you had on last week."

"I have one even more revealing," I reply, teasingly.

"Stop. I'm at my parents."

"Well, maybe we can finish this conversation when you come home."

"Believe me, we will. I gotta go. We're going out to eat. Call you later. I love you."

"I love you too." We disconnect, and I take a moment to reflect on how my life just changed within a day. I look around the house and suddenly it doesn't feel like home any more. I'm finally closing this chapter and walking into a new one, with Carter.

Chapter
TWENTY-TWO

XAVIER AND I TOOK A ride to Jewels house Sunday and spent the day with her and Casey. They asked him to be the ring bearer in their ceremony and he agreed. Jewel is moving in with Casey in a few weeks and I told them that I was turning in my two weeks. Jewel flat out quit. She knew I was going to take the job with Carter and after the abrupt ending to Friday nights poker game, she told Vic she was done. She's been in lover's heaven since that night. If I didn't text her that we were coming over, she'd still be naked and under Casey. You can see the look of love on their face as we enjoyed dinner.

Here it is Monday morning and after getting my little love off to school, I walk into the offices of the casino and hand Vic my letter of resignation.

"So, you're taking that job?"

"Yeah. The money was too good to say no to."

"I imagine the boss must have one hell of an incentive package." He smiles when he makes that comment and I laugh. "Well, you don't have to work these next two weeks. I have filled those positions already. So, consider it a vacation. And trust me, Mr. Jackson left enough money in his house account to cover you and Jewel's pay plus bonus."

"Well, I can help out with the cage if you want," I offer my assistance because I don't want to sit around my house and do nothing. I did that until five months ago.

"As tempting as that is, I don't have anyone going on vacation, so I won't need the help. Then you'll be sitting around here doing nothing."

"True. It's just that, for the first time since my marriage and after my divorce, I was finally doing something to be independent. Now I feel like I'm going back into that dependent status."

"But, doll, you'll have a job." Vic tries to get me to understand that I will still be employed, but I just don't feel like it's the same.

"Will I really? I mean I'm dating my new boss," I reply. He chuckles a bit and encourages me to sit down.

"You don't know Carter very well, do you?" I shake my head in an unsure way of why he's asking this question or if there is some deep dark secret I don't know about.

"Carter is a work-a-holic. When he hires someone, it's not a fluff job. He expects nothing but the same one-hundred and ten percent he gives. He doesn't care whether you are sleeping with him or not. So, you can be assured, this isn't a pacify position just to get you out of the casino. He expects you to work and will have no problem firing you even if you are banging him." This conversation oddly makes me feel better about taking the position with Carter. I don't want any favoritism or special treatment.

"Well, then that's good. I take my job seriously and I finally get a chance to do what I went to school for. Corey kept me at home after Xavier was born and during my pregnancy, so I never got the chance to be me. So, if he's as ballsy as you say, then this will be perfect."

"Yeah, you saw how those guys behaved at the game. Carter can be downright ruthless. And just think, his temper has calmed from when I first met him. Normally, Damien would've been swallowing his teeth." Hearing this aggressive side of Carter has me intrigued. I think back to the times when we were intimate and when we were fucking, he made sure to leave his mark on me. But he was also calm and sweet which resulted in the love making difference. There was also the time when I swore he was going to break that guys arm for touching me. I guess I should've put two and two together. The cow crew comes in to transport money, so I decide to follow Vic's advice and go home.

"Victor, I just want to thank you for giving me a shot at my independence. It means more to me than you know." I give him a hug and he responds with a gentle bear squeeze of his own.

"Sure, doll face. We will see each other again. Carter may not be having his games here, but he is paid up on that villa for a while. This time, you can use the main entrance to come in instead of the employee one." I swat him on his arm and hand him my badge. He pins it to his wall of valuable employees right next to Jewel's. I waive to the rest of the team and instead of going home, I go shopping for new work clothes.

SATURDAY MORNING...

"Now, Ashley is staying the weekend with you since your dad and Nessa are at the hospital with the baby. She has my number, Carter's number and auntie Jewel's number. The house is to remain locked and your dad has the key. He will be by to check on you at night. Meals are prepared and in the freezer. We will only be gone until tomorrow afternoon, so behave."

"Mom, I got it. Ashley will take good care of me and the cameras are on in the house and you will be watching." I've never left my child if I was traveling to another state. Carter said we can take them both, but Corey agreed to stay the night here to help keep an eye on things. He and Vanessa welcomed their daughter Wednesday and he started his paternity leave. He will spend tonight at this house and take his wife and child home tomorrow. By then we should be on the way back here if we aren't here already." Ashley is going over all notes which includes updated numbers to Carter's cell and his house in LA, the hospital where Corey is at, and Casey. I truly appreciate her being a part of our lives and yes, she invited us to her graduation.

"Mom, just go already. Mr. C. is waiting for you outside," Xavier pleads. He has his Lego's set and ready to build. I give Ashley a hug and thank her then give my cupcake a kiss.

"Ms. Lang, I have the video app on my phone too. Just use my email address and I will be able to connect with you."

"Thank you. That will help with my anxiety so much. Maybe once when we land and then before his bedtime."

"That sounds good."

"Alright, you two. I'm off to LA. Back tomorrow afternoon." I walk out the door and stand back until I hear all locks click. I check the app on my phone and see that they went straight for the cookies and milk. I laugh at my little monster as I see him take his plate to the play area and start on his new build. Carter must own stock in these things because he buys him one every week.

"Come on, baby. It's only an overnight stay. We'll be back tomorrow, and I will take you both out for dinner," Carter says trying to ease my nerves.

"Okay," I reply. I get into the car and we head to the airfield where Casey and Jewel are waiting for us. Carter called Wednesday and asked if we wanted to fly out to LA for the day. He needed to go by the office and he figured we'd see his place that he's selling and the main office for his firm. We thought it'd be cool to tag along and at the time, I knew Xavier would be with his dad. But life threw a monkey wrench in that plan. The good thing is Ashley is available and has stayed at the house many times, most of them due to my work schedule.

"Stop looking so sad, I'm sure everything is fine."

"I've just never been without my baby, that's all. I've always been within a certain radius or at least knew he was with his dad."

"You can stay if you like, I won't be upset or mad." He strokes my cheek with his thumb and it calms me. I check in on the app one more time and they are busy constructing his new set. Ashley is helping him, and my doors and windows have not been opened.

"No, I'm good. I want to see the place that you are selling. Does it still have a bed?" Carter slims his eyes at my statement and I flash my sinful smile.

"Come here," he calls to me to come sit on his lap. The driver of the SUV adjusts his rearview mirror so that he can't see into the back seat. He must've experience this before. I straddle him and lock onto his lips as he palms my ass like a basketball. I'm wearing shorts so there is no easy access, but it doesn't stop him from feeling me up. He starts with my nipples while I gently bite and tug at his lips and slow wind on his dick. His khaki shorts are made of a lightweight material and I can feel how hard he is through my clothes. It's been a little over a week since we last had sex and my body is craving him. He unbuttons my shorts and snakes his hands into my panties and plays with my clit.

"Ah," I let out a soft moan into his ear making him rub faster. He manages to get one finger into my pussy and he squirms when he feels how wet I am.

"Fuck. Why do we have to be in a fucking car?" he exclaims. I smile and continue to ride his finger until he removes it and inserts it into his mouth.

"That's the sweetness I've been craving," he says as he nuzzles at my ear. My stomach tightens, and I know that tonight, with or without guests, he's going to fuck me good. I lap at his lips sampling the remnants of my own juices until the driver interrupts.

"Excuse me, Mr. Jackson. But we are at the airfield. I look at him and his face is stone, his eyes are lustful, and he's biting on his bottom lip. The driver hops out and grabs our overnight bags out the back before opening the door. I sit down and smooth my hair back into place while he adjusts himself before we step out onto the tarmac.

"Carter? Did she spaz out about leaving Xavier at home with Ash?" Jewel asks as we join them.

"Just a little. I told her she could stay home."

"And miss a chance to fuck you? She'd have lost her mind." Jewel is insane and no longer my friend.

"Hi Casey," I say giving him a hug and a peck on his cheek.

"Um, bih, you can't ignore me because I tell the truth," Jewel says to me pulling me away from Casey.

"Jewel, you are insane and so not right about why I chose to go. I'm doing this for the future business he's opening." I stand by my statement until she calls my bluff.

"Then why are your shorts unbuttoned?" I hate her. I mean I love her, but she takes jabs and points out shit that no one else should. I turn away to fasten my button and Carter is having a good laugh thanks to Jewel's quick wit and timing.

"Whatever. Just get on the damn plane." I storm up the stairs trying to hold in my own laugh and sit in my seat. When she enters she comes and sits on me trying to kiss me and make me feel better. I love the relationship she and I have. Best friends for a long time and the only sister I've ever had, blood or otherwise.

"Come on, Tiff. Give me a hug and I'll get up," she bargains. I hug her and in true Jewel fashion, she lands a feel of my tits when my arms open. "There, now you feel better." She gets up and takes her seat by Casey who is trembling with laughter. Carter is too.

"You two have a secret relationship I need to know about?"

Carter asks as he buckles his seat belt. His attendant checks on each of us and asks if we need anything.

"No. She's always been my closest friend and always off the collar. You never know what's gonna come out her mouth or what she is going to do."

"I'm only interested in what my mouth wants to do at this moment."

"Carter, you are such a perv," I say smiling hard and pushing on his arm.

"What? I was talking about drinking my water. I think you have the perverted mind, Ms. Tiffany." He takes a sip of his water and I feel rather shameful by my assumption.

"Oh. I guess I jumped the gun."

""It happens to the best of us." The attendant takes her seat and we take off heading towards LA. Once we get at our cruising altitude, the seat belt comes off and Carter's tablet comes out. He scours through emails and replies, Jewel and Casey are watching the inflight movie on the screen installed on the plane and I'm playing games on my phone.

"Hey, do you mind looking over these payroll files and make sure they are entered correctly?" Carter asks. I'm taken off guard for a minute and he hands me another tablet with the accounting software loaded.

"Sure. Is this an audition?"

"Um, no. The job is yours, but I got an email from the bank saying that the taxes didn't add up. The spreadsheet is under this tab." He taps on the tab label payroll taxes, like I couldn't figure that out, and goes over the entries. I ask a few questions pertaining to the calculations used to figure out the taxes and if anyone changed their exemptions recently and correct the error on the spreadsheet.

After a few entries and some corrections, I find the difference and send it to his email for his records but discuss it with him now.

"Okay, all done." He looks it over and compares what was sent in for his tax payment against what I corrected and the amount the bank said that it should be and notices that his tax payment was shorter than he requested. I try to calm him down when I see that vein pop in his neck, but it doesn't work.

"Damn it. I knew my payments looked a little off, but I didn't think about it too much until the bank emailed me. So, now I have to fire my payroll person and go with one of those companies until you start."

"I can help if you want. I don't mind, and it will give me something to do during the week." Vic was right. Carter is about his business and no level of relationship will compromise his principles when it comes to work.

"I may take you up on that offer. It'll save me some time and I already have a lot going on this week."

"Anything else I can help with?"

"Well, I was kinda waiting to discuss this with you alone, but it looks like the engaged couple is engrossed in that movie, so now will be okay." I sure hope he doesn't ask me to marry him. That, to me, seems like his natural progression of thinking, but I wouldn't want to shoot him down and I don't want to say yes out of obligation. He reaches into his pocket and I know he's going to pull out a ring box. My stomach turns in knots anticipating his long drawn out proposal.

"Carter, please don't..." In his hand isn't a ring box, but a business card.

"Don't what?" Having to backtrack my thoughts has been my thing today. I think I should stop assuming things of others, especially him.

"Don't you think that you should relax a little and we can discuss things later. You have so much on your plate already." He nods his head in agreement and puts the card away.

"Yeah, you're right. Unless one of my clients call, I should just relax over the next two days. Even when I was with my folks I stayed glued to my phone and tablet." I'm curious to know his drive and why branching out now.

"What changed? I mean, why did you decide to slow down now?" He looks over at me with a smile on his lips and twinkle in his eyes.

"You. You changed me from day one. I know I've said it and you may find it hard to believe, but yes. That one embarrassing moment of my Jack and Coke spilling all over me, changed me. I don't know, but that made something in me click and I said I had to have you. I'm thirty-five years old and it was time I started listening to my first mind and not live so carefree. I want a wife and kids."

"Kids? Like more than one?"

"Usually that's what the 's' on the end of a word means, plural. Why? Do you not want anymore?"

"I mean yeah, I do. But before you I wasn't thinking of settling back down."

"And now?"

"I don't know. you've changed me." I smile using his words against him. He laughs in response. "So, how many kids did you want?" I ask continuing our conversation.

"I always wanted one of each. If I had more, that would be good, but definitely two."

"Me too. Just to balance out the number of hormones in a household." He takes my hand and places a kiss upon the back of it. I bite my lip as he lays his head on my shoulder nuzzling just under my chin. I can feel his breath on my neck and it sort of entices me. Who am I kidding. It's downright making me horny. I squirm down and away a smidge as to not feel most of his air expelling from his nose.

I hear soft snoring sounds and realize he has fallen asleep. I recline a little and manage to move the armrest between us giving him a more comfortable position. He settles even more, and his mouth opens just a bit. I wanna stick my finger in his mouth, but he may bite it so that may not be a good idea. I crane my neck and see Jewel and Casey taking a nap as well. The onboard map says we have about forty-five minutes left till we land in Pasadena. I allow my head to fall back as I stare at the plane's ceiling. I think of how I presumed he was going to ask me to marry him and how disappointed I was when he didn't. But why? I mean, I tell myself and everyone else I'm not doing that again so why feel hurt when a ring box wasn't pulled out from his pocket? I run my fingers through his black with a few spots of grey hair and he settles even more taking in a deep breath as he relaxes.

I turn my head to stare out the window but catch my reflection instead. I'm looking at the woman who's responsible for her own happiness and needs to remove her won'ts, so her wills have a place in her life. She knows she wants it all and it's time she rewrites her fairytale. Who said Prince Charming has to be your first love?

Chapter

TWENTY - THREE

I WAKE HIM WITH A kiss on his forehead when we land at Bob Hope in Burbank. He stirs a little before sitting fully upright.

"Mmm. This site I can get used to."

"What? Waking up on a plane?"

"No. You know what I mean. I've told you before."

"I know. I just like poking fun at you. Come on, let's go see your bachelor pad." I unbuckle my seat belt and go tap the other two on their heads waking them up. The attendant pushes the button to open the door to the plane and the stairs. We disembark and jump into the awaiting SUV. Carter takes the front seat beside the driver and I sit in the second row with the two sleepy heads. In true friend fashion, Jewel lays her head right on my lap. The trip is about thirty minutes, so she has time to sneak in a nap. Casey tries to pull her to him, but she jerks her arm away.

"It's best to leave the bear sleep. Trust me, she's not a pleasant person when she's awakened."

"You two are pretty close, huh?"

"Well, Casey, I think you know our relationship."

"No, I mean, you have this different bond that transcends a normal friendship. Even her parents asked about you when we called them to tell them about the engagement. They were like, 'where's my other daughter?'"

"Yeah, they are good people. After meeting them I'm sure you wondered why she was working at a casino."

"Just a little, but I'm glad she did. I would've never met her, and I wouldn't be getting married." He rubs on her arm gently, careful not to wake her. I can see the love he has for her in his eyes. In fact, I've always seen it. I make a mental note to ask him why he decided to propose. I look out the window and see we've arrived at our destination.

OUR FIRST STOP IS TO Carter's offices. We meet a few people who are in there working on some new contracts and other things for their boss. They were a bit surprised when they saw him come in the office on a Saturday.

"Well, Carter Jackson as I live and breathe," the blue-eyed brunette says as she steps from her office. She steps over to Carter where they give a friendly, two second, hug. *Yes, I was counting.*

"Donna, didn't think you were going to be here."

"Well, my boss is selling his condo and opening a new office in Vegas, someone had to make sure all the filings were in order. Did you and this mystery woman decide on what you want in the new house yet? I still want to know who she is, so I can tell her that she's taking away my most valuable player."

"Well, as luck has it, you just told her. This is Tiffany, my girl-friend. Babe, this is my personal assistant Donna Mabry. She will be the one to go to with any questions about anything, really." She extends her hand and we shake. Carter introduces Jewel and Casey too, so he doesn't feel left out.

"It's a pleasure to meet all of you. So, Carter is showing you his old place before the new owner takes over?"

"Yeah we decided to tag along since we didn't have anything to do this weekend." Her smile is warm and inviting which eases my mind and tension. I thought she was making a play for my man. I look her over while her and Carter look at some papers she has in her hands and notice she has a ring on her finger. Jewel is looking at the computer at the receptionist's desk and makes notes on a notepad. She's already mentally going to work, and we haven't officially started yet.

"That's good. Here, let me show you all around this location. I imagine you two will be working in the Vegas office, but in case you have to come to LA, you'd have a feel for the land."

"Sure," I reply. She takes us on a short journey to some of the partners offices and gives us the names of their assistants. We end up in her office where she politely asks us to give her a copy of our ID, so she can go ahead and scan them in the system since we are here. I can tell she's efficient and thorough with her job which I know to be a big deal in Carter's book. I only hope I can live up to it with my out of practice self.

"Where do y'all want to eat tonight?" Carter asks entering Donna's office.

"Why not cook at your place?" I respond. I mean we have a bomb-ass bartender, I cook a little, and well, we have Jewel." She raises her hand and flips me the bird causing us to laugh.

"Well, I guess we can do that. I'll have Franklin, take us by the store so we can grab a few things," he says.

"Well, bye Donna. I will be in touch. Any paperwork just express it to the hotel, same suite."

"Okay, Carter. Hey, it was nice to finally meet you two. Carter has been going on and on about his favorite Vegas beauties."

"It was nice meeting you too, Donna. We will be in touch I'm sure." We all shake hands and head back out to the waiting SUV. Carter instructs the driver to our change of plans and we go to the grocery store for a little shopping.

"So, WHAT DID YOU HAVE in mind?" I ask once we arrive and walk in.

"I'm surprised that you even have to ask." I stand with a confused look on my face as he approaches the counter. "Yes, can I have three pounds of shrimp?" He asks the meat clerk. I smile when I recall how he went crazy for my shrimp tacos the night of the 90s party and how he said he could eat them every day.

"Wow, I thought you were just being courteous when I made those."

"No, I've been wanting them ever since. I tried some in Tennessee and they were awful. I'm glad you suggested eating in. Now I can have what I've been craving." He rubs his nose against mine giving me warm and fuzzies.

"Well, this will be nice. The four of us, all in new relationships, new life paths, new found love, having dinner. I don't think I've ever done that. When I was with Corey, the most interaction with others that we had were those boring lawyer association functions and parties. Jewel never had a serious relationship then, so she was at the house every Sunday for dinner and girl time."

"Well, I promise you can have whatever you want. We can go on couple dates, family dates, or friend dates. I want to make you happy. You deserve it after all you've been through." *Oh God, I love this man!* I think to myself. I pull him into my arms and plant my hands in their favorite place. The distance isn't that great being that I'm five-eight, but compared to his six-two frame, it's enough. He kisses me on my nose and I go for his mouth.

"Ick. I mean like, can you two get a room? First it was in the car on the way to the airport now it's the seafood counter at the store. I already know I will hear noises tonight. Just geez." Casey and Jewel come back with three bottles of white wine and some dessert toppings, ice cream and bananas.

"Well, I see we have our after dinner treat ready," I say looking into her basket.

"Yeah. I was thinking about that one night in college when we stayed up all night listening to music and gossiping about everything. I figure we'll do that tonight and have fun. I know you are down, I just wonder if these old fogies will be up to the challenge." She pushes Carter, playfully of course, when she makes that statement as a playful tease on his age.

"I'm sure my man here can handle anything you two divas can throw at him," Casey chimes in defending Carter.

"Case man, are you calling me old?" Carter humorously questions. The counter clerk hands me the shrimp and I place it into the basket and we all walk away laughing and playfully making jokes with each other. We walk down the aisles being goofy and this makes me feel even more relaxed. Him in a non-restricted light is a great contrast to the day I met him when he was livid about something he was discussing on the phone. I wanted to leave that day, but Jewel fought me on it and I'm glad she did. We're at the checkout and as the items are being put up on the conveyor belt, I realize a few things are still needed.

"Oh, shit. I need to go get the tortillas and some limes. I'll be back." I turn to step out of line and Carter says he will cover these items and meet me back at the car.

"Casey baby, why don't you go with Tiff and grab an extra caramel sauce and some apples for later." She presses her body against his and I know she's planning something naughty. I roll my eyes and wait for him. This gives me the chance to ask Casey that question I want answered.

"So, you guys are tying the knot. Are you excited?" I help him grab the right apples to pair with caramel sauce and notice a pause in his actions. "Casey? You're not getting cold feet before you even start planning the wedding, are you?" He looks at me with his eyes wide and I begin to swing on his arm. "I will beat your ass if you hurt my friend," I exclaim so loudly that a few onlookers laugh as they pass by.

"Tiff. Tiff! Wait! Stop hitting me woman. I'm not going to hurt Jewel. I wouldn't do that." His breaths are quick and rapid from him staving off my combat and him laughing.

"Explain before I throw this apple against your head." I toss the fruit up and down waiting on him to spill.

"Ugh, she's gonna kill me, but we're already married."

"What?"

"Yeah, we went to the courthouse and did it when we were in Reno." I stand and look at him with my head tilted not comprehending what he just laid on me.

"But, you guys asked Xai to be your ring bearer," I say confusingly.

"And he will be. We wanted to have a big ceremony and reception but we couldn't wait. I proposed to her at the poker game to not only make it real for everyone around, but to give her the ring she deserved. Those were real tears."

"We're y'all drunk when you did it?"

"I had never been more lucid." I put the produce down and give him a big hug.

"Well, congratulations." Tears well in my eyes and he helps to wipe them away. I always knew how sweet and attractive Casey is, but in this moment, he has a light about him that is a beautiful glow and I know he is happy.

"I, uh, guess we better go check out before we're accused of messing around," he says comically.

"I don't know about Carter, but Jewel wouldn't mind," I reply. He laughs thinking I'm joking, but I'm not. She's that experimental. I've never done anything like that, except her random kisses and grabs. I take the few moments left before we two become four again and ask that question that has been on my mind for a while. Despite learning that they are already married.

"Hey Case, let me ask you a question? When did you know that Jewel was 'the' one?"

"I guess it was around the time we started dating. I'm not sure if you know much about how we started dating or not, but there was the terminal issue at work and then the magical night happened. It was raining, and her battery died. I gave her a jump and followed her home to make sure she was safe. As a thank you, she invited me in and dried my clothes for me." He laughs at the memory and I can't help but smile as he continues.

"There I was sitting on her couch in her little pink short silk robe and a pair of her unopened special undies to try to contain my little soldier. It was so funny. She made me a preventive hot toddy and we talked all night. In fact, we fell asleep on that couch. When I woke up, she was laying on my chest wrapped in my arms and it felt perfect. That's when I knew. So, when I asked her to move in with me, months later, I took a great leap, and it worked out."

"Had you been in relationships before?" I ask, curious to know what his life was like before Jewel stormed into it.

"Well, I was a bit of a playa," his tone is boisterous and funny. "But, it's kinda like Carter said to me about you, when the spirits align, you will know, without a doubt." He smiles, and I allow the silence to fall between us. I pay for the last-minute items and we grab the bag and walk back out. Before exiting, he stops and turns to me.

"You do know Carter is extremely serious about you, right?"

"I -I know he loves me and he knows I'm not rushing to jump the broom or anything."

"Yeah, but that just stagnates your relationship. You know, put it in a box. Waiting is his only option for now, but he wants forever." He turns and walks out the store and I follow putting my shades on to hide my expression.

"What the hell took y'all so long?" Jewel says taking inventory of the bag.

"Sorry, we were discussing wedding ideas when I saw a few bridal magazines." I concoct a half-truth, so she won't know that I know her huge secret. Casey catches my gaze and he nods with his approval as we head to the condo.

It took me an hour to prep our dinner and while we waited for the shrimp and pickled slaw to marinate for the tacos, I made my avocado, cilantro-lime, sauce to go with the meal. During that time, we went through two bottles of wine. Carter's condo is huge for two-bedrooms. If the entry doesn't captivate you when you walk in, then the rest of it will. He has an office, a family room, and a dining area with a table for eight. The kitchen is my favorite. The island with the sink plus enough space to sit five chairs around. This is a great entertaining spot.

"Okay guys, time to eat." I place the food on a plate and set them on table, so we can each serve ourselves. We are nowhere near formal tonight with all the laughing dancing, and off-key singing we're doing. I do insist on washing hands before we eat.

"Dang. You are such a mom," Jewel complains as she washes her hands.

"Why did you say that? Now she's gonna grab her phone and check in on Xavier." Carter says. He has a bit of a buzz going so it's funny to see him this relaxed. But, he isn't lying. I did grab my phone and I had no missed messages, calls, or house alerts. I check the in-house cameras and they are watching a Disney movie, so I put my phone away.

"Baby, come sit down. Xavier is fine." Carter puts his arm around me and escorts me back to the table. But he makes me sit in his lap where he rubs my arms to comfort me. I take a shrimp and pop it in his mouth and watch his expression as he enjoys the savory taste.

"Oh, babe. This is better than the last time. Give me another." I laugh and pop another one in his waiting mouth.

"So, Carter. How much are you selling your house for? Furthermore, why are you selling it?" Jewel asks.

"Actually, it's already sold. This is my last time here and I get to share it with y'all."

"What about all your stuff?" I ask while I fix him a few tacos. I'm bent over in front of him reaching for the food, giving him the perfect view of my ass.

"That ass is fat, ain't it?" Jewel asks Carter and I catch on to what's happening behind me. I roll my eyes and finish putting the toppings on his tacos before setting his plate down in front of him. "I mean damn Tiff, you had this man assmitized." We all laugh, and I throw my napkin across at her.

"As for my belongings. I have someone coming to sell them for me and then what isn't sold will go to a donation center. My clothes will be shipped to the hotel back in Vegas."

"Why not ship it to Tiffany's since you guys will be moving in together when you get the new house?" Casey adds his question.

"Well, then he'd have to be at the house everyday just to get a change of clothes. That's too much." I reply to his question.

"Oh. I thought he was moving in with you. My bad." Jewel slams her shot of tequila and Carter and I look at each other awkwardly.

"I mean, I guess, it never came up, actually," I mention in response to Jewel's statement.

"Yeah that may be too much for little man to have a non-father figure living in his home," Carter replies. We're still looking at each other like it isn't a bad idea.

"Yeah, maybe. but aren't you guys moving into a custom-built home once it's done?" Silence falls because it does make sense for him to stay with me. I know Xavier will love it. I just need to check with him first since his best interest is at heart.

"We never discussed that as an option. Besides, it may be too much for all involved," Carter says.

"Um, it's Tiffany's house, little man likes you, you're over there often anyway. Sounds like a no brainer to me." I hate when Jewel is right. We hadn't spoke about this and considering the fact that we will be moving in together, maybe this isn't a bad idea. He looks over at me and all I can do is shrug my shoulders. Again, the room is quiet. I take the dishes to the sink and begin to clean. Jewel joins me, and the guys step out onto the patio. The music continues to play as we put away the dishes and the food.

"So, what are you going to tell Corey about Carter moving in to the house?"

"I haven't even thought about that, but I figure he knows about the relationship and he approves. He knows we are moving in together and he's okay with that too."

"But moving another man into his house, that may be a bad look."

"Then why the hell would you bring it up in the first place?"

"Tiff, you know me. I operate with no filter in all aspects."

"Maybe it's time you try to use filters, Jewel. You are going into a new life and you can't be so damn carefree anymore. It's like you create opportunities to one-up people."

"How you figure?"

"You casually throw the moving in with me quip then add the whole what would Corey think scenario. That's fucked up. If I'm going to allow another man back into my life and my child's, I don't need any two-sided views. This decision is hard enough and as my friend, I figure you'd be the one to support me and not play devil's advocate." I slam the cabinet door and it catches the attention of the men outside and they come inside to see what happened.

"Is everything okay, T&J?" Casey says, entering cautiously.

"Fine," I say with a bit of an attitude. "You know what, I think I'm going to go take a shower and lay down." I storm off to the bedroom hearing Jewel call out for me. I'm so angry right now that I can't talk to her. I grab my overnight bag and open it to pull out my pajama set. I hang my dress in the closet to allow the wrinkles to fall and place my shoes in there too.

"Hey, " Carter says walking into the room. "You okay?"

I look at him and nod my head yes. "I'm fine. Just, Jewel can be so inconsiderate at times and has no concerns for others. It's been like this forever, so I should be used to it, and I suppose I am, but this isn't something to take lightly. Us moving in together is a major move and I'm ready. I want you in the house with me and Xavier and have a normal relationship and not sneak around."

"I want that too, but don't do anything to upset anyone. If you need to talk to Corey I can stay at the hotel. It's not an issue. Now, go talk to your friend before she jumps in the shower with you. On second thought..." He flashes a devilish grin and I shake my head. I walk back out to the kitchen area where I find Jewel in Casey's arms bawling her eyes out. I take her from his arms and pull her into mine.

"I'm really sorry, Tiff. I didn't mean to hurt you," she cries. Her tears, at least I hope they're tears, are soaking my breasts and that shower is even more needed. I hug her tighter and hold her until she pulls herself together.

"You didn't hurt me, Jewel. You made me mad. I'm doing exactly what you always tell me to do. I'm moving on with my life, but you keep bringing up my ex-husband and reminding me of my failed marriage. Like, why?"

"I don't know. I just want you to be happy and not be afraid to move forward. I didn't realize I was being an asshole."

"More like a bitch." She looks at me with shock before she bursts out into laughter.

"So, you two have made up?" Carter asks while taking me into his arms.

"There wasn't anything to make up for. Tiffany just needed to put me out her business and into my place."

"Correct!" I reply with emphasis.

"Okay, so from here going forward, we will allow each other to make their own decisions about their respective relationship unless the other finds the decision to be detrimental or catastrophic. At that time said friend may either confront the partner or subtly advise. Agreed?" Carter's proclamation has the three of us looking at him with raised eyebrows.

"Tiffany, does he ever not act like a lawyer?" Jewel asks.

"He's a boss at all times, even in the bedroom," I reply.

"Which is where I'm about to take you. Casey, you and Jewel have a great night sleep. See you in the morning." He hoists me over his shoulder and we go to the bedroom where we talk a little and love a lot all night long.

Chapter TWENTY-FOUR

W E ARRIVED BACK IN VEGAS yesterday morning and while Jewel and Casey went home to finish up their weekend, Carter and I took Xavier and Ashley out for breakfast. We talked about her upcoming graduation and what her plans were for after college. This made me think that I will have to get another sitter, in case one is needed for when Carter and I want to go out. She said she'll be available on weekends, but she had a job lined up at a children's center, concentrating on working with kids on the autism spectrum. I applauded her dedication to kids and she actually made me proud when she told of her future plans. Of all the decisions Corey ever made, outside of marrying me, this was definitely one of my favorites.

Today I'm meeting with both Carter and Corey so that we can discuss the plans pertaining to Carter moving in to the house temporarily. I didn't tell Corey that Carter is joining us because I wanted to speak with him alone first.

Carter selected the restaurant and agreed to meet us there around 2:00 pm. Giving me twenty minutes to ease him into the meeting and changes. I keep searching around to see if I see him coming in, but each time you hear that tiny bell alerting to a new arrival, it's not him. I'm on my third glass of water when, in true fashion, he arrives late.

"Hi, Corey," I say as he is escorted to the table with a bit of attitude in my tone. Not too much to start trouble but enough to let him know that I was becoming agitated.

"Sorry, Tiff. I had baby duty last night and I over slept during nap time." I apologize for my behavior and pass him a gift that I purchased for the new bundle of joy.

"I'm sorry. I should've known that it was important. So how is the baby and Vanessa?" I'm genuinely happy for them. I discarded my bitter pill when I decided to move forward.

"They are good. Real good and I know Nessa is going to love this gift." A brief moment of silence falls between us as he pretends to go over the menu. I drum my fingers absent mindedly on the table trying to think of the best way to introduce the topic.

"I need to..."

"What's the meet..." We both attempt to break the silence at the same time and laugh a bit.

"You go, Tiffany," he concedes.

"Well, I wanted to talk to you today about a change in my living arrangements." He sits up with a concerned look on his face, lays the menu down, and gives me his full attention.

"Oh, so you and the lawyer are splitting up?"

"No. Everything is going well in that relationship. In fact, he sold his home in LA, which is one of the reasons why we were done there this past weekend."

"Mmhmm, go on." I get the sense that he knows what I'm about to say and he's waiting to drop a big fat argument in my lap.

"I offered to have his things shipped to my house so that he wouldn't have to pay for unnecessary storage."

"Okay. And?"

"Then Jewel bought up the idea of Carter moving in with

Xavier and I until the house is complete. Now out of respect, Carter and I both thought..."

"That's fine, Tiffany." For a moment I thought I was talking with a clone. I examined his face for sarcastic facial impressions but found none.

"Excuse me. What?" Still shocked by his open agreement with the moving in situation I had to ask him to repeat his words.

"Tiffany, we've been divorced a year now and I have a new child and wife. I know earlier, before you started working at the casino and shortly after you started dating Carter, I tried to get back in, but that was wrong of me. Had you not put me in my place the way you did, I probably would've been out here sleeping with someone else and raising a fuss over what man is in my house. The reality is, that's your and our son's house. If he agrees with another, non-father, male being there all the time, who am I to step in and say otherwise. I wish you all the happiness you can handle. God knows you deserve it." He holds my hand for a minute and I feel free of our past. He reaches across the table to embrace my face and follows it up with a napkin tossed right at me making me laugh.

"Thank you, Corey. That means more to me than you will ever know."

"You're welcome." We pass friendly smiles at each other before perusing the menu. A weight has been lifted and I feel liberated.

"Hi, babe. Sorry I'm a tad bit late," Carter says as he kisses me. Suddenly they taste even sweeter.

"Corey, nice to see you," he says as he extends his hand for a shake. Corey stands to greet him and returns the gesture.

"Mr. Jackson, nice to see you again." I look to see if there is a measuring contest going on with the eyes, but there isn't. They are both warm and inviting towards each other making me all the more pleased.

"Have you ordered yet?"

"No, we just completed our short conversation and was just about to when you arrived." The waiter arrives to take our order.

"Oh, yes, I'll have a Coke and rum, make it a double. Corey, what can I get you?"

"I'll take a vodka and Sprite."

"Okay and you, Tiffany? A peach sangria?" They both answer at the same time and they laugh. My drink choices are simple, but I didn't think I was predictable. I let them have their fun before ordering a peach margarita. Carter orders an appetizer for the table and the waiter dashes off the put in the order. Meanwhile, it seems that a shared laugh about my drink preference is the common ground that they needed to strike up general conversation. Over the course of the afternoon lunch, they talk about sports and legal things both entertainment and otherwise. I was left to play games on my cell phone or text Jewel and annoy her. This all came to an end when Corey's wife called with a list of things to grab on the way home.

"Well, I had a great time with you two. Carter, it was great getting to know you, truly."

"Likewise. And if you need anything or any recommendations on some of these businesses, let me know." They shake hands for a minute and Corey starts off before turning around.

"Hey, Carter?" We both turn to look towards Corey.

"Be sure you take care of her. Trust me, you won't find another."

"I plan on it. And I won't ever try to replace you in Xavier's life. I will make sure that I establish that boundary. I'll even call you before making any major decisions." Corey nods his head in agreement and heads on out the door.

"See, that wasn't bad," Carter says as he takes a drink of his water. I cut them both off after three drinks. This wasn't a sports bar or male bonding time.

"I guess it wasn't. You seem like you rather enjoyed his company."

"I did. He's an all-around good guy, I guess. I know what you have been through, so your opinion may differ, but overall he seems okay." I shrug and finish off my water. The waiter brings the check and Carter sees that it is already paid.

"Why is the balance zero?" Carter asks.

"Oh, Mr. Lang paid for it on his way out and said to tell you both ygt. Whatever that means." I laugh and they both look at me with questionable expressions.

"Tiff, what is ygt?"

"That was our code for you got tip. If one of us paid the bill, the other got the tip. Funny he still remembers that."

"I have to remember that." Carter pulls out a crisp one hundred-dollar bill and hands it to our waiter.

"Thank you for wonderful service." He takes my hand and we drive over to my place to talk to Xavier. I know this boy is going to be super happy.

"So, MR. C WILL BE STAYING here every night until we move?" Breaking the news to Xavier was just as I imagined. He goes through all the emotions from cheering, jumping up and down, and yelling. It's almost the same reaction when he found out he was at Disneyland.

"Unless he has a business trip, or he wants to stay over at the hotel, yes he will stay here with us."

"Cool! Now I can have someone here to play with me."

"Uh, son, I play with you."

"Yeah, but you're my mom. He's a man like me." He flexes his little arms like he has big muscles causing me to roll my eyes and Carter to laugh. I grab him into my arms and tickle him until he has a pause in sound. I let him go so he can catch his breath.

"I guess you are okay with me staying here?" Carter asks Xavier to get a clear understanding.

"Yes," Xavier says as he jumps up and down. "Are you staying tonight?"

"Well, I would but I have to go to the hotel to pack my things and take care of some business. I will be back tomorrow after I finish with work. Your mom and I are going to go see the new office building in the morning after she takes you to school."

"Aww, man. I wanted to show you the Lego set you gave me."

"I can see it tomorrow, okay?"

"When can I see James Durant again?" The kid flips thoughts like a remote control.

"Well, he's busy with the playoffs, but I'll see what I can do."

"Mmkay. Mom, can I go play on my tablet?"

"Sure, why not, but bedtime is coming in an hour."

"Okay. Bye Mr. C. See you tomorrow." He scampers off to his room where he grabs his tablet and plays Minecraft. Carter looks around to make sure no little eyes are watching and pulls me into his arms for a big embrace. We stand there for a few moments enjoying the relief that has blessed our relationship and that we are free to be us with no potential issues. He strokes my hair back and tilts my head up, so I can swoon over his looks.

"You feeling okay?" he asks.

"Yes, I'm great. Never better." He lowers his head to kiss me and for a moment I feel like there is no one around. I mean technically, there isn't, but I really feel the world disappear around us. I let out a deep sigh when our lips part and he smiles.

"I got a call in the morning so let me get back to the hotel. I will text you the address to the new building and what time we will meet. Dress comfortably because you will be required to wear a hard hat due to the renovations going on. Jewel should be there too since she's overseeing IT. Call her and let her know." One thing I notice is that Carter can flip to business at the drop of a hat.

"Okay. Let me walk you out before I entice you to stay." I tease grabbing him by his hand. I holler at Xavier that I was walking outside, and he comes to wait for me in the living room after giving Carter a hug and a high five. Once we are at the car, he opens the door and pulls out a little black box.

"Still buying him gifts?" I say with an irritated tone.

"Oh, no. That's not for him. I had those ordered for you and they came in today. Go ahead look." I open the box and inside are customer business cards with my name, Tiffany Lang, Chief Accounting Specialist. They have a satin finish and are somehow holographic with the company's logo.

"Thank you. These are beautiful."

"Glad you like them. Jewel has a box too. I will bring them tomorrow. I can't wait to see you."

"Can't wait to see you. He gets in the car and closes the door."

"Goodnight, my love." I kiss him on his cheek and he heads back to the hotel for what I hope will be his last night there.

JEWEL MET ME AT MY house twenty minutes before we were to head to the new building. When she walked into the house, I almost didn't know who she was. She was in dress slacks, a button-down shirt and some flats. She toned down her accessories and lightened up on her color palette for makeup. One thing she wasn't without was her engagement ring.

"So, we get to see our offices today. I'm excited, are you?" She asks while I finish applying my makeup.

"Yeah, a bit nervous actually. What kind of security are you going to have on the computers? Like, will we be able to share files, or will you use a cloud-based server?"

"Um, I know Carter has more clients than the A and B-listers we know about and their information is just as important as the celebrities. So, I think I'm gonna use a double firewall which is easy for those within the company but hard for those outside to hack. I have to talk with Carter about the file sharing. That's a good question, Tiff."

"Well, I couldn't sleep last night thinking about today and stuff. So, I had time to think and research. Looked up all the tax laws so that I can keep my mind fresh and some of the payroll changes."

"Yeah, I know what you mean. The day the job was positioned, I went research crazy." I step out of the bathroom and she's laying on my bed with her arms behind her head staring at the ceiling.

"Is everything okay? You're not your usual vibrant self."

"Casey and I are thinking about..." She stops herself and I wonder if she's about to tell me that they are already married.

"About?" I encourage her further. She turns and looks at me before speaking.

"Getting a dog. We also looked up a few of those last night. I was thinking about a toy variety. What do you think?

"I think whatever you two decide is fine with me. No other opinions matter." I grab my keys and tell her to come on, so we won't be late. I lock up the house and we climb into my car where she immediately starts fidgeting with the radio settling on the eighty's station.

"So, when is your live-in D moving in with you?" Just like that she's back to normal.

"I'm hoping tonight. It's really on him at this point. Corey is okay, in fact they were chummy by the end of the brunch and of course Xai is okay."

"Hmm. Are you okay? I haven't heard or think anyone has asked you how you feel. We just all assumed you'd be okay with this.

"Yeah, I'm okay with it. I've dreamt about it, to be honest. I imagined us together raising Xavier and having lots of family time."

"Do you see a future with him? Like beyond what you just said?"

"I think I have a mental block on marriage. I'm sure if it comes up, I'd marry him but not right now. I need time."

"Tiffany, you dated Corey since you were a freshman. Four years later you two were married and you still ended up divorced. Time is not the answer my friend, love is."

"Okay, who are you? You're dressed fresh out of a working woman magazine and you are spitting knowledge. Where is my crass and rude but fun-loving friend? Has marriage changed you already?" I realize my slip of the tongue and hope she didn't catch it.

"What did you say?"

"I said has marriage changed you already? As in you're not even married yet and already changing."

"Oh. Oh yeah. Well, no it hasn't, but this job has. I can't be Jewel of the Nile any longer, I have to be Ebonee." She moves her head to the tune of the music currently playing while she sings along. I focus on the GPS directions and clear my mind of any other thoughts. We exit the highway and continue on the highlighted route displayed. When we arrive to the location, there are workers outside repairing and restriping the pavement, working on the new building sign, and installing covered car ports for rainy days, when we get them. Jewel and I walk in and find Carter talking with a contractor about expanding some of the offices and working on the bedroom suite upstairs. He spots us and waives us over to where he is standing.

"Tony, this is Tiffany the chief accountant and Jewel the IT manager. This is Tony the foreman in charge of the renovations. If these ladies call you or email you, you treat them with the same urgency as if it were me directly. They will be in charge when I'm not in town." We shake hands and greet each other accordingly.

"So, what do my two favorite ladies think of the place?" Amongst the dust and noise, this is shaping up to be one attractive office.

"I think it's great. Lots of renovations going on," I reply.

"Do you have a separate room for your server or servers since you will be sharing information with your home office in LA?"

"Yes, we will have a separate location for the server. In fact, you see that man there with the blue shirt on and white hard hat, he's designing the space for the servers. Feel free to go introduce your-self and make sure you have what you need." Jewel wastes no time going over there to input her two cents. I smile at her eagerness. It's almost like watching Xavier at Christmas.

"Come here, I want to show you something." Carter takes my hand and we walk up the stairs to the draped off area where the workers are updating the executive suite.

"Can you gentlemen give me a few minutes?" The men excuse themselves and I walk about the room looking at the layout. It's nearly like a loft apartment up here. There is a full bath complete with shower and a lounge area. He pulls me into his arms as I look out of the blinds at the street below.

"Do you think you can help me decorate in here?" His kisses trail down my neck to my shoulder blade instantly relaxing me and I lean my head back giving him even greater access.

"I'd love to. What do you have in mind?" He turns me facing him and picks me up. I wrap my legs around his waist, a position I can never get tired of, and he presses me against the wall.

"First, we need something that I can lay you on when we have late nights at the office. He unbuttons my pants and slides them past my hips exposing my ass cheeks since I'm wearing a thong.

"Well, I can find a futon, but how often do you think we'll be in here?" I ask my question in between his steady fingering of my pussy and my moaning.

"As many times as we want," he replies in between sucking on my neck while fidgeting with his belt.

"In that case, a sleeper sofa is best," I answer. My hips grind harder against his fingers and this thong is no longer good to wear.

"Okay, look into that. Meanwhile, let's go to the bathroom and see what we can do in there." We enter and before I know it, he has me bent over the sink and is stuffed tightly within my walls. I can't scream like I want, but I'm enjoying every thrust he's driving into me.

"Carter," I moan out. Reaching behind me I grab his thighs and dig my nails into his skin. He pounds me harder and faster not caring about our location or who may accidentally walk in on us.

"Call my name again," he grits out.

"C-C-Carter," I stammer out as my legs begin to tremble with my orgasm. He places his finger on my clit and rubs as I continue to come...hard. I don't think I've ever had an orgasm this intense. Not even with him. Maybe it's the excitement of knowing we can get caught at any moment. He frees his hand and grabs my hair instead snapping my neck back where his other hand gently caress with my throat. His fingers play with my mouth and I nibble on them as they pull at my bottom lip.

"You are mine forever, Tiffany." He takes one more push and he comes. I feel the quivering of his thighs against my ass and the beating of his heart as he collapses onto my back. We are sweaty and out of breath from a crash course in office fucking. Always the one who is prepared, he pulls out a duffle bag with a towel, soap, and a fresh pair of thongs with the tag still attached. We clean up and not a moment too soon as Jewel and the other workers come in.

"Hey, what are you two doing up here?" She asks.

"Nothing, discussing how to design this to make it feel relaxing and at home for some of his clients who may need a bit of privacy.

"Oh, smart idea. So, Carter this is what we came up with for the server room." Jewel takes Carter away to discuss the plans for the server room and I share my ideas of changing the tile and adding some crown molding to the room with the builders. I catch Carter looking at me and he smiles. Just thinking this is forever gets me all excited again. Guess I'll have to wait till we get home.

Chapter

TWENTY-FIVE

ONE MONTH LATER

THINGS MOVED RATHER FAST AFTER Carter gave us the tour of the new office. He did stay over that night, but in the guest room, citing that he was uncomfortable sleeping in the room with me because he didn't want to set a bad example for Xavier. That not only was the sweetest thing ever, it also made me want him even more. The few times we have had sex has been crazy hot. We even snuck in some adult time at the movies which is something I've never done.

His assistant, Donna, came up from LA to train me on the software for payroll and all finances. Jewel implements new firewall protection and gets everyone up to speed on how to access the cloud base servers. They are only accessible from in office. No more working from home without a token to sign in on a secure VPN. She's a boss at the things she does. For the past week, she's been in LA updating that office and making sure all employees update their personnel files so that the paper copies can be destroyed. That didn't stop her from video chatting with me while she worked. A few clients came in and she'd absolutely fangirl over them. I knew how she felt after my meltdown at the party a few months back.

This is the first time that I've been alone in years. I always had Jewel somewhere nearby but with both her and Carter being out of town and Xavier is out of town with his dad and new family visiting his parents, I'm left solo dolo. I'll be in this lane until Thursday when Carter returns from the UK. Jewel is out of town for a month. Casey is meeting up with her tonight and will be burning his bounty of PTO.

"Ms. Lang, here is today's mail," Natalie our receptionist says as she enters my office.

"Thank you, Natalie. If you haven't taken lunch already, you may do so now since the phones are quiet.

"Yes, ma'am. Thank you." She heads to her desk and clocks out for lunch. I shuffle through the piles of letters, magazines and other advertisements. One piece of mail is addressed to Carter Jackson Law, but to my attention. I examine the envelope and notice the address is from the real estate company in Pasadena that is selling his condo. I open it and find a check for two point six million dollars. *Holy shit*, I say to myself as my hands tremble with nerves. Corey made his first six figure bonus off a lawsuit, a HUGE lawsuit, and I trembled then. This guy sells his home and it is two times that amount. I lock my computer and go over to Carter's office where I place the check in his safe. I do not want to be responsible for that kind of money.

"Ms. Lang," a voice calls to me when I lock Carter's office door. "There's an older gentleman out front needing assistance. Since Natalie is at lunch, I just had him to wait in the lobby."

"Okay, Courtney. Thank you." I head out to the reception office and my eyes are in shock.

"Daddy? What are you doing here?" Like a child I run over and hug him tight. I don't get home often, but then again, my parents are travelers, so timing isn't ever right. I'm just glad he's in town.

"There's my cupcake. Your mother and I decided that we should come see your new office. I must say, it is quite impressive. Your boss must be one of those ambulance chasers." It's safe to say that if I didn't see them often, chances are I didn't talk to them often either. When daddy mentions my boss and the probability of his characteristics, I cringe knowing that they don't know about the man that is living with Xavier and I and having a house built.

"No, he's not one of those attorney's. He's an entertainment lawyer."

"Oh, you mean one of those lawyers to get the celebrities out of jail."

"Well, none of his clients have ever been to jail, that I know of, but yes daddy, one of those lawyers."

"He seems to do handsomely." I escort my father to my office where we can have a sit-down chat.

"So, where's mom?" I ask handing him a bottle of water from my fridge.

"She's coming. She had to stop at one of those machines to grab a water." He looks at me and smile only the way a father can look when he sees his little girl.

"Did you guys just fly in? I could've had someone to pick you up, you know."

"Oh, no baby. We've been in town since last night. We are here with Ginger and Tomas."

"Oh, okay. A couple's trip. That's nice." Natalie lets me know she's back from her lunch and alerts me to my mother's presence. I go out to the lobby and meet her.

"Mommy," again I run like a four-year-old to greet her.

"Cupcake. Look at you big accounting executive. I'm so proud." We walk and talk back to my office where she joins dad.

"Now, where is my grandson?" she asks.

"Well, he's with his father visiting his family with their new baby."

"Oh, really? Well we didn't have any idea. If you'd call us we'd know," Dad says.

"Baby, are you okay? That has to be difficult for you?" Mom rebuts shaking her shame finger at my dad.

"Mom, I'm great. Couldn't be happier for him." They look a bit befuddled and before I can explain, my video messenger rings. I look and see that it's Carter and think of how I'm going to answer.

"Mr. Jackson, good afternoon. I hope your trip is going well." He looks concerned and fucking delicious since he is laying in the bed shirtless and wrapped in a towel still wet from his shower. I quickly plug in my headset so that my parents can't hear him, making it easier for me to disguise.

"Mr. Jackson? Did I do something wrong?" His eyebrows arch up and I know I'm going to hear it later.

"No sir. Everything here at the office seems to be going smoothly. You did get that letter from California about your property. I put it away in your safe."

"Okay, why all the code talk, Tiffany? Are you in trouble?" he asks after I continue faking a professional conversation.

"Oh, no sir. No trouble at all. Just sitting here talking to my parents." I close my eyes for a second and when I open his look is exactly as I imagined.

"Oh, you haven't told them about me or our plans. I see. Well, how long will they be in town?"

"That I'm not sure of. But I will let you know soon."

"Okay. Well call me later, if you can." He disconnects, and I feel like the biggest asshole of all time. He introduced his parents to me over video and they knew about us before he went out there and I haven't even mentioned him to mine.

"Is everything okay? Your boss sure asks a lot of questions."

"Yeah, well, that's because there is something I haven't told you two." I get up and close my door before I spill the news to my parents.

"Mom, dad, I haven't been honest with you. See, there are a lot of changes I haven't quite told you about." I shrink away when they give me the infamous parental look that says nothing but everything all in one stare. I wait a few seconds to see if they are going to ask a question before I continue with my explanation.

"Um, Carter Jackson, isn't just my boss, but he's my boyfriend. We've been dating for about four months now and as of last month, he moved in with Xavier and I. That's only until his new house is complete in which we all will be moving in there. Corey is aware of the situation and is okay with how things are." I sit and wait for the question and lecture series to begin. For one moment, nothing is said. They look at me and then to each other before they come back to me.

"So, you mean to tell your mother and I that you've been dating and that Xavier likes this man you're seeing and that he's also your boss?"

"Yes, sir."

"Why didn't you tell us?"

"It took me a minute to grasp what was actually happening. I was so stuck on being alone that I didn't want to be open to dating anyone. He just kinda forged his way through my walls. Plus, he's really good with Xavier. I'm sorry. He told his parents about me and I even met them on a video call when he went home to visit a few weeks back. I should've told y'all and even worse, I should've introduced y'all."

"Baby, it's okay," my mom says.

"The hell it is. My daughter is dating some stranger and we don't know anything about him. Not okay, Eleanor." My dad's eyebrows furrow and I know he is livid.

"George, you know that my father never approved of you even after we were married," she reminds him.

"Mom, I'm not marrying the guy. We are just in a serious,

committed relationship." I feel like I'm on display. The stares from their eyes knowing they know that I've also slept with him.

"One that you neglected to mention to your parents." I know I'm going to hear the same thing from Carter, but to get a preview of what's to come isn't enjoyable.

"Mom, dad, I know that I owe some form of explanation, but I'm not sorry for not telling you anything about my personal life. And you should know that Jewel is going to investigate and check out a person before I even think of dating. Besides, she's known him longer." This will surely take the heat off me some since they know Jewel well and treat her like a daughter.

"Oh, how did she meet him?" My mother asks.

"He once hosted private poker nights at the casino. She had been working the parties for a long time before I came along."

"Well, that makes me feel better. I don't know about your father. But still, we would've liked to have known."

"I know and I'm sorry. He got James Durant to come to Xavier's game one day and co-coach." I know this will win brownie points with my dad since he's a big sports fan.

"Really? He knows James?" My dad's eyes widen and the wrinkles around them appear as the corners of his mouth turn from a frown to smile.

"Yes, he does. And a few others too."

"Well, will we get to meet him?" Mom adds.

"He's mad at me for not telling you so, I will have to smooth it over first. Will you be here Thursday? You can have dinner with us."

"We'll be there. Do you need help in the kitchen?"

"If you can make your peach cobbler mom, that'll be amazing!"

"Okay. Just call us and tell us what time, cupcake. Come on Eleanor, we have plans with the Thomas'."

"Oh yes. I guess we should be going. I love you darling." Mom kisses me on my cheek and dad circles back with a hug. I escort them to the lobby and they leave. Now, off to call Carter and flash a little boob to cool him down.

THURSDAY...

"BABE, WHAT TIME WILL YOUR folks be here?" Carter calls from the closet. I just finished putting the final touches on the pot roast and it is resting on the stove along with the string beans and red potatoes. Mom already has the cobbler made it just needs to go in the oven when they arrive. Carter uncorked the wine earlier allowing it time to breathe and I had two Mike's peach lemonade to ease my nerves.

"Mmm, smells good," Carter raves as he makes his entrance into the kitchen buttoning up his white shirt. He's going for a casual look tonight, with khaki shorts and boat shoes. He looks and smells like sex on a stick. He wraps me into his arms and I melt. There isn't a doubt in my mind how I fell about this man. After my parents left the office on Monday, I video chatted with him to explain why I was so delayed with telling them about us and our plans and that they gave me the parental stare. We joked about how only parents can give you that look and suddenly you know you are in trouble.

"You smell good," I reply turning to face him and still a little make out time before my parents arrive. The kissing starts with simple pecks before it turns into full on tongue action. That only heats things up and he descends to my neck before picking me up and sitting me on the island counter by the sink.

"I love you," he softly speaks while capturing me with his eyes.

"I love you too. In fact, I know I do because I thought you were going to propose to me when we went to Pasadena, but instead you pulled out a business card and I convinced you to postpone any talks."

"Oh, that explains that funny look on your face. Now, we already said that we're not rushing things, so I don't plan on popping the question anytime soon."

"I agree. It was just so awkward. It felt like the natural thing to do."

"I think it may have been the moment with Casey and Jewel that led you to those feelings."

"Or maybe it's something that I want."

"I want it too. But I think we should wait until you are comfortable."

"I am comfortable."

"No. I don't think you're there yet."

"Oh? And what makes you an expert on who's ready for commitment and who's not?"

"I'm not an expert. I just don't think you're ready."

"What if I said I were?"

"I wouldn't ask." I don't know if I should be insulted or relieved. Am I asking him to ask me to marry him and he's telling me no? My doorbell rings and I know it's my parents. He helps me down from the counter and I take my spray and wipe it off before we go to the door together to answer. He stands to the side and I swing the door open.

"Mom, dad. So glad you made it."

"Here let me take that for you," Carter offers as he relieves my mother of her famous cobbler. I'm sure the smell enticed him.

"Thank you, dear," mom says as she hands off the dish.

"Mom, dad, this is Carter Jackson. Carter, this is George and Eleanor Arnaud."

"Nice to meet you, young man," my dad says as they shake hands on the introduction.

"Pleasure to meet you sir, and you too, Mrs. Arnaud." He hugs her and takes her by the hand escorting her to the living room. I take the cobbler from him and go pop it in the oven while my dad sits next to mom on the couch.

"Can I get you something to drink?" Carter asks of my parents.

"I'll take a Jack and Coke if you got it." That was music to Carter's ears. He rushes to the bar and fixes my dad a cocktail and I take mom a bottle of water before joining in them in conversation. Mom and dad ask all the basic questions about how we met and what were the plans for our future, to which I rolled my eyes and Carter answered just as we were discussing earlier, no immediate plans for marriage. When the cobbler is finished, we head to the dinner table and enjoy our meal. Mom and dad share sweet and embarrassing stories of me as a child and she even has a baby picture of me in her phone. Carter begs her to send it to him and she does.

"Well, cupcake, I think we should be heading back to our room. We have an early breakfast with the Thomas' and then we are going to catch some shows tomorrow afternoon."

"Okay, dad. Call me tomorrow when you get a break. Xavier should be back and maybe Corey can swing him by your room, so he can spend some time with y'all."

"Oh, I'd love to have my snuggle bunny," mom exclaims.

"Where are you staying?" Carter asks.

"Oh, we got a room over at the big hotel with the lion."

"Oh, really. Okay. Give me a second." He pulls out his phone and has a brief conversation before coming back. "Okay, I upgraded you and your friends to a suite and I will cover it."

"Son!" My dad exclaims, humorously, of course, but it brings laughter to the room.

"That was mighty sweet of you, Carter. Well, we are off. Pleasure meeting you. Be sure you take care of my daughter. Love you, cupcake," my mom says.

"Love you too, mom. Goodnight, dad."

"Goodnight, sweet pea." I give my parents a kiss on the cheek before they head to the car. Carter escorts them both and I watch as he opens my mom's door and walks my dad around to the driver side. He pulls out his wallet and hands him a business card. I know by that gesture, they have become friends. Carter sees them off and when he comes back in, I'm already in the kitchen cleaning up.

"I really like your parents," he says as he rolls up his sleeves and washes the dishes while I put the food away.

"I can tell they genuinely like you. Corey had to go through a lot before he even received permission to ask my dad to marry me." Carter laughs but I'm serious.

"Well, when the time comes, I won't have that problem." This conversation is circling the room tonight. I choose not to respond but instead, I stand behind Carter and begin to unbutton his shirt.

"Baby, what are you doing?" he questions.

"Well, parents are gone, Xavier is away with his dad, what do you think I'm doing?" I unbutton his shorts and they fall to the floor. I begin massaging his junk and it responds to my touch almost instantly. He rinses his hands and turns around placing me back on the counter. He doesn't waste any time undressing me. He pulls at my shirt and the buttons pop off revealing my demi cup bra and the spillage that is on display. We engage in a deep lip lock and he slides my pants over my hips and they fall to the floor.

My ass cheeks are cold from the granite but soon two large and firm hands slide under my hips and lift me. He carries me to our bedroom and lays me onto the bed pulling my thong off with ease. His lips do a graze of my thigh before they find a landing on my clit. He softly sucks applying enough pressure to make me squirm. Locking my legs down with his hands, he continues to work my pussy with his mouth. His tongue circling and then going in and out of my sweet hole at various speeds bringing me immense pleasure until I can't hold it in any more. I erupt hard and loud with my hands tugging slightly on his hair.

Once my legs stop quivering, he kisses me from my belly up to my breasts where he pops open my bra. Taking them into his mouth he teases me by playing with my nipples. his mouth his so warm and that tongue is getting another work out. He takes a deep thrust into me, feeding my still hungry pussy his full, thick, ten-inches of dick working me over for another orgasm. We don't speak any words just allow our bodies to speak for us. He tells my body what to do, and it follows his commands right up to the last orgasm in which we both come at the same time. That explosion alone left scratches on both of us since I'm the one on top. I collapse on him and he pulls the sheet over us where we fall asleep. Good thing we are not in the office tomorrow and I already ran payroll because I will be sleeping in.

Chapter
TWENTY-SIX

COREY AND VANESSA CAME BACK Friday afternoon and after spending one hour with my baby, Carter took him over to spend time with his grandparents. Meanwhile we went to meet with the builder of the new house and finalize the colors and design. Jewel and Casey are coming home for the weekend, especially since she knows my mom is here and she's craving her lemon cake. I'm glad they're coming. I miss my friend, plus Xavier has his championship game today and all of his support team will be there, including the Thomas'.

"Mommy, my tummy is feeling funny," Xavier says coming into my room and climbing in bed with me. Carter went to grab some things for the game today and should be on his way back.

"What's wrong? Did you eat too much candy yesterday?" He shakes his head no and snuggles closer to me. I check his head for a fever and he feels normal. No other signs of an illness.

"Does it hurt when I do this?" I tickle him, and he kicks and giggles with excitement.

"Mommy stop that tickles," his laugh is infectious, and it brings me peace within. I should record it to have for days I need a pick me up.

"Do you feel better now?" I ask trying to gauge what's bothering him. He takes a big breath and releases it before responding.

"This is a real big game and I hope I don't mess up," he confesses.

"Son, you're going to do great no matter what."

"But what if we don't win?" I can tell he's real nervous about this game and his tummy issues are probably little nerves.

"If you don't win, that just means you come back harder next year. It doesn't mean that you aren't good, or the other team is better. It just means that it wasn't your time to win." I hug my baby tighter and he puts his little arms around me and gives me a big hug too.

"I love you, mommy."

"I love you too, cupcake. Now go wash up for breakfast and then we will get ready to go." I kiss him on his forehead and he runs to his bathroom while I go to mine and shower. I turn on the Bluetooth speaker in the bathroom and begin listening to some slow jazz creating a space of relaxation and my kind of meditation before I start a busy day. I run through a mental checklist of all the things I need to grab and jot them on my waterproof tablet I keep in the shower. I step out and autonomously I wrap my hair in a towel then my body. I go to grab my toothbrush and I notice a small white leather ring box. I gasp at the sight and my hands find my mouth.

"That look is the one I had hoped to see if you had spotted the box," Carter says from the door frame. I didn't even see him standing there since I was on autopilot. Words are lost with me and all he can do is read my expressions while I fight past the lump in my throat.

"I put the box in here when I came back and seen that you were in your mental zone and making lists in the shower. If you open it, you won't find the actual ring, but I wanted to let you know that

I'm so serious about you, us, our family. And when you are ready, I have the ring that goes in that box for you." He takes my ring finger and places a kiss on it. Words finally find their way back to me and I figure I better say something before they leave again.

"Why? I mean why'd you do it this way?"

"Well, Thursday, you had that same look on your face as you did when we went to Pasadena, disappointment. I just don't want to rush this. I'm in love with you and Xavier. You both fill in what I have always needed. A strong woman who takes no shit, including from me, and who is the best mother I've ever known. Ours excluded of course. And Xavier giving me a chance to be a strong positive role model for him and I get to exercise my parenting skills. And being thirty-five, I find myself wanting to settle down and have a family and someone to grow old with, and that's you."

"I'm not getting old," I joke. He closes the door and drops my towel.

"That body most certainly isn't getting old."

"Boy, stop." I grab my towel among our laughing outbreak.

"That reminds me, what do you want to do for your birthday? Xavier will be starting football camp so maybe we can take the day and do something."

"Like what?"

"Anything you want, cupcake."

"No, sir. That name is only to be used by my parents. By the way, since everyone is here in town, I figured we can have a family dinner tomorrow, if you don't mind. That's what we can do for my birthday."

"We can do that, and I will plan something for Tuesday. I'll call Natalie while you get dressed and have her to shift everything from Tuesday to Wednesday and change my next trip to next week." I've learned that there is no wiggle room for him as he always presents a strong defense. I agree with his plans and get dressed for today's game. I begin to lotion up when I see a t-shirt with Xai's basketball picture on the front and his number on the back next to my jeans. Carter walks back into the room and gives me the thumbs up when I hold up the shirt while he is still on the phone giving orders for the week. I complete getting dressed and meet him and Xavier in the kitchen.

"Okay guys, are you ready?" I ask as I grab a kolache from the box that Carter had delivered early this morning.

"Yes, ma'am," Xavier says as he puts his cup in the sink dragging his duffle bag. I load the rest of the breakfast dishes and begin the dishwasher and we head out to meet the rest of the family at the high school gym

MY PARENTS MEET US IN the parking lot so that we can all sit in the same section. Jewel and Casey pulls in shortly after us. I look around and see that Corey and Vanessa are already here.

"Hi, mom and dad," I greet my parents with a hug while Carter shakes my dad's hand and gives my mother a kiss on her cheek.

"Momma Eleanor," Jewel calls as she comes up to greet them. She hugs them both and they awe over her ring.

"What a big rock on your hand, Ebonee. So beautiful. When is the big day?"

"Um, well, we haven't really decided on one yet, but as soon as we do, your invitation will be in the mail."

"It better be. This must be the fiancée," my mother says looking over Casey.

"Yes, ma'am. This is Casey McIntyre. Casey, these are my adopted parents."

"Hi, dear. We're Tiffany's parents, Eleanor and George."

"Hello, nice to meet you both." Casey shakes their hands and Carter passes out the remaining shirts.

"Look at this, these are nice," my dad says of the new shirts.

"I had a client press them up for me. I hope I got the sizes right. I just used the picture we took Thursday when Tiffany wasn't looking."

"Mom, can we go in now? I need to warm up," Xai pleads.

"Yes, baby. Let's go in." I walk ahead with my son while Carter takes my mother's hand and escorts my folks into the gym.

Corey spots us as we walk through the door and rushes to greet my parents. I plead with them to behave since they are still carrying a bit of anger towards them.

"Carter, you made it." Corey says trying to establish that these two get along in front of my folks.

"Of course. Can't miss my little man's big game."

"Mr. and Mrs. Arnaud. Nice to see you." Corey extends his hand to my dad and he accepts it under my stare. Mom is a little more callous, but she shakes his hand as well.

"Corey, good to see you. I hear you have a new baby. Congratulations." My mom forces those words out and I'm thankful for the attempt at peace. I know it's not easy with these two.

"Thank you. Well, I guess I will get back over there to Vanessa. Nice seeing you all. You too, Jewel."

"Fuck off, Corey," she bites back.

"Jewel!" I whisper shout. "There are babies around. Mind your mouth." She nods her head and Carter steps in to diffuse the situation.

"Oh Corey, wait. Here's a shirt you can have for today's game. I'm sorry. I didn't know your wife was coming."

"Oh, thanks Carter. Well, see you guys after the game." He heads back to where Vanessa and the baby are seated. After that tense moment, we take our seat and Carter goes over and talks to the coach alongside Corey. I can say that I'm glad they get along. I don't want any issues between them two for the sake of Xavier.

"So, they really do share a calm relationship?" My dad asks as my mom and everyone else looks on.

"Yeah. We had a lunch together and those two put egos aside and for the sake of all involved, agreed to have a workable co-parenting relationship. No toes are stepped on and no one pulls rank higher than the other." Everyone looks back to the side court and see them laughing about something.

"Well, don't expect me to invite them to my reception." Jewel makes a slip and I have to pounce on it.

"Don't you mean wedding?"

"No. The wedding will be for friends and family only. The reception will be open." *Good recovery, Jewel. But I will catch you,* I think to myself. The announcer signals the start of the game and we watch those little boys dribble the ball from end to end shooting basket after basket. I can't help but cheer loudly when my son has the ball. In fact, I'm probably the loudest parent here. I can see Carter and Corey shaking their heads and probably making comments about my behavior. My dad joins in when the other team starts fouling and the refs aren't calling it. My mom sends dad down to the side with Carter and Corey and Casey follows not wanting to be the only man in the hen coop. We continue to cheer on the team but especially Xavier who is showing out today. He hasn't missed one shot including his free throws and that makes this momma bear proud.

"Excuse me. We'd like to see our son play too," this lady behind me says with a bit of attitude.

"Then might I suggest you stand up like the rest of the parents or better yet, move." Jewel looks at me with shock because normally I'm having to calm her down.

"Tiffany, just sit down," my mom chimes in.

"No, mom. I will not. I will cheer for my son the way I feel like cheering for him and no one is going to tell me otherwise." The lady gets up with her husband and walks out the building..

"Are you okay, Tiff? You never go off like that." Jewel questions.

"I'm fine. It's just something about the way she spoke to me that grated my nerves the wrong way." The lady re-enters and takes a seat in the section on the side of us and I continue to cheer for my baby. By the end of the game, our little bulldogs won 59-55. Each participant gets a trophy and gift card to Game Yield which will make my son all too happy.

"Mommy, mommy. We won! Look at my trophy!" Xavier runs to me screaming.

"Wow, that will look good in your room."

"Yeah in my new room with the trophy case that Carter is going to get me." I realize that he stopped calling him his usual name.

"Hey, you didn't call him Mr. C. Why?"

"He told me I can call him that. I figured that Mr. C sounded like a baby name and I'm a man now." I can't even think of anything to say I just let him go to his grandparents. I grab his duffel bag and we all leave the gym and go to our respective cars.

"So, I was thinking, for my birthday, we can all get together and have dinner at my house tomorrow, since mom and dad are leaving Monday," I say to crowd of us.

"Oh, hell yeah! Momma Eleanor, I want my cake." Jewel makes her request first and I know that my mom will make sure she has her request. She says her goodbyes and they leave for the casino where Casey is putting in his two-week notice. They decided that with her salary from her new job, he can work on getting his business license and open his sports bar.

"Okay, baby. Tiffany, we will stay at your place Sunday night if you can give us a lift to the airport."

"Sure dad, that's no problem. I'm thinking maybe we can meet around 6 P.M. Mom, I know you will be there earlier. Dad, you, Carter, and Xavier can play miniature golf while we prepare the meal."

"Just make sure I have my beer," dad says as he puts in his request.

"I'll make sure the fridge is stocked," Carter adds while putting Xavier's bag in the car.

"Tiffany, this one is a keeper," dad whispers to me as he gives me a hug. I laugh a little and inside, I'm pleased to know that my dad approves.

"Bye, dear. We're going to go have dinner with our friends and catch a show," mom says. I kiss her on her cheek as Carter, ever so the gentleman, escorts her to their car. My mom is taken by him too and my dad mouths "keeper" to me again. I waive him off and make sure Xavier is buckled in before strapping myself in.

"Okay, so, what do we need from the grocery store and I'll make sure to have it delivered tonight," Carter says as he gets into the car and we drive to the house. My head hurts a little so I'm slow to reply.

"Tiff, are you okay?" He must see the grimace on my face when I mentally try to figure out why I have this pain.

"Yeah, I think I have a severe headache coming on. I didn't eat my usual for breakfast and with the adrenaline of the game, I might just be hungry."

"Well, let's go home and order some pizza. That's what Xavier told me he wanted for dinner."

"Of course. It's his favorite. But yes, I will put the list together and place the order. Do you have any special requests?"

"No. I'm waiting on your mom's cake. The way Jewel described it to me sounds like a dream."

"It is. My mom is known for it. You know what? I'm glad you and my parents are getting along." I make the list out on my phone and send it to him via text message.

"Me too. I have a little surprise for you when we get home. Well, it will be there in about thirty minutes. Don't worry, I didn't spend any money." It's not even a fight with him any longer when it comes to him and his finances. I can always tell him no, but he's a man that will get what he wants.

"I can't wait to see what it is." My eyes lighten with happiness because his surprises are always good.

"I will need to use one of the extra bedrooms to keep it in."

"That's fine. It must be pretty big if you need to use a room for it."

"Yeah, this isn't something you can put away in a closet." Now he has my interest piqued. I look in the backseat and my little basketball player is knocked out cold. I guess all his adrenaline finally ran its course. We pull into the driveway shortly after and Carter takes him inside and puts him in his bed. I grab his duffle bag and trophy and take it to his room where Carter intercepts them from me.

"Go lay down so that headache can go away. I'll take these to the little king's room." He kisses me on my forehead and I follow his orders and go take a nap.

Chapter

TWENTY-SEVEN

Y ESTERDAY'S NAP TURNED INTO A full on five-hour sleep. When I woke, it was 9:00 pm and my surprise was sitting in the living room with Carter and Xavier. He arranged for his parents to come down and have dinner with us since my folks were here too. This still made me think he was planning to propose. Emma insisted on letting me sleep once they arrived and Xavier took over hosting duties giving her a tour of the entire house. I alerted them to my presence when I turned on the light in the kitchen looking for a piece of pizza. From that point forward we stayed up past 1 a.m. getting to know each other even more. I kept thinking to myself if Carter ages the way his father has, I'm never letting him go. Damn, his dad is fine. At times I found myself looking at him and my mind going into a school girl stupor. After boring them with my stories, we decided to turn in, so his folks can get some rest. This morning when I woke, a huge country breakfast was made, and my kitchen was clean.

"Morning, mommy," my toothless angel says when he sees me appear.

"Hi baby. Carter, why didn't you wake me?"

"Oh, I'm sorry. But when my mom cooks, I don't have time to be chivalrous. It's my weakness."

"That's good to know." He points to the seat next to him and I take my place beside him and start fixing my plate. She made Sausage, eggs, country gravy, biscuits, bacon, and hash browns. I look at Xavier clean his plate and actually ask for more. His dad pours me a glass of orange juice and I begin to dig in. All you can hear is the sound of knives and forks hit the plates. No conversation is being had. This is a first for me. My son isn't drilling me with a bunch of questions and Carter isn't on his phone dealing with business matters. I'm taking all of this in stride because who knows when I will have this again. The doorbell rings bringing me from my blissful state. Carter goes to answer and it's my parents.

"Mmm, Tiffany must've got up early to fix breakfast. It sure smells good in here." My dad says as he brings mom's groceries into the kitchen. He looks and sees Carter's parents and stops his yammering.

"George, Eleanor, these are my parents Emma and Vincent Jackson. Mom, dad, these are Tiffany's parents, Mr. and Mrs. Arnaud." His parents stand to greet mine and they shake hands.

"Please, there is plenty here. Join us for breakfast." My dad wastes no time getting to the table and fixing him a plate.

"Mom, do you want some breakfast?" I ask.

"Yes, baby. I'd love some. I take it you didn't prepare this breakfast."

"No. Ma'am. Mrs. Jackson did." Carter offers my mom his seat and she takes it while I place her plate in front of her.

"Nana, you want some juice?" Xavier offers holding the pitcher and waiting to pour. He loves his grandparents, but his Nana is his favorite. I finish my plate and get up to load the dishwasher and prepare the chicken for today's family meal. I look over and see our parents conversing and I smile. I never thought about this situation unfolding in front of me, but Carter is laying it all on the line. He reminds me of a kid who gets the highly sought out toy for Christmas and has to tell everyone.

His eyes beam when he laughs at our parents' stories about us growing up as kids. Xavier is helping me in the kitchen by making sure all the dishes are loaded from breakfast as our parents retreat to the outside lounge area. Carter helps Xavier finish clearing the table while I start preparing the side dishes. I love cooking family dinners but this one is by far my favorite. I get to meet my boyfriend's parents in person and mine are here for a visit. I knew they'd do something to celebrate my upcoming twenty-ninth birthday. The last year of my twenties.

"What are you in so deep thought about, baby?" Carter asks slipping his arms around my waist and stealing kisses from my neck.

"I'm turning twenty-nine. The end of my twenties. That's a big deal."

"Ah, yes. The dreaded birthday is lurking around the corner. I have a great day planned for us so don't go sulking now. Wait till afterwards." A loud outburst of laughter comes from the back and we look to see what the commotion is about.

"They are having a great time, huh?" I say to Carter.

"Yeah. I think it's great but look at the body language. They are truly comfortable around each other. I tell you, we are a match made in the heavens."

"You think this was meant to be? Two people, one who is a playboy the other a divorcee with child, were meant to be together?"

"Yes. You can't tempt the fates or question them, my love." He puts the plastic wrap over the chicken and sets it in the fridge while I start boiling the macaroni.

"I see. So, it's like a course correction. Like this path was destined to be but we both had to find our way to each other. Me the cocktail waitress and you the high roller."

"Exactly." He tilts my head back giving him full access to my lips and we lock in a lovers kiss."

"So, when are you two getting married?" His dad asks as they walk in from the outside. Carter closes his eyes and whispers, *I'm sorry*, before turning to answer his dad. From the looks of it, inquiring minds want to know.

"We're not exactly running to the church. Tiffany just came out of a marriage and we aren't rushing. She knows my plans are to marry her, but when she's ready. I mean, we've only been dating for four months."

"Well, Carter, your dad and I were engaged and married within six months. I think we turned out fine."

"Tiff, I asked your grandfather for your mother's hand within the first three months of our dating. He told me no, but I kept going back until he softened."

"Those are sweet stories, but that's what worked for you all, no disrespect. This is what is going to work for Carter and I. Sure Corey moved on with no problem, but that's him. This is my choice. Carter has a ring for me, but when I'm ready." I leave and go to my room to take a breather. I don't like being pressured and I feel like that there is a lot of intimidation for us to get married. Carter comes in behind me and sits on the foot of the bed.

"You okay?"

"I'm good. I just knew my parents would be the ones to spear-head a campaign to get me re-married. I don't feel like I need a ring to seal my relationship. Why can't we just be us for a while. Yes, I know. We're living together and there's a gorgeous ring waiting for me when I'm ready, but I love just being with you. I want to enjoy what I have. Is that so wrong?"

"No, it's not. And I'm with you. We just have to let our parents know that when we get married, they will be the first on the invite list and to please not bring it up again. I hate when you're mad. I'll talk to them. Give me a few minutes to get them back outside and then come out."

"Thank you." He kisses me on my forehead and leaves the room. I think about how my words may have been a bit harsh or bratty, but this is exactly why I didn't want to introduce him to my folks. I think they feel that I can't be happy unless I'm married or that I'm miserable because Corey moved on. I was, at one point at time, but I'm not now and I owe that to Jewel for pushing me.

I go back into the kitchen and finish prepping and finally cooking tonight's dinner. Carter's mom and mine enter the kitchen and put on aprons.

"What do you need me to help with, dear?" Emma says placing a loving mother's hand on my shoulder.

"My kitchen is open to you. Whatever you want to cook, please feel free."

"Okay." My mother takes out her ingredients and starts on her deliciously moist cake.

"I'm sorry if I stepped out of line with you all this morning. I just couldn't take any more of the subtle and not so subtle hints to get married. It's not what we want at this moment."

"No, dear, you are right to feel how you do. We agreed that maybe we are all too excited about your relationship with Carter. You two complement each other so well. This is the happiest we've seen him in a while." Emma says as she makes up dough for what looks like a pie.

"We know this is the happiest you've been, ever." My mother adds. "But we're sorry cupcake."

"What a cute nickname. Carter's is dumplin." They giggle as the continue making their desserts. I heat up the oil in my fryer for the chicken and check on my macaroni. We are three women busy in the kitchen while our men are outside playing miniature golf with Xavier.

"I bought the libations," Jewel shouts as she comes in.

"Good. Pour me a glass, wash your hands, and get in here and help." Jewel loves it when I ask her to help in the kitchen.

"Girl, let me tell you about last night Casey and I were in

the...oh, hello." She stops mid sex story when she sees Emma and mom.

"Oh, Carter's parents are here. This is Emma, and his dad, Vincent, is outside. This is my best friend Jewel."

"How do you do, dear?" Emma says, placing a kiss on her cheek as she continues to roll out her dough.

"Ebonee, hand me that butter over there, would you love?" My mom asks. She passes me the wine, mom the butter, and grabs an apron and starts grating the cheese. Three hours later, the meal is prepared, desserts are tempting, and we finish the third bottle of wine.

"Dinners ready," I yell from inside. The wine has me a bit inebriated and the men come in at the sound of my voice and all the giggling. Carter sees the empty bottles on the counter and shakes his head as he puts them in the recycle bin. We all take a seat, Xavier says thanks, and we begin to eat and toast to the last year of my twenties.

CARTER NEEDING THE ROOM FOR my surprise was also a rouse for my birthday gifts. My parents bought me a diamond drop necklace with exactly twenty-nine diamonds. His parents bought me a set of diamond studs. Jewel and her dirty minded ass bought me two sets of very provocative lingerie and some sex toys. Carter seemed very pleased with that gift. And Carter, let's just say we now own matching his and hers AMG E 63 S Sedans. That lingerie wasn't even needed that night. I've said it before, but I've never been so happy to have a sound proof bathroom.

Today we are back to work as usual. Carter doesn't have any

trips coming up soon so he's here today as well. He has clients coming in to the office today and I've been asked to stay away so I don't fangirl over any of them. I told him it was okay since I had reports to run and deposits to check and account for. Numbers are my thing and I love my job. I stay with my head in spreadsheets and bank accounts all day. If I have time to talk it's because I'm either coming or going. My time in between is spent at my desk.

"Hey, babe. I just got off the phone with the builders and they start the groundbreaking today." Carter says as he enters my office. I'm in a cash reconciliation zone, so I don't really express excitement.

"Oh, wow. That's good news," I say rather dry. Carter pulls me and my chair away from my keyboard forcing me to interact with three-dimensional people.

"Tiff, did you hear what I said?"

"Yeah. They are making ground beef today. If you find that to be good news, then I'm happy for you." He laughs, and I laugh at my own statement. "Okay, so maybe I need you to repeat what you said."

"I said, they are breaking ground on the house today." With the repeat, I understood him better and become super excited.

"Oh my God! That is great. Did they get all the changes in and approved?"

"Yes, they did. I have the updated plans on my desk and we will go over them tomorrow while we enjoy our day off to celebrate your actual birthday."

"Well, I don't think I can go tomorrow."

"Why? Is something wrong with the accounts?"

"No. See, my future fiancé has this huge day planned for me and I'm sure he's going to take me to the site of our new home build, so I don't think I should hang out with my boyfriend."

"That's one lucky man. If he can have all this beauty and brains to himself."

"Mmmhmm. I think I'm the lucky one. He makes sure me, and

my son are taken care of and in the bedroom, he always pleases me. Never a disappointment." I bite him on his bottom lip, which is a trigger for him, but a phone buzz interrupts.

"Ms. Lang?"

"Yes." I say through my giggles while he kisses me on my neck and tickles me.

"Please let Mr. Jackson know that Kane is here to see him."

"Okay will...did you say Kane?"

"Yes, ma'am."

"Okay. Send him to my office and make sure he has a drink. I'll be in there shortly," Carter takes over the conversation since I again find myself speechless.

"If I were your fiancé, I'd be worried about your girl crush on my client. By the way, that one actor guy you like, the one who did those two movies about male strippers and now they have a show here? He'll be here today too. Just stay in your office. I'll bring him to see you." This job has such great benefits. Carter kisses me, and he goes back to his office to work. I calm my inner fangirl down and get back to my daily duties.

Chapter

TWENTY-
EIGHT

"HAPPY BIRTHDAY, MOMMY!" MY LITTLE angel runs into my room and wakes me with his adorable little voice and a big wet kiss on my cheek. He takes my phone from the charger and snaps a birthday selfie of us. A thing we have done for the past three years. "Come on Carter. You have to take the selfie with us too." We squeeze together, and Xavier takes the picture. Our first picture together as a family of sorts.

"Okay now go wash up and get dressed so you can go to your dads for the day and help him watch the baby." School has been out for a few weeks now, so he spends more time with Corey and the new baby and doing summer activities.

"Okay, mom. I hope you have a great day. I love you!"

"Love you too cupcake."

"Good morning, my beautiful birthday girl." The nuzzles on my neck makes me want to stay at home in bed all day with him. Thanks to the dancing client, we went to the review show last night and was actually part of the show. We stayed up a little later than I like, but I'm excited to see our property in its infantile stage.

We get up and eat breakfast with Xavier before Corey arrives to pick him up. I make sure he has all his things packed and pick out his outfit for the day.

Carter is on the phone as usual and I begin to clean up the breakfast dishes. Corey arrives on time, which is odd for him and he brings me a card.

"Happy birthday, Tiffany." He hands me the card and I thank him with a hug lasting two seconds. No mixed signals or mistakes for affection will be had here today.

"Thanks. I appreciate it." I call out to Xavier and he comes to meet his dad in the living room.

"So, you ready to put this house up for sale?" he asks.

"Um, no. Not yet. They broke ground yesterday, so I think if we wait to list around forty-five days before ours is complete, we will be ready."

"Okay. Just let me know."

"Hey, Corey. How are you?"

"Carter, man. I'm good. I heard your house broke ground. Congratulations."

"Thanks. We are excited. I'm taking Tiffany to see the land and I have a little brunch spot to take her to."

"Sounds nice. I guess we'll get out of here and let you two to get your day started."

"Make sure you have my son home by dinner, Corey."

"Yes, Tiffany."

"Bye mommy. Have a great birthday and save me a piece of cake."

"Okay. I will." They leave, and Carter carries me to the bathroom where we take advantage of the alone time and make love in the shower before getting dressed for the day. I have to make sure our new bathroom has a shower bench. It comes in hand for so many things and positions. I pull my white sundress out of the closet and put it on along with my sandals. I accessorize with my birthday jewelry and pull my hair up into a banana clip.

"I'm ready to go," I say to Carter as I enter the living room where he is waiting.

"Seeing you in that dress, I'm not sure I want to go anywhere but here." He's such a flatterer. He takes my hand and kisses the back of it. "You look like a goddess."

"Thank you. I'm excited for today. First time I've been excited about my birthday in a while. Also, the first time I'm celebrating without Jewel."

"Changes are happening for both of you. I love the new security she's done..." I place my finger over his lips stopping him from talking.

"No work talk today, okay?"

"Right. No work. Let's go." We get into his car, since he knows where we are going, and we leave for our first stop."

AFTER A FORTY-MINUTE DRIVE, we arrive at our home site. There's a little basket sitting there and when we pull up, the workers take their lunch.

"You planned this? Very Nice."

"I wanted us to break bread over our new property so that we can have many meals and a happy and blessed life in this house." He reaches inside the basket and pulls out a peanut butter and jelly sandwich. In a Jackson-Lang ceremonial break, we pull apart the sandwich and eat the half that we hold. Kind of like the wishbone tradition. This is fun. We walk around the acres that are attached to the site and talk openly about plans to develop that land into a garden for fresh fruits and vegetables. He wants a pond on the property somewhere with protective fencing around and of course

290 | ML PRESTON

a full basketball court for Xavier. We make our way back up to the lot for the house and while looking at the plans, we walk over the spot marked for each room.

"This right here is our living room and over here the open dining area with kitchen attached." He says as he gives me the virtual tour.

"Okay where are the bedrooms?"

"This will be Xavier's, near us but not too close. Over here is the office we both share. And this spot, our bedroom. Then about three guest bedrooms from what I see here." He survey's the property looking around and taking in the scenery.

"Hmm, so if Xavier is here and we are over here, where will the baby go?" He looks over the plans like I just said something that actually had a designated area then it hits him. He tilts his head to the side before speaking. His facial expression is of confusion.

"Excuse me. What?" he says.

I smile before I restate my question.

"Where will our baby's room be located? Will he or she have their own room, or will they sleep with us?"

He takes a few steps back and looks at me perplexed.

"I'm sorry. It sounds like you're asking where our baby will be. I assume you mean when we decide to have one will we turn one of the rooms into a baby room." His hands are shaking, and I can tell that this news is knocking the usually calm Mr. Jackson for a loop.

"No, Carter. I'm telling you that in about seven to eight months, you will have your first-born child." I pull out the pregnancy test that started my downward spiral over the last few days and the confirmed blood test that I had the results rushed to me after going on my lunch break yesterday. He was in a meeting and it was the perfect time for me to get in to my doctor and have an HCG test performed.

"Bullshit!" he shouts. "No fucking way." He lets out a big scream, picks me up and spins me around. "Fuck baby. Really?" The crack in his voice leads way to the tears that follow only for a moment when all the questions come back. "I thought you were protected. How far along are you? How did this happen?"

"I apparently missed an appointment to get my protection updated and when we had breakfast at my house that one time after fighting, that's when your little men broke through the golden circle because the defenses were down. We are about six weeks along and I go to the doctor next week for another checkup and then the week after." He squats down with his hands collapsed together and resting over his mouth as if he was praying.

"Holy fuck, baby. I-I just can't..." He takes a few deep breaths before rushing me and kissing me with fervor. "I'm going to make love to you all night. No, wait. Will that hurt the baby?"

"No," I laugh.

"Good because I want to love you so much right now. I can't believe I'm going to be a father. This is your birthday, how is it that I got the gift?" I laugh because he is so flustered and not thinking sharply and has all these random questions and words coming from his mouth all because he is happy. "We must tell our parents."

"No, Carter. They will most definitely want us to get married and we will. I think we should just announce that we are having a baby to everyone in about three months.

"You know Jewel will know before we tell her. She's nosey like that." He reminds me.

"Yeah. I have a little time to work on a plan for her." He takes my clip out of my hair allowing my hair to fall around and frame my face.

"Fuck. You have no idea how happy I am. Let's go home. I'll scrap today's plans. I can't think of anything else right now, I just want to take you home." We get into the car and drive back to the house where we lay in bed, cuddling for the rest of the day. This is officially the best birthday ever.

To Be Continued...

About

THE AUTHOR

ML PRESTON, WAS VOTED ONE of the Top 50 Sexy Writers by Publishing Addict 2015. Her Undeniable Series, (Unthinkable, Untouchable and Unbreakable), is evident of the heat she can bring. She also has 4 short stories in her Southern Charm Series that rival the heat of her debut. Born and raised in Oklahoma City, she learned early on that she had a gift for bringing worlds to life with her words. An avid and voracious reader, she was encouraged to nurture her active imagination and quickly found a passion for storytelling. Inspired by her own personal love story, she began to write the voices in her head, embarking on a journey to share her stories. She spins tales of passion and romance where the lines between race and creed, physical perfection and social norms disappear in the face of love. Tales of real love; erotic connections with a heart and soul that everyone can relate. ML writes to escape from the mundane day-to-day. Well, that and a few glasses of wine. She makes a home in Texas with her husband and three children, who keep her grounded when the voices call on her to tell their story. And they never stop calling.

Other Books By

ML PRESTON

THE UNDENIABLE SERIES:

UNTHINKABLE

UNTOUCHABLE

UNBREAKABLE

SOUTHERN CHARM SHORT SERIES:

SUMMER STORM

SOUTHERN COMFORT

SAVANNAH NIGHTS

SWEET SOLSTICE

ANTHOLOGY:

BEAUTIFUL SKIN

FIND THESE TITLES HERE:

Author.to/allmychildren